SPIRITS ONSTAGE

ALSO BY ALICE DUNCAN

The Mercy Allcutt Mystery Series

SPIRITS ONSTAGE

A DAISY GUMM MAJESTY MYSTERY
BOOK 9

ALICE DUNCAN

ePublishingWorks!
love what you read.

April 2019
Paperback ISBN: 978-1-64457-063-0
Hardcover ISBN: 978-1-64457-064-7

ePublishing Works!
644 Shrewsbury Commons Ave
Ste 249
Shrewsbury PA 17361
United States of America

www.epublishingworks.com
Phone: 866-846-5123

My wonderful beta readers did overtime work on this book, and I can't thank them enough: Lynne Welch, Kathleen Birmingham, and Sue Krekeler. I honestly don't know what I'd do without you.

ONE

The night of Mrs. Pinkerton's dinner party, the one she'd begged Sam Rotondo and me to attend, Sam picked me up on the dot at seven-thirty p.m. My state of astonishment that he'd accepted Mrs. P's invitation still hadn't lessened. Sam isn't the most socially jovial person I've ever met. That's putting it mildly.

But perhaps I should introduce myself. I'm Daisy Gumm Majesty, widow of the late love of my life, Billy Majesty, who was shot and gassed during the Great War. After he came home from that catastrophe, he was miserable. He was confined to a wheelchair and could barely breathe. He finally managed to kill himself with the morphine syrup he had to take in order to relieve the pain in his body. However, Dr. Benjamin, our wonderful family physician, knew what was what and reported Billy's death as accidental, resulting from the injuries he had suffered in the war. Doc Benjamin was right, except about the accident part. I still blame the Kaiser.

Even though I knew in my heart that Billy wasn't long for this world when he came home from Europe, I was devastated by his death. Which just goes to show that one can know almost exactly what the future will bring and still be crushed when it happens. To this day, my insides ache for Billy. And for me, too, actually. I was only seventeen when we married, and only twenty-three when Sam drove me to Mrs. Pinkerton's house the evening of the party I was surprised Sam was attending.

Mrs. P's dinner party took place about a year and a half or so after Billy's demise. She pleaded with both Sam—who had been Billy's best friend and at one time my worst nightmare—and me to attend her function. This was mainly because Sam and I had solved a problem for her the week prior. Actually, I'd done most of the solving, but never mind about that. Mrs. Pinkerton appreciated the both of us, and that's the important part.

Um…maybe I'd better explain that last comment, too. You see, ever since my Billy had come home from war a ruin of his former happy-go-lucky, vibrant, healthy self, I'd been the primary breadwinner in our family. The family includes my mother and father, Peggy and Joe Gumm; and my aunt, Viola Gumm, widow of my late uncle, Ernie Gumm, who was Pa's older brother. Vi lost her only son, Paul, during the Great War, too, so every once in a while things got a trifle glum in our house. But I didn't mean to digress. I do my breadwinning as a spiritualist-medium to wealthy matrons in Pasadena, California. In other words, I conjure up and chat with dead people for a living.

Do I believe what I do is for real?

Good Lord, no! I mean, I'm not an idiot. However, most of the people for whom I work, while probably not technically idiots, have far more money than sense. And thank God for it, I say, or my family would have to struggle a whole lot more than it does. I make a really good living as a phony spiritualist, I'm excellent at what I do, and my clients appreciate me for it.

A slight amendment is called for here: one time, and one time only, a real, honest-to-God ghost appeared through me during a séance. The phenomenon has never happened since, and if it ever recurs, I do believe I'll be compelled to take up another line of work, even though that would mean a hefty dent in the family's income. More like a gaping gash, perhaps.

But anyway, Sam picked me up smack on time, and we drove from my family's lowly bungalow on South Marengo Avenue to Mr. and Mrs. Pinkerton's grand mansion on Orange Grove Boulevard in Sam's big, black Hudson automobile. Not only that, but Sam was dressed appropriately for the occasion!

Sam usually looks at least slightly rumpled. Not that night. That night, he wore a pristine black dinner jacket along with creased evening trousers and a stiff white shirt with a stiff white collar. His shirt even had gold cufflinks. The fact that he'd agreed to Mrs. P's invitation had amazed me. The fact that he actually had the appropriate duds to wear to such a shindig left me in a state of utter flabbergastation. If that's a word.

Sam doesn't care much about the social graces, but they're my bread and butter. I strive to maintain a sober and elegant façade to my clients. That evening, which was the first Tuesday in October, 1923, I wore a perfectly gorgeous blue velvet evening gown that came to my ankles and was tubular in shape, even when I wore it—I'd lost a lot of weight after Billy died. I used to have more curves than were strictly fashionable. The dress had a short train, and both the dress and the train edges had been embroidered by my own skillful fingers. Well, heck, the entire ensemble had been made by me, using the White side-pedal sewing machine I'd given to my mother one Christmas, but which I used pretty much exclusively. I'm a whiz at sewing. I'm also a whiz at spiritualist-mediuming.

My dinner companion worked as a detective for the Pasadena Police Department. Sam was a New Yorker of Italian extraction, tall, large although not fat, somber, and about as light on his feet as a slab of granite. Sam was solid. My Billy had been long, lean and limber. Sam was long, wide and marble-like. Although Sam and I used to be at each other's throats all the time, for the past year or so we'd been getting along quite well. Sort of. On one memorable occasion when we'd been hollering at each other, he'd brought the argument to an abrupt halt by saying he loved me. Neither one of us has explored that admission much since, but we did get along better now than we had earlier in our acquaintanceship.

My parents and Aunt Vi were rooting for a romance to spring up between Sam and me. I wasn't so sure I wanted one, although I did notice that I missed the big lug when he wasn't around for a day or so.

"I'm surprised you agreed to come to this dinner party, Sam," said I as we tootled along Pasadena's streets.

"So am I," he said grumpily.

"I figured you'd back out."

"So did I."

"Why didn't you?" I peered at him, but it was too dark to see much except his profile, which was rather good-looking. I wasn't used to thinking of Sam in terms of his physical appeal, but I have to confess, if only in this journal, that he had some. Physical appeal, I mean.

His shoulders lifted in a slight shrug. "I keep my word."

He would have to say that, wouldn't he? I vividly remember the day shortly before Billy succeeded in killing himself when he'd asked Sam to take care of me after he (Billy) was gone, and Sam had agreed. I hadn't meant to overhear their conversation, and I'm often sorry I did. But oh, well. Too late not to hear it now.

"I appreciate you joining me, Sam. I have a feeling Mrs. Pinkerton didn't invite us merely as a thank-you gesture."

His big head turned, and his dark eyes gleamed in the deeper darkness of the interior of the automobile. "Yeah? How come?"

"I don't know. But she's been really excited for the past week, and I'm afraid that might bode ill for one of us. I suspect me."

"I thought you said she just wanted to thank us for getting the Ku Klux Klan off her back."

"That's what she said, but I'm not sure that's her only reason."

Very well, I suppose I'd better explain that Klan reference, too. For weeks Mrs. Pinkerton's gatekeeper, Joseph Jackson, a Negro fellow and all-around good man, had been harassed by members of the KKK who had come all the way from Tulsa, Oklahoma, to do mischief to his brother, Henry. They'd even shot Joseph Jackson and blown up Mrs. Pinkerton's mailbox. But they'd been foiled, mainly by me. I say that in all modesty, but it's the truth.

Jackson was now out of the hospital, but he still wasn't yet able to resume his gate-keeping duties at Mrs. Pinkerton's mansion. Sam and I both noticed the face of a newly acquired gatekeeper when we stopped to tell the fellow our names. He only nodded and, I presume, pressed a button so that the huge, black iron gates swung open. They'd been repaired admirably after having been partially blown to bits. Sam drove his Hudson up the deodar-lined drive to Mrs. P's gigantic circular drive, where several more automobiles were parked.

We arrived precisely thirty minutes before dinner was to commence. We were both factually and socially on time.

I brightened when I saw Harold Kincaid's bright red Stutz Bearcat. Harold is Mrs. Pinkerton's son and a particular friend of mine. Mind you, our relationship is strictly platonic, and it probably would have been even if Harold hadn't been...Oh, dear. I see I've hit another slight snag.

Harold and his...well, his lover, dang it, Delray Farrington, lived together in a gorgeous home in San Marino, a wealthy community a very few miles south of Pasadena. Many people believe Harold and Del's relationship to be sinful, if not downright criminal. Recall, if you will, the late Mr. Oscar Wilde. As far as I've been able to determine, neither Harold nor Del—nor, I presume, Mr. Wilde—ever had a choice in the matter of that particular branch of their personalities. So phooey on those who consider them less than human. They were my friends. Well, Oscar Wilde wasn't, but...Oh, nuts. You know what I mean.

"Harold's here," grumbled Sam at my side. He was nowhere near as ecstatic to see Harold's machine as was I.

"Yes," I replied with much more animation than he'd showed. "I'm so glad. I never know who I'm going to meet when I go to a do at Mrs. P's house, and Harold always relaxes me."

"Who's going to relax me?"

"Pooh, Sam. You're never ruffled, no matter whose company you're in."

"Huh."

Typical Sam comment.

"I wonder if Del will be here, too. They helped capture that awful man, you know. If Del hadn't gone through the banking records, he might have escaped."

"Not after you bashed his head in with a baseball bat, he wouldn't."

He would have to bring that up, wouldn't he?

"Nonsense. Del helped pin the crime on the correct man."

"I guess so."

5

The "correct man" of whom I spoke had been the exalted cyclops of Pasadena's chapter of the Ku Klux Klan. I'm not making that up, either. That's what the KKK called their leaders. Talk about idiots.

Quincy Applewood appeared before us. Quincy and his wife, Edie, were old school chums of mine, and they both now worked for the Pinkertons. Edie was Mrs. Pinkerton's lady's maid, and Quincy took care of Mr. Pinkerton's sons' horses. He also doubled as a car-parker during dinner parties, which was why he strode up to Sam's Hudson now, wearing a broad smile.

"Hey, Daisy. Hey, Detective Rotondo. Glad to see you. There's sure a lot of folks dining at the Pinkertons' this evening. Your poor aunt had to hire two other girls to help her with the spread."

"Yes, she told me," I said, as Quincy opened my door and guided me out politely. Sam opened his own door and stomped around to my side of the car. There he more or less wrenched my arm from Quincy's.

"Vi's cooking the feast?" Sam asked, sounding almost happy for the first time since he'd showed up at my door.

"She sure is," I said. "I can't remember what all she said we're going to be dining on, but it's sure to be delicious."

"I'm sure it will be."

Sam knew all about Vi's excellent cooking skills, since he dined at our home almost every other day.

Have I mentioned Vi's particular talent? I shall do so now. My aunt, Viola Gumm, is the best cook in the entire City of Pasadena, if not the entire United States of America. I've never known her to fix a flop. I, on the other hand, can sour milk just by looking at it, and my mother's not much better at cooking than I am. A shame, that, but Ma and I have our own talents. I've already mentioned mine. Ma is the chief book-keeper at the Hotel Marengo, which is a darned impressive job for a woman. Well, it would be for anyone, but a woman having a job like that in 1923 was special. Pa used to work as a chauffeur for rich folks in town until he had a heart attack and the doctor told him to knock off the driving.

The family would have been in the soup if it hadn't been for its enterprising females, by golly.

But that's incidental to this story. At that moment Sam took my arm,

Quincy took Sam's key and drove the Hudson somewhere to park it, and Sam and I walked up the marble steps, past the two lounging marble lions, and across the marble porch to the enormous double front door of the Pinkertons' gigantic home. Sam picked up the knocker dangling from an iron lion's mouth and whacked it against the brass knocking plate.

Featherstone, the Pinkertons' fabulously correct butler—he even had an English accent, for crumb's sake—opened the door to us, and we walked in and down the hall to join the melee in the drawing room. The drawing room is what we plebeians in the middle-class world would call a living room, by the way.

TWO

"Daisy!"

I jumped a little, but smiled when I saw Harold Kincaid hurrying over to greet Sam and me.

Perhaps another explanation is needed here. Mrs. Pinkerton's last name used to be Kincaid when she was married to her first husband, a scoundrel named Eustace Kincaid. For good and sufficient reason, Mr. Kincaid now resides in San Quentin Prison. After divorcing him, and after waiting a suitable length of time, Mrs. Kincaid married Mr. Algernon Pinkerton, known by his friends and family as Algie. He's a very nice man, but I don't know that I'd like to be called Algie, which reminds me of moss and slime and other types of pond scum. But that's neither here nor there. I was overjoyed to see Harold.

"Harold!" I cried with equal vigor.

Sam said, "Kincaid." He would.

"Glad to see you, too, Detective Rotondo," Harold said with a wicked twinkle in his eyes.

"Boy, there sure are a lot of people here. Are they all staying for dinner?" Poor Vi. As I peered out over the crowd, I figured there must be thirty or thirty-five (or thirty-six, in order to keep the numbers even) people there, including Sam and me.

"Yes, indeedy. Nothing's too difficult for my mother," said Harold with a wink. "That's because Mother doesn't have to do any of the work. I feel sorry for your aunt." See? Told you he was a nice man.

"I don't think Vi's worried," I told him. "She's been excited all week, telling us about the menu for tonight's dinner. And according to Quincy, she has hired a couple of people to help her."

"It sure smells good in the kitchen," Harold said wistfully. He's a little plump, is Harold. "I know, because I peeked in and Vi kicked me out."

I laughed. "Harold! I don't blame her. She must wish she had eight arms right about now."

"I offered to stir something for her, but she only yelled at me." He faked a sniffle. "Didn't even give me a stalk of celery."

"She's serving celery?" Sam squinted at Harold.

"Not your average, every-day stalks of celery, Detective. Daisy's Aunt Vi fancied them up a good deal." He tipped me another wink. "I peeked."

"I'm glad of that," said I. Not that I don't care for celery, but it's not my favorite vegetable, which is probably the lowly carrot. Or maybe the even lowlier rutabaga.

Sam, who couldn't seem to help himself, glared around at the guests. "I'm not used to eating this late. I'm hungry."

"Featherstone will announce the meal soon, Detective," Harold assured him. "In the meantime, would you like me to introduce you to the folks you don't know?"

"No," said Sam.

"Sure!" said I.

With another laugh, Harold said, "You can lounge in a corner, Detective. I'll escort Daisy around the room."

"I'll come with you," growled Sam.

"Happy to have you," said Harold. He probably meant it, too, but only because Sam amuses Harold. As for Sam, he doesn't care for Harold because of what he is. I've told him a thousand times that people like Harold don't choose their preferences, but my nagging hasn't done any good.

"You already know Mrs. Bissel," Harold said, stopping beside a large woman wearing an eggplant-colored evening dress that didn't much become her. Well, her dressmaker probably said the color was *aubergine*, but that's just a French word for eggplant.

"Oh, Daisy!" Mrs. Bissel cried, delighted to see me. Mrs. Bissel had given us our dog, Spike, a black-and-tan dachshund. Spike had made Billy's last couple of years on this earth almost bearable. "I'm so glad you're here!"

"It's good to see you, Mrs. Bissel," I said sincerely, shaking her hand. We both wore gloves. Mine were black. Hers were eggplant-colored.

"And good evening, Detective Ro-ro—" Mrs. Bissel's face flamed to a color that clashed with her gown.

"Rotondo," I supplied. "I'm amazed Sam decided to join us." I probably should have left that last part out.

To my surprise, Sam executed a small, sharp bow and said, "How do you do, Mrs. Bissel?"

"I'm fine, thank you." She held out her hand and Sam shook it just as a gentleman would have done.

"But you need to meet some other people. I'm sure the two of you can talk later, Daisy." And Harold hauled Sam and me away from Mrs. Bissel and toward a woman whom I didn't know.

"Oh, Harold," whispered the woman, a tall, skinny lady in a straight up-and-down red dress. She had a cigarette holder in her right hand and looked languid—if you know what I mean. She had flaxen-blond hair that I would have bet came straight out of a bottle. She seemed to have stationed herself in a pose meant to reflect boredom.

The image of boredom was something the too-rich strove to project in those days after the war, when nothing seemed to matter and the world appeared headed straight to heck. Harold's horrible sister, Stacy, used to try to look languid and bored, but lately she'd taken up a tambourine and joined the Salvation Army. I don't expect this phase of hers to last. She'll be back to drinking and smoking and getting picked up in raids on speakeasies any old day now.

"Good evening, Mrs. Lippincott. Please allow me to introduce you to Mrs. Majesty and Mr. Rotondo."

"Oh!" Mrs. Lippincott actually stood up straight. "Are you the spiritualist-medium, Mrs. Majesty? Madeline"—Madeline is Mrs. Kincaid's first name—"has told me so *much* about you!" She held out her hand, and I shook it. Then she offered it to Sam, who also shook it. "And you are? I didn't catch your name, I fear."

"Detective Sam Rotondo," said Sam stolidly, not avoiding the issue of belonging to so ignoble a profession as that of policeman. "Pasadena Police Department."

Mrs. Lippincott's eyes widened. "Oh, my. We'd better be on our good behavior this evening, isn't that so, Harold?" She giggled, which sounded incongruous coming from so languorous and sophisticated a specimen.

"You betcha," said Harold, who was undaunted by much of anything, bless him. "Sam's a tough customer."

"Ahhhh," said she, drawing out the one word into three syllables. I wanted to snatch Sam away from her before she dug her claws into him. She looked as if she'd be pleased to devour him—or do other unmentionable things to him.

Fortunately, Harold was on the job. He said, "Aha! Here are some other folks you know. Mr. and Mrs. Hastings."

Oh, dear. I did indeed know Mrs. Hastings. I'd never actually met Mr. Hastings, although he'd banned me from his law offices a year or so prior, when I was in pursuit of a murderer. Not that I pursue murderers on a regular basis, you understand. It just worked out that way.

"Mrs. Majesty! How lovely to see you this evening." Laura Hastings, whose only son had died several months before this—which was why I'd been in Mr. Hastings' law offices—was delighted to see me. I could tell.

"It's wonderful to see you, too," I said, trying to ignore her husband's scowl.

"And here's Detective Sam Rotondo," said Harold, not mincing words this time.

I saw Mr. Hastings' lips writhe a little before he unbent. As well he should have. If not for Sam and me, he'd have been fleeced of a good deal of money, and his son's murderer would never have been apprehended.

"How do you do, Mrs. Majesty. Detective Rotondo." His voice softened when he spoke Sam's name. "I appreciate the good work you people did in breaking up that land swindle."

"You're welcome," said Sam. Stolidly, I'm sure I needn't add. He shook hands with both of the Hastings.

"And let me introduce you to Mr. and Mrs. Miller—Malcolm and Veronica, that is to say. Mal, come over here and meet the spiritualist and her detective friend. The two of them haunt the streets of Pasadena, seeking out villains to prosecute. Or persecute."

I whacked Harold on the arm. "We do not!"

With a laugh, Harold said, "That's true. They don't have to go to so much trouble. Villains are just attracted to Daisy. Kind of like steel shavings to a magnet."

I held out my hand to Mrs. Miller and said, "Don't believe a word Harold tells you. He's fibbing."

"I have no doubt of it," said Mr. Miller in a rumbly voice, shaking my hand after his wife had let it go. He then shook Sam's hand. "I admire the work you do, Detective Rotondo. I've seen you in the paper a time or two. You've solved some mighty complicated crimes."

"Thanks," muttered Sam.

"Oh, and there are Connie and Max Van der Linden!" Harold cried with glee, yanking me away from the Millers. Mrs. Miller smiled and waved us off. I guess she understood Harold's personality.

He hauled me over to a younger couple. I resisted slightly, but only because the couple's last name sounded German to me, and I'd held a grudge against Germans ever since they all but murdered my Billy. Irrational, I know. But I'm just a lowly human, and humans are irrational creatures.

Harold, who knew me well, leaned close and whispered in my ear, "It's a Dutch name, so you're free to like them if you want to."

I poked him in the ribs, but didn't respond. Sam, the rat, smiled slightly. I saw him. Well, I guess it was better than his usual scowl.

Harold said effusively, "Connie and Max, please allow me to introduce you to Mrs. Majesty and Detective Sam Rotondo. Daisy's the one I told you about, Connie."

The Van der Lindens were an attractive couple. He was tall and lean, and she was a little taller than I am—I'm five feet, four inches—and also lean. They both look fresh-faced and as if they didn't strive to achieve boredom. I instantly liked them for it—and the fact they weren't German—and smiled.

"How do you do?" I asked them both together.

"I'm so very happy to meet you, Mrs. Majesty. Harold has told us all about you. I understand you sing!" Mrs. Van der Linden grabbed my hand and pumped it as if she expected water to gush from my mouth.

Her words startled me. "Sing? Me?" Harold often told people I was a spiritualist-medium, but a singer? I glanced at Harold, puzzled, but he only grinned more broadly.

"She has a good voice," said Sam. That startled me, too. Sam wasn't given to complimenting people, especially me.

"Sing? Well...I sing in the choir at First Methodist-Episcopal Church, but I'm only an alto."

"Hmm," said Connie Van der Linden, tapping her chin with a lovely manicured finger, "Can you manage mezzo?"

"Mezzo? Isn't that a soprano?" I felt like an idiot. "Um, I sing alto. I've never even tried to sing soprano."

"Mezzo's lower than a coloratura," said Harold.

Whatever that meant.

"What about contralto? I'm sure you can, if you sing alto in your church choir," said Mr. Van der Linden. He, too, appeared rather avid.

What was going on here? And what in the world was a contralto? I vaguely remembered reading about a contralto in a Sherlock Holmes story, but darned if I could remember which one.

"I...I don't know. What's a contralto?" Then I felt stupid.

But the Van der Lindens only laughed. The mister said, "I'm sorry. You must think we've gone 'round the bend. But you see, we're interested in putting together a little musical operetta company. We're thinking of staging light operas like *The Merry Widow* and perhaps some of Gilbert and Sullivan's works."

"And a contralto is, basically, an alto," said Mrs. Van der Linden. "Non-opera people have just chopped the C-O-N-T-R off the word contralto. We're hoping to stage some operettas soon."

"What fun," I said, still confused. Did they want the lowly *me* to sing in their operettas? Actually...that *did* sound like fun. "I loved *The Merry Widow*, when I saw it at the Shakespeare Club last year."

"Daisy is a wonderful seamstress, too," said Harold, sounding coy.

Was he volunteering me for something? I slipped him a glance. He looked innocent. I considered this a very bad sign.

"Oh, how marvelous!" cried Ms. Van der Linden, clasping her hands to her more or less nonexistent bosom.

"But—"

Didn't work. Harold interrupted me. "I'm a fabulous baritone," said he with his customary modesty (I'm joking).

"Yes, you are," said Mrs. Van der Linden, giggling. On her a giggle sounded just about right.

"Do you sing, Inspector?" Mr. V asked Sam.

"Detective," said Sam. "Not really."

"I beg your pardon. Detective. You have a deep voice. I'd bet, if I were a betting man, that you'd sing bass."

"Maybe," said Sam, as voluble as ever.

"Let's discuss this more after dinner," Harold suggested. "I want to introduce Daisy and Sam to a couple of other people."

He tugged on my arm and whispered, "Connie is fabulously wealthy, but she's sweet anyway."

"How nice for her," I said, wondering what Connie Van der Linden's wealth had to do with anything. I lurched after Harold, bringing Sam along with me. "Harold Kincaid, is this why your mother has been in such a lather this past week? Does she want to get me to sing in some stupid operetta?"

"That would be telling," said Harold with a laugh.

I wasn't sure I approved of this nonsense, and I was positive Sam didn't. His glower could have wilted roses.

"Del! Here are Daisy and Sam!" Harold chirped as we approached his better half.

Del's smile could have made a woman who didn't know his deepest secret melt into a puddle of slush. As tall and lanky as my late Billy, Del was the opposite of the shortish, plumpish Harold. But the two men loved each other, and in my book, love trumps looks any old day.

I gave Del one of my best smiles and held out my hand. "It's so good to see you again, Del. Harold has been hinting at dire doings involving singing. Do you know anything about this?"

He chuckled as he shook my hand and then Sam's, who deigned to give Del's hand a short little shake. He didn't like Del for the same reason he didn't like Harold. Silly man.

"Don't look to me for enlightenment. I can't carry a tune in a basket," said Del. "But I think Harold, the Van der Lindens, and Mrs. Pinkerton have been up to something. I suspect you'll learn all about it before long."

"Oh, look over there," said Harold nodding to his left. "There's someone you probably know, Detective."

I heard Sam mutter something under his breath, but darned if I know what it was.

"Chief Kelley," Harold said, yanking me over to a portly gent who looked out of place. A stout woman stood next to him. She appeared slightly overdressed and nervous. Chief?

A glance at Sam told me all I needed to know.

"Chief Kelley," Harold said again once we stood before the couple. "Please allow me to introduce you to Mrs. Majesty, who has received two…whatever you call thems from your department for helping the city's police officers solve crimes."

Wishing I could disappear, I pasted on a gentle smile—I excel at gentle smiles because they go well with my line of work—held out a hand and said, "How do you do?"

"Uh. Oh, yes. Mrs. Majesty. Good to meet you. Again." He nodded at Sam. "Detective Rotondo."

"Chief," said Sam. His hand lifted slightly as if he were going to salute, but he remembered he was in dinner garb and not his uniform, and he didn't.

"Please," said the chief stiffly, "allow me to introduce you to Mrs. Kelley." He tipped his head toward the ill-at-ease woman at his side.

I did another hand extension and another howdy-do. Only in my wafting spiritualist's way.

"Good evening, Mrs. Majesty. I've heard about you," said she in a slightly nasal voice.

Oh, dear. I only smiled at her. I feared she'd heard about me, all right, and probably not in very flattering terms. Some people—Sam among them—thought I poked into too many corners I should stay away from. Nuts to them. I got things done.

"Daisy!"

I recognized that shriek, felt a second of reprieve from the hands of the law, and braced myself.

Sure enough, I turned around just in time to have Mrs. Pinkerton fling her arms around me. We'd probably both have hit the floor if we hadn't bumped into Sam, who was more or less an immovable object. He put his hands on my shoulder to steady Mrs. P and me.

"I'm *so* thrilled you could come this evening, Daisy! And you, too, Detective Rotondo. Thank you for coming!"

She usually called Sam Mr. Rotund. She must have been practicing his name.

"Thank you for inviting us, Mrs. Pinkerton," I said politely, trying to wrest myself from her embrace. "How's Jackson doing? I understand he's out of the hospital now."

"Yes, he is. He's recuperating quite well. His mother…"

Here Mrs. Pinkerton paused, as if she weren't quite sure what to say about Jackson's mother. I understood. Mrs. Jackson was a voodoo mambo from New Orleans, and she was not your typical Pasadena matron. And that was even besides her not being white and rich. If you understand what I mean.

"I've met Mrs. Jackson. She's an unusual woman."

"She certainly is," said Mrs. P. "But she brought us some marvelous pastries."

"Ah, yes. Her famous beignets. She gave Aunt Vi the recipe, if you want her to make some for you."

Mrs. Pinkerton smiled enormously. "Oh, how wonderful! I must admit to having been slightly…startled by Mrs. Jackson's appearance."

"Understandable," said I, meaning it. Mrs. Jackson wore the brightest colors I've ever seen on a person, and always had her hair covered by a vivid turban. She also made little voodoo dolls, which she called jujus. I still wore the one she made me when I could. That evening, it wouldn't have gone well with my lovely gown so I'd left it at home.

As things turned out, I probably should have worn it anyway.

THREE

By the time Featherstone appeared in the drawing-room doorway and announced, "Dinner is served," my head was spinning, and I couldn't remember anyone's name. I was sorry Mrs. Pinkerton was such a stickler about table etiquette, because I knew I wouldn't be sitting beside Sam, but probably stuck next to some stranger. I hoped it wouldn't be Mr. Hastings, who didn't like me much.

I was in luck. Harold sat to my right and Mr. Van der Linden to my left. Poor Sam was seated between Mrs. Hastings and Mrs. Lippincott, who fairly drooled over him. I disapproved, but I tried not to show it. Anyhow, Sam was as stoic and impervious as ever, so her wiles seemed for naught.

"Before the first course is served," announced Mrs. Pinkerton, rising from her chair at the head of the table—Mr. Pinkerton sat at the huge table's foot. "I want everyone to know that this dinner party is primarily in celebration of the excellent job Detective Rotondo and Mrs. Majesty did of foiling the dastardly villains who harassed my household during the past month or so. Thank you both."

She sent first me and then Sam a brilliant smile and lifted her water goblet. I suspect that if the chief of police and his wife weren't present that evening, she'd have had Featherstone dust off a couple of bottles of wine from the cellar and used that for her toast. But Mrs. P wouldn't flout Prohibition in front of the law. Maybe she would in front of Sam, but not Sam's boss.

I felt heat rush up my back and neck and invade my cheeks. The trouble with being a redhead is that we tend to blush at the slightest provocation. When everyone else at the table rose and lifted their glasses to Sam and me, I wanted to crawl under the table and hide. However, having been consorting with rich people since my tenth year, when Aunt Vi brought home Mrs. P's aged Ouija board, I knew how to act my part. I sat serenely, hoping the candlelight would hide my blushes, and smiled in my most demure fashion. When I looked in Sam's direction, I saw him shut his eyes in pain for a moment before he, too, nobly rose to the occasion and pasted on a phony smile. His boss, who sat near Mrs. Pinkerton, frowned. Then his dinner partner, whose name I didn't recall, elbowed him—I saw him jerk, so I know that's what happened— and he lifted his own glass and rose, rather belatedly, to toast Sam and me.

Thank God *that* didn't last long. After a dithery little speech and after one and all had drunk from their water goblets, Mrs. P let everyone sit down, and the meal commenced. I noticed Mrs. Bissel had lent her houseboy and Mrs. Hastings had lent her maid, so we were served by a young Japanese man named Keiji and a young Chinese woman named Li.

The meal began with stuffed mushrooms. Boy, were they good! I don't generally like mushrooms because they taste like dirt to me, but these were wonderful. Vi served them with the already-mentioned celery, but the celery sticks were stuffed with creamed cheese and, I think, chopped pecans. Yummy. Then came a squash soup, which I know sounds strange, but it was very good. After that came some kind of delicate white fish served alongside a salad I think Aunt Vi calls a Caesar salad, although I'm not sure what Caesar had to do with it. Went really well with the fish. After that the main course, roasted lamb done to perfection along with roasted potatoes and gravy, about stuffed me to the gills. Small wonder Mrs. Pinkerton was hefty, if she ate like this every day. I mean, Aunt Vi cooked for my family, but we generally had a meat course and a couple of vegetables. Soup and salad and some dinner rolls would be a meal for us. Oh, well, it was sure good.

I almost forgot to mention the dessert, which was some kind of lemon pound cake with a lemony sauce. I was really too full to eat most of it, but I did my best. Delicious!

And then, after the last bite had been swallowed and folks were beginning to moan slightly from over-stuffedness, Mrs. P rose to lead the ladies out of the room. This act was a relic of the past, when the ladies would leave the gents to their port and cigars. This evening, I imagine the port would be replaced by tea or lemonade or some other non-alcoholic beverage. They'd probably smoke cigars, though.

Because I knew the first floor of the house by heart, having been practicing my trade there for lo, those many years, I made my way down the hallway to the kitchen. I didn't want to annoy my aunt, but I did want to let her know how much Mrs. P's guests had enjoyed her fabulous dinner. I gave the swing door a tentative push and saw dishes piled up everywhere and my aunt more or less collapsed at the kitchen table, as many minions washed up. She held a glass of iced water in her hand and took a swig before turning to frown at the door. When she saw me, she smiled.

I scooted in and sat beside her. "Oh, Aunt Vi, you're the best cook in the world. That was the most delicious meal I've ever eaten."

"It was probably the biggest you've ever eaten, at any rate," said my aunt, who must have been exhausted, because she wasn't given to irony as a rule.

"You're right about that. Shoot, I'm glad we don't eat like that at home every day. We'd all blow up like balloons."

"Not even the Pinkertons dine like that every day, Daisy. This was a special party, and Mrs. P put it on for you and Sam, so you'd better get yourself out there and mingle."

"I will. I just wanted you to know how delicious everything was."

"Thank you, sweetie. Now, get going."

So I went.

The men must have been released from durance vile—or cigar smoke vile, at any rate—because by the time I entered the drawing room, everyone had gathered there. Harold spotted me at once, as did Sam, and they both converged on me.

"Where the devil did you go?" Sam demanded.

"Oh, Daisy, come over and chat with Connie and Max for a minute," said Harold.

"I went to thank my aunt for her superb meal," I snapped at Sam. To Harold I said, "Are they going to make me sing? I don't think I can sing in front of a bunch of people, Harold."

"You sing in front of a bunch of people every Sunday," said Sam, still sounding grumpy. Then again, he almost always did.

"Yes, but I don't sing solos," I pointed out.

By that time Harold had begun dragging me across the drawing room floor, dodging people here and there. Like a Saint Bernard—or maybe more like an elephant—Sam clomped along behind us. He loomed large, did Sam Rotondo.

"Fiddlesticks," said Harold.

I looked a question over my shoulder at Sam. He only shrugged as if he didn't know what Harold was talking about, either.

"Connie and Max!" cried Harold at the couple standing before the fireplace. "Here's Daisy. Do your worst."

"Harold!" I cried, aghast. I wasn't going to be roped into doing something I didn't want to do, darn it!

"Don't pay any attention to him," said Connie Van der Linden with a smile for me and then one for Sam. "We're not going to lock you up and force you to sing or anything. But Max and I—and Mrs. Pinkerton —are interested in putting on *The Mikado*, by Gilbert and Sullivan, and Harold said you'd be perfect to sing the role of Katisha."

My mouth dropped open. I read music and liked playing the piano in our living room at home. I'd also checked out the score of *The Mikado* from the Pasadena Public Library not long ago. I'd played the music and loved it, and I thought Mr. Gilbert was exceptionally clever with words and Mr. Sullivan equally clever with music, but...*Katisha*?

I turned on Harold. "Harold Kincaid, Katisha is an old, ugly, mean-tempered, nasty, vindictive, *horrible* person!"

Sam mumbled, "Sounds perfect for you."

I shot him a glare.

Before I could say more, Harold said, "But the part is in your vocal range. I've heard you sing, Daisy."

"You have?" I was astonished. To my knowledge, I'd never sung a note in front of Harold.

"Yes, my dear. Perhaps you aren't aware of it, but you sometimes sing when you think you're alone. I've heard you. Right here in this room. A couple of times. When you've been waiting for my mother to show herself so you can conjure up Rolly for her."

A word of explanation is called for here. I made up Rolly at the same time I made up my role as spiritualist-medium. He's supposed to be my spirit control, and he's a Scottish chap who lived in about the eleventh century. According to the story I made up to go along with him, Rolly and I were soul mates who'd been married in Scotland in ten-something, and we'd had five sons together. He'd followed me through all my incarnations to this very day. Rolly had been a soldier in life, also according to my story, and had never gone to school, so he couldn't spell worth beans. That had been more than ten years ago, and I'd since learned how to spell quite well, but I couldn't change the story now, so Rolly remained illiterate.

Back to the drawing room.

"I...I didn't know that."

"You sing duets with that other woman at church all the time," said Sam.

Sam's comment annoyed the heck out of me. "Sam Rotondo, I've introduced you to Lucille Spinks fifty million times! You can't even remember her name?"

"It hasn't been fifty million times," he grumbled. "And you sound good together."

"So you're against me, too?" I all but hollered at him.

"I'm not against you. I just think you have a good voice. That's all."

"Well..." My voice trailed off. What could one say to that? I mean, it was a nice thing for him to have said. I couldn't very well be mad at him for having said it, could I?

"We really don't want to apply pressure, Mrs. Majesty," said Mrs. Van der Linden, smiling sweetly. "And you certainly don't *look* like Katisha."

"Pish-tosh," said Harold. Then he laughed. "Which is the name of one of the characters, actually."

"It's Pish-Tush, but you're close," said Mr. Van der Linden with a chuckle of his own.

"But the fact that you don't look like Katisha is why God invented makeup," the irreverent Harold plopped into the conversation. "I think you'd be swell in the part. I," he said, preening slightly, "am the Lord High Executioner." He took a poker from the fireplace-implements thing and brandished it. I had to leap out of his way. "'I have a little list,'" sang he. I remembered the song well. Harold replaced the fireplace poker and smiled at me. "You and I get married in the end," he said.

"Is that meant to be an inducement?" I asked, snarling a bit. I instantly reminded myself that I was a spiritualist-medium, and that spiritualist-media—or mediums. I don't know which is correct under the circumstances—didn't snarl. It was hard, though.

Harold only laughed.

"Will you at least give us a try?" asked Mrs. Van der Linden with another sweet smile.

Frustrated and feeling as though the whole world were turning against me, I said, "Where will this operetta take place?"

Mrs. Van der Linden and her husband exchanged a guilty glance.

"Um…" said Harold.

"Well…" said Mr. Van der Linden.

Good heavens, what did this mean? Perhaps they really *were* plotting against me.

"You guys are ganging up on me," I said, trying to maintain my spiritualist persona, but feeling like hitting someone.

"Actually, we've received permission to stage the show at the First Methodist-Episcopal Church you attend," said Mrs. Van der Linden.

My mouth fell open yet again.

"Mr. Floy Hostetter has agreed to play the role of Pooh-Bah, the Lord High Everything except the executioner, which is who Harold is."

"M-Mr. Hostetter? *He's* going to be in the show?" Mr. Floy Hostetter was our choir director. He was *my* choir director, for crumb's sake!

"Yes, indeedy," said Harold, rubbing his hands with glee. "And another member of your choir…what's his name?" He glanced at Mrs. Van der Linden.

"George Finster," she supplied with alacrity.

"Yes. He's going to be the Mikado. He's got a good bass voice, or so I've been told."

"Yes," I said weakly. "He does."

"So you'll consider it?" asked Mrs. V with strong appeal in her voice. The woman was a good actress; I'd give her that.

I glanced at all the people ranged against me: Harold, Max Van der Linden, Connie Van der Linden, Sam. Sam? Good Lord! Even *Sam* wanted me to sing in the stupid operetta! And I gave up.

"Yes," I said, feeling as though my heart were being squeezed by a giant's fist. "I'll consider it."

To judge by the joy emanating from my companions, you'd think I'd just achieved world peace. I felt as though I'd just sold my soul to Satan.

FOUR

As Sam drove his big, black Hudson from the Pinkerton palace to my humble abode on South Marengo Avenue, I was still sulking.

"Darn it, Sam Rotondo, that was a sneaky thing to do, agreeing with the Van der Lindens and Harold like that."

He shrugged. "It wasn't sneaky. I think you have a good voice, and if the part is in your voice range, why not do it?"

"I'm not a soloist!" I cried.

Another shrug. "Give it a try. Broaden your horizons. Who knows? Maybe you'll enjoy performing."

I'd once told Billy I wanted to broaden my horizons. He'd looked at my hips and told me my horizons were broad enough. But that's not the point.

I wasn't sure precisely what the point was. In actual fact, I *did* enjoy performing. In truth, I earned my considerable income performing. Only I was comfortable in my spiritualist act. I didn't mind singing duets with Lucille Spinks, who had a beautiful soprano voice and who sang in the choir with me, but I'd never sung a solo before. At least not before anyone but my family. And, according to him, in front of Harold, but that was by accident. If it were true, and I didn't know it for a fact. Harold didn't mind stretching the truth from time to time.

"Give it a try," Sam repeated. "Can't hurt. You might enjoy it."

"Will you try out for a part in the chorus?"

"Hell, no. I can't sing."

"*I* don't know that! In fact, you just lied. I heard you sing when you came to our house on Christmas Eve. You sang with the rest of the family when I played the piano." I crossed my arms across my chest and glared at what I could see of him, which wasn't much, the night being dark and all.

"That's not singing. That's just playing around the Christmas tree."

"Piffle."

"Pish-tosh."

I glared at him harder. But it was no use. Sam was impervious. "Maybe Pa would like to sing in the chorus."

"He might. He has a pretty good voice, too."

Sam was right about that. My father liked to sing, and he did so with abandon around the house. Guess I'd inadvertently picked up the habit from him. *If* you wanted to believe Harold.

Just then Sam pulled his machine to a stop in front of our bungalow, so I dropped the argument. There was no point to it anyway.

However, because I was still peeved, I opened my own door and didn't wait for Sam to do it for me. A small rebellion, but it felt good—for about a second and a half, and then it only felt petty. Nuts. I couldn't win.

"Feel better now?" asked Sam as he walked me up the pathway to our porch. He knew I'd been rebelling, the rat.

"No."

All at once, a racket began in the front room of our house. Spike, the absolutely perfect black-and-tan dachshund I'd got to keep Billy company during his final years—I never admitted to myself that they were his final years, even though I knew in my heart they were—started barking as if the house were on fire. I loved Spike. He was not merely a darling, loyal, friendly, playful dog, but he was smart as a whip. Approximately a year and a half prior to that evening, I'd taken Spike to one of the Pasanita Dog Obedience Club's obedience classes. They were held in Brookside Park every Saturday morning for several weeks running during the summertime, and Spike had come in first in his class!

Thanks to Spike's greed, Pa and I had also taught him to add, subtract, multiply and divide. I'm only kind of kidding. I'd begun by asking him, "Spike, what's two plus two?" When Spike began barking, I'd make a big gesture when he barked four times and thrown him a piece of food—Mrs. Hanratty, the woman who taught Spike's obedience class, called these treats "bait"—and Spike would stop barking and grab his goodie. He'd become so good at spotting signals that by this time, I could barely wiggle my little finger, and Spike would stop barking at the appropriate time. I hadn't yet dazzled Sam with Spike's mathematical genius, but I'd do so one of these days. I was too mad at Sam that night to give him any treats. No matter how much he barked. So to speak.

I opened the front door and cried, "Spike!" I bent down and caught Spike as he leapt at me, happy to be with a being that didn't want anything from me but affection. Well, and food. "I'm so glad to be home!"

"Rough night?"

I looked up to see Pa smiling down upon my dog and me.

"Harold Kincaid is making her sing in an opera," said Sam by way of explanation.

Naturally, Pa looked puzzled.

I said, "He is not! Well, he's not *making* me. I just...well, I agreed to try out for a part in Gilbert and Sullivan's operetta, *The Mikado*. It's not an opera. It's an operetta, which is different, although I'm not sure how. He did apply a little pressure," I admitted because I saw Sam open his mouth and wanted to beat him to the punch.

"*The Mikado*? Isn't that the music you brought home from the library a couple of weeks ago? The one set in Japan?"

"That's the one, all right." I excused myself to Spike and rose from the floor. I did so with a grunt, and embarrassed myself, but that meal had been *huge*.

"That sounds like fun," said my father, grinning broadly. "You like to sing. You should do great."

"That's what Harold and Sam said. Mr. Finster's going to play the role of the Mikado." I thought of something and brightened minimally.

"Oh! Maybe Lucy Spinks can be in the play. That would make it not quite as awful as it might be."

We all, including Spike, strolled into the dining room and sat at the chairs surrounding the dining room table. Well, Spike sat on the floor, but we all took turns petting him. The dining room led to the kitchen, which led to my room. The other bedrooms were on the side opposite the kitchen, down a hallway. Aunt Vi had a darling little two-room suite upstairs. Our bungalow basically looked like a house with a very tiny other house on top of it. Several of Pasadena's bungalows did, too. Ours wasn't unusual or anything.

"I hope Spike didn't wake up Ma," I said, feeling guilty that I hadn't taught my dog better manners. Heck, if I could teach him arithmetic, I could surely teach him not to carry on so loudly when a family member came home from an evening out.

"You mother sleeps like a rock," said Pa. "And it's not that late. Heck, your aunt isn't even home yet."

"Good Lord, do you mean to tell me she's still working at the Pinkertons'? I thought they'd have had someone bring her home before now. The poor woman must have worked herself to death today!" I felt guilty, mainly because I should have asked Vi if she wanted to ride home with Sam and me.

"Don't work yourself into a lather, Daisy," said Pa. "Vi called about forty-five minute ago and said that Harold was going to drive her home soon."

Bless Harold's heart! "Oh, that's so nice of him!"

"He's a nice fellow," said Pa, who either didn't know or didn't care about Harold's...what would you call it? Eccentricity? Well, that's as good a word as any, I suppose.

Sam didn't have time to grunt a rebuttal, because Spike tore off to the front door again and began his "I'm so happy you're home" routine. I walked to the door, told Spike to hush, Spike hushed, and I opened the door. Vi all but fell into the house. Harold, who had accompanied her, winked at me and stepped into the house, too.

"Thank you again, Mrs. Gumm," said Harold as he walked Vi into the dining room, Spike cavorting at their heels.

"Stop thanking me, Harold Kincaid. You know I love putting on shindigs."

"Yes, but I'm afraid Mother about worked you to death over this one."

"It was for Daisy and Sam, and that made it all worthwhile," said my delightful aunt. Naturally her words made me feel even guiltier.

"Delicious meal, Mrs. Gumm," said Sam, who had stood when she came into the room, almost as if he were a real gentleman.

"My brother knew a good thing when he found it," said Pa, smiling fondly at Vi.

"Get along with you, Joe," said Vi, flapping a hand at my father. "I'm going to get myself a glass of water, and then I'm going to climb those stairs and might never wake up again."

"You'd better wake up again," I told her. "How would the family survive without you?"

"Well, *that's* the truth," said Vi. "Neither you nor your mother can cook a lick."

"Oh, I forgot!" Harold cried. And darned if he didn't dash to the front door, fling it open and hurry on outside.

"Don't worry," said Vi, taking note of our various startled expressions. "He's just going to carry in the box of leftovers I brought home. We can eat them for lunch and dinner tomorrow."

I know it's stupid—I was positively stuffed to the gills—but my mouth began to water. "Oh, Vi, thank you! I'm so glad!"

She laughed and marched to the kitchen. "I know you are, Daisy, but you really should thank the Pinkertons. They're the ones who paid for all of it. There's plenty, so we'll all eat well tomorrow. Mrs. Pinkerton gave me the day off."

Harold, huffing slightly as he carried in a large cardboard box from which emanated enticing aromas, said, "As well she should have. You worked like a slave for my mother, Mrs. Gumm. And for days and days, not just today."

"Your mother is a special woman, Harold. I enjoy my job, and I try to give satisfaction."

"You more than give satisfaction. You've helped my mother through almost as many rough patches as Daisy has."

With a chuckle, Vi appeared at the door between the kitchen and the dining room holding a glass of water. "I doubt that. Daisy has a special touch with hyst—er…with your mother."

"With hysterical women, you mean," said Harold with a knowing grin. "And indeed she does. She's going to be singing in light opera soon, too."

"Harold!" I frowned ferociously at him.

"I heard about that," said Vi.

I stared at her.

"Mrs. Pinkerton told me, sweetie. She said you'd be perfect for some part named after a cat."

"Katisha," said I, my voice sagging with doom.

"Strange name." Vi turned, took her glass to the sink, rinsed it out and set it on the counter. "Well, I'm off to bed. Sleep tight."

"Yeah," I said, feeling gloomy. "Don't let the bedbugs bite."

"Daisy!" said my formerly wonderful aunt. "The things you say."

"Good night," came a chorus from Harold, Pa and Sam.

Silence reigned for a moment or two as we watched my aunt open the door to the hallway and shut it behind her. We heard her heavy tread going up the staircase. She must have been awfully tired.

For that matter, so was I. Yawning, I said, "Thanks for coming with me, Sam. Even if you are on Harold's side."

"I'm on Harold's side, too, if he wants you to sing in the play," said Pa.

"Don't worry, Daisy. You'll be a spectacular Katisha." Sam winked at my father.

"Thanks. She's nasty, mean old witch."

"Perfect part for you," said Sam.

"Absolutely," said my father.

"Nuts to both of you. I'm going to bed." I stomped off to my room amid a chorus of masculine chuckles. Spike trotted at my feet. I could tell he was offended on my behalf. Well, I pretended he was, anyway.

I slept late on Wednesday morning, not rising from my warm and comfy bed until almost eight o'clock. When I grabbed a robe, shoved my feet into my tattered old slippers, and stumbled into the kitchen, I saw that Aunt Vi had also slept in. She stood at the stove in her own bathrobe, and had just lit a burner under the coffee pot. She glanced at me.

"Good morning, Daisy."

I wasn't ready to agree to anything yet, so I merely said, "Hi, Vi," and plunked myself on a chair at the kitchen table. A bowl of oranges sat perkily on the table, and I resented it. Why should those oranges be perky when I could barely open my eyes?

"Coffee will be ready soon. Would you like some eggs and toast?"

"You don't need to cook anything today, Vi. I can survive with some toast. I don't even burn it any longer, now that we have that keen electrical toaster."

"Nonsense. I like to cook. I guess your father and mother rose early. I'm sure Peggy's on her way to work, and I suppose Joe's taken Spike for a walk."

Startled, I glanced around the kitchen. Sure enough, no Spike wagged at me. "Shoot. I didn't even feel him jump off the bed."

"You were tired."

"Not nearly as tired as you."

"Pooh. I'm used to cooking for armies."

"Hmm."

I'd probably have thought of something more cogent to say to my excellent aunt, but at that moment the telephone on the kitchen wall started ringing. I turned my head and scowled at the instrument of torture. The ring belonged to our household. In those days, telephone rings were doled out individually. Ours was two long rings and a short one. Nuts. That stupid 'phone never rang in the morning unless Mrs. Pinkerton was on the other end of the wire—and I'd just left her house last night! Surely she couldn't have encountered a crisis this early on the day after her very own dinner party. Could she?

Thinking back over my long acquaintanceship with Mrs. Pinkerton, I knew it was entirely possible for a crisis to have arisen in her life overnight. She attracted crises like flowers attract bees. With a grunt, I shoved myself up onto my slippered feet and trudged to the 'phone.

It took a great effort of will to assume my low, soothing spiritualist's voice when I lifted the ear piece, stuck it to my ear, and said into the receiver, "Gumm-Majesty residence. Mrs. Majesty speaking."

"Daisy!"

I closed my eyes and prayed for patience. "Good morning, Mrs. Pinkerton. I'm surprised you're up and about so early this morning after that swell party you put on last night."

"Well, I'm just so excited, you see!" She was all but burbling. Generally when she called me, she wailed with distress. This sounded like a burble of pleasure. Instantly, I suspected *The Mikado*.

"Oh, but Harold told me you've agreed to play the part of Katisha, and I'm *so* thrilled!"

Darn and heck, I'd done no such thing! Feeling pressured and aggrieved, I yet held onto my spiritualist's voice. "I agreed to try out for the part," I said soothingly. Not that she needed soothing. I was the one with the ruffled feathers.

"Nonsense, dear. I know you'll be a perfect Katisha."

I paused for a couple of seconds, afraid that if I spoke, I'd shriek. After I knew I had myself under control, I purred mildly, "We'll see."

"Mr. Hostetter will tell you all about it at your choir rehearsal tomorrow night. I'm so excited about this!"

She even knew when I had choir rehearsal? Maybe I should change my name and move somewhere else. Somewhere far, far away from Mrs. Pinkerton. I'd liked Turkey. Maybe I should move to Constantinople. I could probably learn the language pretty easily, and Turkey was a pretty nice place. I'd visited it once, with Harold. Except for being sick and pursued by villains, I'd kind of enjoyed myself. The food there was really good.

But no. Mrs. Pinkerton had been my best client ever since I began my spiritualist career. Besides, I couldn't leave my family. "I'll be interested to get all the details from him tomorrow, then," said I.

"This is going to be so exciting!" And she rang off.

I carefully replaced the receiver and turned to find my aunt looking upon me with trepidation.

"Daisy..."

"Don't worry, Vi. I'm not going to holler or throw anything."

"Mrs. Pinkerton can be a trial sometimes."

"*Sometimes!*" Very well, so I'd just lied to my aunt and hollered. "That blasted woman is determined to ruin my *life*!"

Vi opened her mouth, thought better of speaking, shut her mouth again, and turned back to the stove.

I plunked myself down at the kitchen table once more and buried my head in my arms. Only when Vi placed a plate filled with bacon, eggs, and toast in front of me, did I decide I might as well bow to the inevitable.

"Thanks, Vi."

Boy, was I ever going to tell Mr. Hostetter what I thought of people planning my life for me tomorrow night!

FIVE

But I didn't get the chance.

As soon as I walked through the door to the choir room at church on Thursday evening at seven, Mr. Hostetter rushed over to me, all atwitter. Mr. Hostetter isn't generally a twitterer.

"Mrs. Majesty!" he cried, sounding extremely happy. "I understand you've agreed to play the role of Katisha. May I say I'm absolutely thrilled. *Thrilled* that you'll be performing in the operetta. I've been wanting to use you as a soloist for the longest time, but I wasn't sure you were ready."

"I'm not," I said.

He didn't seem to notice.

"The Van der Lindens are here this evening, and after rehearsal, you and I can speak with them. There may be other choir members who'd like to try out for parts. I know George Finster has taken a bass role."

He didn't seem to be listening to me, but I spoke anyway, "How about Lucy Spinks?"

His rather small eyes went round. "Miss Spinks? Why, certainly! She has a…nice soprano voice. Perhaps she could be one of the schoolgirls."

"Yes, that's what I thought." The song, "Three Little Maids from

33

School," was one of the perkiest ones in the whole operetta. While I didn't resent perkiness that evening as much as I had the morning before, it still irked me. Worse, "Three Little Maids from School" was one of the songs I liked best in *The Mikado*. I'd sung it at home to my own accompaniment on the piano and had rued my fate to exist in this life as an alto and not a soprano. Now I was sorry I could sing at all.

"Well, come along. Let's rehearse quickly, and then we'll discuss the operetta," said Mr. Hostetter, all but rubbing his hands with glee.

Shoot, I hadn't known the First Methodist-Episcopal Church (North) in Pasadena, California, harbored a repressed actor in our choir director until that very moment. Nevertheless, I followed him to the choir's nook behind the pulpit on the chancel and looked into the sanctuary. Sure enough, there sat Mr. and Mrs. Van der Linden, Harold, and...good Lord. Was that Mrs. Lippincott? I squinted a little harder—the main sanctuary lights weren't on—and saw that it was, indeed, Mrs. Lippincott, and she appeared as bored and languid as the last time I'd seen her. Oh, joy.

I walked back to my own personal chair, the one reserved for me among the altos, and sat, feeling peevish. Not Mr. Hostetter. He looked as if his butt had landed in the butter tub. That's one of Aunt Vi's expressions. Not quite sure what it means, but I can speculate.

He tapped his baton on his music stand and cleared his throat. Loudly. "Ladies and gentlemen, we're going to have a rather short rehearsal this evening. We've sung our Sunday's anthem before, and we've worked on next week's for a couple of weeks now, so we don't need to practice too much. There's something else I need to discuss with you after rehearsal." He smiled broadly at his choir.

So we only went through our anthem, "Praise to the Lord, the Almighty," twice. That's one of my most favorite hymns, even though it was written by a German. He was long-ago German, however, and had had nothing whatsoever to do with Kaiser Bill. Then we sang our next week's anthem, "It is Well with My Soul," only once. That's another goodie, but we aren't here to talk about hymns. Darn it.

After Mr. Hostetter had rushed us through those two hymns, he told us to look up Sunday's hymns in our hymnals so that we'd be prepared when we gathered on the Sabbath. Then he said, "And now, it is my great pleasure to introduce you to Mr. Max Van der Linden, who will explain why he and his group are here with us tonight."

So he did, and Mr. Van der Linden did, and all heck broke loose in our choir alcove. Actually, by that time we'd spread out onto the chancel. I decided to heck with it, and went into the sanctuary to sit with Harold. Mrs. Lippincott sat next to him on his other side and gave me a languorous smile.

"Good evening, Mrs. Majesty," said she.

"Good evening, Mrs. Lippincott," said I.

Then I turned to Harold. "You know, Harold Kincaid, I think it's mighty rotten of you to go behind my back, to my own *choir director*, for Pete's sake, and drag me into singing in an operetta I don't want to sing in." I sat back on the pew and crossed my arms over my chest.

"Nuts. You'll be great. Anyhow, Hostetter is beside himself with glee. Look at him." Harold gestured to the chancel, and I saw he was right. I'd never seen Mr. Hostetter look so happy.

"Huh," I grumbled, sounding a good deal like Sam.

"Oh, get over it, Daisy. It'll be fun, and you know it. Won't it, Gloria?"

He'd asked the last question of Mrs. Lippincott, so I guess her first name was Gloria.

"I believe it will be fun, yes," she said.

"What part will you be playing, Mrs. Lippincott?" I asked. Then I was irked with myself. I didn't want to talk to that woman about *The Mikado* or anything else.

"I'm Pitti-Sing, one of Harold's wards. Well, Ko-Ko, I mean, since that's the role he'll be playing."

"I see."

I glared at the commotion going on in my church and felt almost betrayed. Perhaps I'm not the most sanctimonious of human beings on this earth, but to bring a musical comedy into church seemed…I don't know. Blasphemous or something. I was probably just being grouchy.

Harold nudged my shoulder. "You're just being grouchy, Daisy. It'll be fun, and you know it. Besides, it's for a good cause."

How come he always knew what I was thinking? Bother.

"What good cause?" I asked, but Harold didn't have time to answer.

"Mrs. Majesty!"

I jerked to attention and saw Mr. Hostetter gesturing for me to join the choir members and the Van der Lindens on the chancel. Or onstage, I guess I should call it at this point. So I did, my feet dragging slightly.

"Good evening, Mrs. Majesty!" Mrs. Van der Linden sounded and looked just as sweet as she had at Mrs. Pinkerton's party. If I didn't watch myself, I might end up liking her.

What a stupid thing to say! Chalk it up to my mood.

"Good evening, Mrs. Van der Linden."

"Oh, call me Connie. Please!" She appeared a little pale that evening, but maybe that was because of the lighting, of which there wasn't much.

Huh. "Thank you. Please call me Daisy."

"Mr. Van der Linden is going to play for us at the piano," said Mr. Hostetter.

I instantly glanced at the piano, prepared to see Mrs. Fleming, our organist/pianist, in a snit. But no. She seemed as smiling and happy as the rest of the choir. Either they were right and I was wrong, or I just didn't want to give up a good grump.

Mr. Hostetter went on, "And we'll have various choir members sing various parts in the operetta."

"Lucy should try out for one of the three little maids," I said instantly. I glanced at Lucy and found her blushing madly. She'd recently become engaged, and I noticed that, as she pressed her hands to her cheeks, she made sure the one with the diamond was foremost. Well, I didn't blame her.

"Very good idea. I understand the role of Pitti-Sing has already been assigned, so why don't you, Miss Spinks, sing from the libretto. You can take...ah..." Mr. Hostetter flipped madly through the libretto. "Ah, yes. You may sing Peep-Bo. Mrs. Van der Linden will sing with you, to give us an idea of how you'll sound together."

So Lucy stepped up, stopped blushing, took the libretto, waited for Mr. Van der Linden to strike a few chords, and she and Mrs. V took off singing. They sounded good together. I could definitely more easily feature the two of them as innocent schoolgirls than I could Gloria Lippincott.

"Excellent," said Mr. Hostetter, going so far as to clap his hands. "Er, what do you think, Mrs. Van der Linden?"

"I think Miss Spinks will make an excellent Peep-Bo," said Connie. That was nice.

Try-outs went on, and pretty much all of the members of the choir who wanted to were tapped to play various roles, most of them in the chorus. They all seemed pleased.

"And now if Harold Kincaid will come up onto the chancel, I'd like to hear him sing with you, Mrs. Majesty. You spend a good deal of time together onstage. I want to make sure you look and sound as good together as I think you will." This, from Max Van der Linden.

Harold, the rat, leapt to his feet and charged to the chancel, taking the steps two at a time. He was *such* a ham.

I heaved a sigh that was probably bigger than I was. "I haven't even looked at the libretto yet. Well, not since I checked it out from the library, and that was over a month ago."

"Not to worry," said Harold. "Here you go. I got one especially for you. I even marked Katisha's part for you."

"How kind of you," I said in a monotone.

"Heck, *I'm* Ko-Ko, the Lord High Executioner. I can do anything."

I only looked at him. But I did take the libretto. He'd opened it to Katisha's first scene, the one in which she interrupts Nanki-Poo and Yum-Yum, the two leads, and tries to spoil their fun.

"This looks high to me," I said, frowning at the libretto. I glanced at the back of the booklet. "Hey, it says here Katisha is a soprano! I thought somebody said the part was in my voice range."

"Don't worry about what the libretto says," said Mr. Van der Linden from the piano bench. "The part is generally sung by a contralto."

"And I can sing contralto?" I asked, confused.

"You are one, Daisy," said Harold, the rat. "We've been over this before. I've heard you sing. Contraltos are altos in disguise."

"I'll already be in disguise, as a nasty Japanese witch." Yes, I was being snide. I didn't want to be there, doing what we were doing. It didn't matter. Everyone was out to over-rule me that evening.

"You can either sing it as a mezzo or a contralto. You can sing an octave lower than the score if you want to," said Max—he hadn't said I could call him Max, but what the heck.

"But I *don't* want to!" I cried piteously.

"Nonsense. You'll be great, Daisy," said Harold.

Nothing mattered. At least nothing having to do with *me* mattered. By the time I finally managed to creep away from the church, it was ten o'clock at night—choir rehearsals generally ran from seven to nine— and rehearsals for *The Mikado* were scheduled to begin on the coming Saturday.

At least Spike was awake to greet me when I dragged myself into the house. Everyone else had gone happily to bed.

Phooey.

Saturday arrived, as it had a habit of doing. I wasn't happy to greet the day. Nevertheless, because I knew where my duty lay, after eating breakfast and tidying the kitchen, I took Spike for a quick walk (my father came, too) and headed to the church. "Eager" wasn't even on the list of emotions I entertained that morning.

I didn't want to sing in the stupid operetta. I did wear my juju, figuring I needed all the help I could get.

Gloria Lippincott had a glorious voice, so I guess her name was appropriate. I still hadn't taken to her by the end of our first rehearsal, although I was certainly getting into my part. For more than half my life, I'd pretended to be the sober, serene, slightly mysterious spiritualist-medium. But boy, the role of Katisha brought out a whole 'nother me. I enjoyed it, too.

We practiced my first entrance, which came just as Nanki-Poo (Mr. Van der Linden) and Yum-Yum (Mrs. Van der Linden) were celebrating their undying love for each other (and a month's worth of marriage before they both died, but never mind that detail). I stepped from the sidelines, held up the arm that wasn't holding the score, and sang as loudly as I could, "'Your revels cease! Assist me, all of you!'"

Connie and Max leapt apart as if the hand of God had separated them. They were wonderful in their parts. I assumed they'd played them before. They both cringed away from me as if I were a witch. I could get used to having this much power over people. Too bad it was all make-believe.

The chorus sang, "'Why, who is this whose evil eyes rain blight on our festivities?'"

And I sang, "'I claim my perjured lover, Nanki-Poo! Oh, fool! to shun delights that never cloy!'"

And on it went. We fumbled around quite a bit, but it *was* only our first rehearsal. The contralto part was perfect for my alto self. A mezzo-soprano is a notch lower than a coloratura soprano, if anybody cares, and a contralto is, as Harold said, what the hoity-toity opera aficionados call an alto. At least I didn't have to sing the part an octave lower than the score. It is, however, a good thing that old Katti was a contralto and not a mezzo, or I'd probably have collapsed.

Harold made a superb Ko-Ko, the Lord High Executioner. He reveled in his part, and when he sang "I Have a Little List," everyone laughed.

Our first rehearsal had begun at ten a.m. It was now a little past one, and I was hungry. I was gathering up my score and my coat and hat, aiming to head home, eat something, and take a nap if I was lucky, when Harold stopped me.

"You were wonderful, Daisy."

"Thank you. So were you, Harold."

"I honestly didn't know you could sing that well."

I gave him an evil-eyed squint. "Then you lied to your friends."

"Don't be nasty. I do believe you're taking this role to heart."

"It's fun being unpleasant," I said. And I meant it. I'd never been cruel before.

"I've always found it fun to be unkind," he said, smirking.

"You said this operetta is for a good cause. What's the good cause?"

"Besides giving the Van der Lindens a step up in their effort to establish a local operatic ensemble, the proceeds of this particular operetta will go to Belgian war orphans."

"Hmm. I guess that's a good cause."

"The best. Don't forget what those nasty Germans did to Belgium."

I glowered my gloweriest glower at Harold. "How could I *ever* forget what those nasty Germans did to anyone, Harold Kincaid?"

"Oops. Sorry, Daisy. I know the war's aftermath was hard on you."

I humphed. "It was a lot harder on Billy."

Harold cleared his throat, then said, "You're being a good sport, Daisy. But I want to talk to you about something. How about I buy you a sandwich and an ice-cream soda, and we can chat over luncheon at the counter at the Rexall."

This time I gave him a real stink-eye. "What are you talking about, Harold Kincaid? If you've lured me into singing in this stupid operetta under false pretences, I'll...I'll...well, I don't know what I'll do, but you won't like it."

He grinned. "Nonsense. You know me better than that."

"I don't, either. I don't trust you. You've tricked me before."

"I have not."

Casting my gaze to the ceiling, I thought about that. Had he tricked me before? He'd shot a man in Turkey in order to rescue Sam from some nasty kidnappers. I guess I still owed him for that.

Nuts.

"Oh, very well, but I'm not going to do anything else I don't want to do for you."

"You won't have to. Come with me. We'll hit the drug store."

"I'd rather not. Hit it, I mean."

"Funny."

I'd walked to the church for rehearsal, since it was only a few blocks north of where I lived, but Harold had his Stutz Bearcat with him, so we rode in that to the Rexall Drug Store on Colorado near Marengo. The day was a cold one, and he'd put the top up on his machine. I was still cold, however, when he found a place to park his car, and we got out and huddled in our coats and hats into the drug store.

When we'd made it to the counter and sat, I said, "I'm too cold for ice cream. I want a cup of cocoa." I thought about food for a minute, looked at the sandwich menu chalked on the blackboard behind the counter then added, "And a chicken-and-almond sandwich."

"Sounds good to me, although I think I'll take a roast beef sandwich with horseradish." When the soda jerk appeared, Harold said, "Two hot cocoas. Heavy on the whipped cream. One chicken-and-almond sandwich for the lady, and a roast-beef sandwich with horseradish for me."

"Coming right up," said the counter boy, and he loped off to fill our orders.

"Now, what's up that you need to talk to me about, Harold? I'm not sure I want to know."

"Gloria Lippincott thinks somebody is trying to kill her."

After goggling at Harold for at least thirty seconds, I said, "I *knew* I wouldn't want to know!"

He only chuckled, the soda jerk set steaming mugs before us, and Harold began to explain. Evidently Mr. and Mrs. Lippincott didn't get along. Mr. Lippincott, according to his missus, had begun an affair with a married lady in the upper realms of Pasadena's society. Mrs. Lippincott claimed her husband didn't believe in divorce, and that he'd been trying to kill her through various despicable means. Clearly, he hadn't yet succeeded.

"What about her? She's a definite flirt. Has she had any affairs?"

"Darned if I know. I also don't know if it matters. She still claims someone is trying to kill her."

Hmm. I'll admit here that I didn't much care for Mrs. Lippincott, mainly because she was pretending to be bored and languid and...well, not my type of person, but I thought murdering her might be an excessive reaction to a nominally unpleasant personality. I said, "Hmm." I sipped my cocoa thoughtfully, and had come to no firm conclusion about anything before the soda jerk reappeared and set our sandwiches before us.

I ate as thoughtfully as I'd drunk my cocoa, and after a couple of bites I said, "What do you think I can do about Mrs. Lippincott's suspicions? I'm not a bodyguard, I'm not a policeman, and I'm not a private detective or a food taster. If she really thinks her estranged husband is out to get her, she should call on somebody else. Like the police. I'm only a phony spiritualist."

"She doesn't want to call attention to her suspicions."

"That's stupid."

With a shrug, Harold said, "Maybe, but she still won't call the authorities or a private investigator. However, you're a keen observer."

He was dead wrong about that. I never observed anything. "That's rubbish. Things can happen right in front of me, and I won't even notice." I shuddered, remembering an incident in which someone had leaned out of a car window and taken a potshot at me. I guess I'd observed him, but it was at the very last minute. If I'd been a split-second slower, I'd have been left bleeding on the sidewalk. "Anyhow, if he wants to get rid of her so badly he'd pay somebody to kill her, wouldn't divorce be cheaper?"

"Probably not. Maybe he doesn't want to pay alimony or something. If she dies, he won't have to."

"Hmm."

Harold patted the hand not holding the sandwich. It was pretty darned good, that sandwich. I'd never have thought about mixing toasted, chopped almonds into a chicken sandwich filling on my own.

"Anyhow, what about her? She doesn't seem like the innocent maiden to me. Maybe her husband doesn't want her infidelities to get out any more than he wants his to."

With a shrug, Harold said, "I don't know. I doubt that Gloria is pure as the driven snow, but from what she's told me about her husband, he's a real poop."

"Nuts. I don't want to do any snooping."

"Dear Daisy. Don't fret. Just keep your eyes and ears open and let me know if you see or hear anything you think is strange."

"Heck, Harold, I think singing in an operetta is strange."

He only laughed again. He should have known better.

SIX

Pa and Spike were there to greet me when Harold dropped me off in front of our Marengo bungalow. I pretty much staggered into the house, more tired than I could remember being in a long, long time. Singing in an operetta takes a lot more out of a person than singing in a church choir does. And here I'd always thought of myself as a lowly alto, but I was actually a bona fide contralto. Would wonders never cease?

As I knelt to greet my darling dog, my father smiled benevolently upon the both of us. "How'd rehearsal go? I expected you home before this time."

I got creakily to my feet. "Harold took me to lunch at the Rexall drugstore. It's cold out there." I shivered.

"That was nice of him. Both your aunt and your mother are taking naps. You look bushed, too, Daisy. I was going to ask if you want to take an s-t-r-o-l-l with the d-o-g, but I think you need your rest first."

"I'd love to go for an s-t-r-o-l-l after I nap a bit, Pa." That wasn't much of a lie. At the moment, I wanted to fall down right where I was and sleep for a hundred years, but I knew my state of exhaustion wouldn't last. Heck, most of it was due to strain and not lack of sleep

43

anyway. Doing new things—like singing a contralto role in a Gilbert and Sullivan operetta—always takes more energy than one expects it to.

So Spike and I headed for my bedroom, I removed my clothes, donned an old, worn-out day dress, and flopped onto the bed. Spike jumped up to join me, and the two of us snoozed contentedly for an hour and a half. My eyes opened at last, and when I looked at my bedside clock, I saw it was 3:30. Yawning, I decided that left time enough to go for a walk with Pa and Spike before I had to set the table for dinner.

So I put on heavy socks and shoes, pulled on an old, lumpy, stretched-out cardigan sweater, and grabbed my warmest coat and an old felt cloche hat that I could pull down to cover my ears, and grabbed my gloves. Spike and I exited the bedroom...

And ran smack into Sam Rotondo chatting at the kitchen table with my father! And me, looking like a war refugee! Darn it all, anyhow!

Pa and Sam glanced up, and I swear I saw Sam's lips twitch.

"I see you're awake," said Pa mildly.

"Yes," I said. Then, glaring at Sam, I demanded, "What are you doing here?"

He stopped trying to hide his amusement and grinned at me. "Just wanted to find out how your first rehearsal went."

"It was all right," I said, sounding sullen.

But really. It wasn't that I wanted to look *good* for Sam. I only just wanted to look...not like I'd grabbed my outfit from a ragbag. If you know what I mean.

Sam eyed my gloves and hat. "Going somewhere?"

"Pa and I were going to take Spike for a—" I caught myself before I could say the word *walk*. Spike knew that word. "A ramble around the neighborhood."

But Spike wasn't fooled. I think he caught on to the "take Spike for" part. He woofed, wagged, and raced over to where his leash hung from a hook on the service porch. Smart dog, Spike.

"Mind if I tag along?" asked Sam, sounding deceptively pleasant.

I squinted at him, but didn't detect any subterfuge. Then again, I've already admitted I'm not a keen observer. I said, "Sure. The more, the merrier."

"Maybe I should just stay here today," said Pa.

"No you don't!" I all but yelled at him. "You're the one who said you wanted to take Spike out in the first place!"

My father held up his hands, as if in surrender. "Very well. Very well. Just…thought I'd see if you'd give me a reprieve from the cold, cruel world."

"Nuts. It's not *that* cold out." Actually, it was, but I'd never admit it.

So Sam and Pa and I and a deliriously happy Spike, who never minded what the weather was like, left our house via the side entrance, and walked down to Belvedere, around the block, and came back to our house. I don't know about the men and Spike, but I was darned near frozen by the time we got back home. And I was dressed for winter in Siberia, for Pete's sake.

Naturally, Sam stayed for dinner that night. Sam very nearly always stayed to dinner when someone asked him to. This time it was Vi, who was up and about and preparing some kind of feast for our dining pleasure. We Gumms and Majestys—well, I was the only Majesty left by that time—always dined at six p.m. We weren't posh.

Before I set the table, I hurried to my room and put on a more suitable day dress, stockings and low-heeled shoes. I even brushed my hair. I didn't mind walking around the neighborhood bundled to the teeth, but I didn't want Sam to think I dressed like that often. Not, of course, that I cared what he thought of me.

Oh, very well, that's a flat-out lie. I *did* care what he thought of me. I just didn't want to.

Dinner that night was delicious. Everything Vi makes is wonderful. That night we had roast chicken and mashed potatoes.

"I love these mashed potatoes, Vi," I said, as I munched on a forkful of them contentedly. "They taste a little different tonight. Really, really good."

"I put some cream cheese in with the butter and mashed everything up together with a clove of chopped garlic."

I lifted my head and stared at my aunt, awe-stricken by her creativity. "Goodness gracious, Vi. You're a genius in the kitchen. I love everything you make."

"I know you do, sweetie. How did your first rehearsal go?"

"Oh, yes!" cried my mother, who worked half days on Saturdays at the Hotel Marengo. "Was it difficult for you to sing that part? Was it too low for you?" She frowned. "Or do I mean too high?"

"The role of Katisha," said I, as if I knew what I was talking about, "traditionally is sung by a mezzo-soprano or a contralto. Mr. Van der Linden, our director, who plays the role of Nanki-Poo, the hero of the story, told me I could sing it as a contralto, which is lower than a soprano. So far it seems to be perfect for my voice range. According to Harold, contraltos and altos are basically the same."

Ma blinked at me. Not the most imaginative woman in the world, my mother, but a dear soul. Plus, she was good at mathematics, which, in my book, makes her a certified brain. Algebra in high school had just about done me in. "Why do they call you an alto in church if you're a contralto?"

"Beats me," I said in all honesty.

"When's your next rehearsal?" asked Sam.

"Tuesday evening. Seven to nine." Then I looked at him, suspicion clouding my mind. "Why?"

"No reason. Just wondered, was all."

Hmm. I wasn't sure I trusted this meek demeanor of his. Had he heard about the domestic trauma extant between the Lippincotts?

"I was thinking, if I got off work early enough, I'd like to see a rehearsal or two," he added.

"That would be fun!" exclaimed my mild-mannered mother, surprising me. "Perhaps we can all go."

"I'd enjoy that," said Vi.

"Me, too," said Pa.

Aw, criminy. "I'd rather you wait a while. We're just learning our roles, and we don't have the blocking down yet." A feeling of panic began to gnaw at my innards. I didn't want Sam Rotondo to see me making a fool of myself, darn it!

"What is blocking?" asked my mother. Good question.

"Blocking is determining where everyone will stand on the stage, and where to move and when."

"Oh." Ma shrugged. "Wonder why they call it blocking."

"I have no earthly idea," I told her in all honesty.

The telephone rang before I could think of any good reasons for my family and Sam not to watch our rehearsal on Tuesday night. Bother. Because the telephone was almost always for me, I got up from my roasted chicken and mashed potatoes (with cream cheese, butter and garlic, by golly) and gravy, walked into the kitchen, and picked up the receiver.

"Gumm-Majesty residence. Mrs. Majesty speaking."

"Daisy, Gloria just called me. She's hysterical. She said somebody tried to run her down when she went to Nash's Department Store after rehearsal." Harold sounded quite rattled.

I was silent for a couple of seconds, then said, "Why is she calling you about her problems? Are you bosom buddies or something?"

"No! I scarcely know the woman! She just seems to have attached herself to me as a sounding board. And she just called to tell me someone tried to run her down!" I could almost see Harold wiping his brow with his handkerchief.

Nuts.

"And you're telling me this because…because…Why? What do you think I can do about it? For that matter, what does she think *you* can do about it? She should telephone the coppers if she thinks somebody tried to run her down, whether she wants to or not."

"I know, I know." Now Harold sounded harried. Harold Kincaid didn't care for ructions in his routine. Can't say as I could fault him for that, especially if they were as idiotic as this one seemed to be. "But she begged me to help her."

"Oh? And how do you aim to do that?" I'll admit my voice held a hint of acid.

"I'm calling you," said Harold. Before I could point out the futility, not to mention the idiocy, of his action, he said, "Which is stupid, isn't it?"

"Yes. It is."

"Sorry, Daisy. I don't know why Gloria's got me so upset about her problems."

"I don't, either."

"You were probably eating dinner, weren't you?"

"Yes. We dine early. We're peasants."

Harold laughed and said, "I'm sorry to have disturbed you. I think I'm going to have to tell Gloria she needs to hire a private eye."

"That's the best idea you've had in days, Harold Kincaid."

"Don't be snide, Daisy. You're supposed to be a soothing spiritualist, remember?"

"I remember." In my most syrupy voice, I repeated, "That's the best idea you've had in days, Harold Kincaid."

Harold gave another bark of laughter and hung up his receiver. I did the same at my end of the wire and went back to the dinner table. I must have looked annoyed, because Pa said, "Something wrong, sweetie?"

With a sigh, I sat at my place and picked up my fork. "Not really. Just Harold. He...he wanted me to help him with something I can't help him with. If that makes any sense."

"My goodness," said Vi. Harold was one of Vi's special pets. Kind of like Sam, actually, drat it. "What's the matter with the dear boy?"

"Nothing's the matter with him," I said after swallowing. My mother scolds me if I talk with my mouth full.

"Then why'd he call?" Sam. The detective. Rats.

"To ask if I could help him with a problem. I can't."

"What problem?"

I eyed Sam without benevolence. "It's nothing, Sam. It concerns another person entirely, and I don't even know why Harold asked for my help to begin with. There's nothing I can do for the person in question."

"My goodness. You sound very mysterious," said my mother.

"I don't mean to be. But Harold said the other person doesn't want a lot of people to know about this problem."

Ma sniffed. "It's not as if we're in daily contact with people like the Pinkertons. Well, *you* are, Daisy, but the rest of us sure aren't."

"Ain't *that* the truth?" said Pa. In case you wondered, the only time he ever uses the word "ain't" is when he's making that particular comment.

"Me, neither," said Vi. "I see Mrs. Pinkerton every now and then, and Harold more often, but they're the only rich folks I talk to on a regular basis."

"True, but I promised Harold," I said, feeling beleaguered.

Then I thought about what I'd just said. *Had* I promised Harold I wouldn't mention Gloria Lippincott's perceived problem to anyone? Pondering our conversations at the Rexall drug counter and recently on the telephone, I realized I hadn't promised him a darned thing. I'd told him I was unable to help him, why, and hadn't said anything about not telling anyone. So I decided what the heck and said, "Gloria Lippincott thinks her estranged husband is trying to kill her. That's what Harold's call was about. She thinks somebody tried to run her down outside Nash's Dry Goods and Department Store after rehearsal today."

If you ever want to stop a conversation dead in its tracks, drop a comment like that before the assembled guests. Everyone at the table sat as if suddenly turned to marble, forks, knives or spoons suspended, and stared at me.

I stared back and smiled at them all.

Then I ate more chicken.

SEVEN

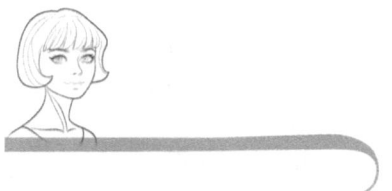

Because I knew he'd make me if I didn't offer on my own, I walked Sam out to his big old Hudson after he and Pa played a few rounds of gin rummy while Ma and I cleaned up the dinner dishes. Vi didn't have to clean up, since she was the cook.

"Damnation, why do people always go to you with their problems?" Sam demanded furiously. Before I could answer, he held up a hand. "I know. I know. Because you're nicer than I am."

"Precisely. However, I told Harold I couldn't do a darned thing for Mrs. Lippincott, and I don't aim to get involved in her problems, so you needn't lecture me, Sam."

"For once," he grumbled.

"Unfair, Sam Rotondo."

"Huh. You always involve yourself in things that are none of your business."

"I have never," I said sternly, "become involved in anything that didn't directly concern me, and you know it!"

"Huh."

"Oh, nuts to you!" I whirled around, but was thwarted in my intent to storm back into the house—it was cold out there, darn it—by a pair

50

of big hands clamping down on my shoulders and spinning me around again.

"I mean it, Daisy. If you see anything at all that looks as if this Lippincott dame might really be in trouble, I want you to tell me about it. All right?"

Although I wasn't pleased to have been manhandled, I agreed with Sam's sentiment on this subject. "All right with me."

"Promise?"

"Promise. I already told Harold she should call the police."

And to my utter astonishment, Sam Rotondo bent down and gave me a quick kiss. On the lips. It felt good.

I stood there, stunned, my fingers pressed to my mouth as his Hudson roared to life. Then Sam tootled on down the street, turned left at the next corner, and, I'm sure, aimed to turn right on Los Robles Avenue. He lived in an adorable little row of courts on Los Robles.

Sam had kissed me.

Sam had kissed *me*.

Goodness gracious sakes alive, as Vi sometimes said. I more or less floated back to the house.

———

On Wednesday morning, I had an appointment for a Ouija-board session with Mrs. Bissel, probably my second-best client, and one of my favorites because she'd given me Spike. Mrs. Bissel lived in a big house on many acres of land in Altadena, a little townlet just north of Pasadena, smack up against the San Gabriel foothills. Her mansion sat more or less on the corner of Foothill Boulevard and Maiden Lane.

Mrs. Bissel breeds and "shows" dachshunds. That means she takes one or more of the dogs she breeds and enters them into dog shows in various places. The height of her ambition is someday to have one of her hounds entered into the Westminster Kennel Club Dog Show in New York City, which is evidently the cat's pajamas of dog shows. To each her own. The height of *my* ambition was to continue making a decent living for my family and me.

Mrs. Bissel's houseboy, Keiji Saito, greeted me at the back door.

Mind you, Mrs. Bissel wouldn't have minded if I'd come to the front door, but in order to do that I'd have had to park on Foothill Boulevard and walk the approximately half-mile from Foothill to her house, up the terraced lawn. It was easier to park in her gigantic circular driveway in the back of her house. A big monkey-puzzle tree sat in the middle of the circle. I don't know if you're familiar with monkey-puzzle trees, but they're odd-looking specimens, and their leaves are spiky and hurt like the devil if you accidently step on one. Their bark looks kind of like the pieces of a jigsaw puzzle, which I guess is how they got their name.

"Good morning, Keiji," I greeted him warmly. I liked Keiji a lot. He'd taught me how to use chopsticks a few months before, and I'd awed my family when we'd gone to dine at Miyako's Japanese Restaurant once.

"Good morning, Mrs. Majesty," said he in his turn.

"Daisy," I reminded him. Heck, if he was Keiji to me, I could be Daisy to him. It was only fair.

He grinned. "Daisy."

"Is Mrs. Bissel ready for me?" I stripped off my gloves and stuffed them into a pocket of my heavy woolen coat, which I'd sewn myself from a bolt end I'd found at Maxime's Fabrics on Colorado Boulevard. After I'd made the coat, I'd decided I'd make a really crummy sheep, because the wool itched like mad. However, the coat was warm, so I used it. But that's beside the point. I handed my coat and hat to Keiji, and he took care of them for me.

"She certainly is. She's in her sitting room upstairs."

"All right. Thanks."

I loved Mrs. Bissel's house. In truth, I enjoyed most of the glorious homes my clients owned. While I lived in a modest bungalow on South Marengo Avenue, which was a nice little house in a friendly neighborhood and perfect for my family, my clients lived in palaces. Mrs. Bissel's personal palace had suites of rooms upstairs, each one complete with a bedroom or two, a bathroom, a dressing room, a sitting room, and maybe a couple of other rooms. Oh, and a huge closet. Heck, the place even had a suite of rooms off the kitchen for the cook and her husband to use.

Must be nice. On the other hand, it must be expensive to maintain. On the whole, I was happy with our bungalow.

Mrs. Bissel wasn't as nervy and excitable as Mrs. Pinkerton. Perhaps that's because she had a bunch of dachshunds to keep her company. I didn't hear any barks coming from upstairs, so I presumed the dogs were in their kennels out back near the stable-turned-garage. The kennel, if anyone is interested, is heated. I swear…But never mind.

I climbed the stairs and knocked lightly on the open door of Mrs. B's sitting room. It was a pleasant room, with a fireplace in full roar on this raw October day, and built-in bookcases lining the walls. The mantelpiece held pictures of Mrs. Bissel's late husband and her grown children and lots and lots of dachshunds. Some of them looked like Spike, and I smiled.

"Good morning, Daisy!" said Mrs. Bissel, coming forward to greet me. She never attempted to run me down, as Mrs. Pinkerton did. Well, Mrs. Pinkerton didn't *mean* to run me down. It's only that she's a large woman and generally in thrall to some emotion or other.

"Good morning, Mrs. Bissel. It's cold out there. Your fireplace is lovely and welcome today."

"Thank you, dear. Please, have a seat over here." She gestured to a card table someone, probably Keiji, had set up at the window-end of her sitting room, which overlooked her rolling front lawn. Two chairs had been placed on either side of the table.

I gazed out the windows at her yard for a moment before saying, "Your grounds are beautiful, Mrs. Bissel." Generally, I entered Mrs. Bissel's house via the back door, so I didn't get to see her front yard—or front acreage—very often.

"Thank you, dear. They aren't as extensive as some, but I do enjoy the bird of paradise plants in front of the porch when they bloom."

"Yes, indeed. That bird of paradise you gave us is thriving."

"I'm so glad to hear it. How's Spike doing?"

I turned and smiled broadly at the dear woman. "He's perfect. I've never had such a wonderful dog. And he's so smart, too! Why, did you know that my father and I have taught him math?"

Her eyes widened. "You've what?"

Laughing, I said, "Not really. But Spike will learn any trick if there's food at the end of the trick."

"Ah, yes. You have to watch their weight, you know."

"Yes, I do know. Dachshunds love to eat, but you have to be strict with them because too much weight is a strain on their long backs. You and Mrs. Hanratty taught me that."

"They'll eat until they just about pop if you don't watch them."

"I know." Actually, I kind of did the same thing, but I didn't mention it.

Pulling my Ouija board out of its cloth bag (I'd made the bag several years earlier), I set it and the wooden planchette on the card table. "Do you have anything specific you'd like to ask Rolly today, Mrs. Bissel?"

An expression of worry crossed the dear woman's face. Mrs. Bissel didn't possess the dramatic personality of Mrs. Pinkerton. Generally a serene person, it took a good deal to worry her. She'd been terrified about two years previous to this, when she'd believed her basement had been invaded by a ghost or a spirit, but I'd solved that problem for her. In another instance, an honest-to-God ghost had manifested itself during a séance at Mrs. B's house, but I was the only one who'd suffered from that invasion. Thank goodness nothing like that has ever happened since.

"Well, it's not specifically my problem," she began. She must have seen me open my mouth to speak, because she hurried to explain, "I know you can't help anyone other than the person on the other side of the planchette."

"Right." Darned right, in fact. Mrs. Pinkerton was forever forgetting that. I was glad to know Mrs. Bissel had remembered.

"But I'm afraid my Dennis is in trouble, and that makes me worry." Dennis was Mrs. Bissel's son.

"Dennis? Rolly can't help—"

She held up a hand. "I know. I know. But perhaps Rolly can advise me. I don't know whether to stick my two cents into Dennis's business, or just remain silent. I don't like to see him getting caught up in a vile woman's clutches." She frowned majestically. Heck, I'm a Majesty, and I can't do that. Probably happens when you're born to money.

"A vile woman's clutches?" I asked. "But isn't Dennis married? I thought he and his wife were happy together."

"They are. Or they were," said she, still frowning. "But there's a woman who's trying to break them up. I *know* she is, although Dennis claims it's all my imagination. And Patsy doesn't even seem to notice what's going on." Patsy was Dennis's wife.

"Hmm. Well, I honestly don't know what Rolly can do to help you, but let's give it a go." I sat in the chair closer to the window. Heck, Mrs. B could look at her rolling lawn any old day. I figured I'd grab the opportunity when it presented itself.

"Thank you, Daisy. You're so sweet to all of us little old ladies."

"Nonsense," I said, laughing. They might be old, but precious few of them were little. Mrs. Bissel, for instance, was a trifle bigger than Mrs. Pinkerton, who was not a small woman. But never mind that. It was nice to know my clients appreciated me.

So the two of us sat at opposite sides of the table, put our fingers lightly on the planchette, and our session began.

"Why don't you begin by asking a question," I suggested. "Try to make it about you and not Dennis."

"Very well." She sat and thought for a minute or two while the planchette perched there on the board, unmoving. Then she said, "Rolly, I'm worried about my son Dennis and his wife. I'm worried that a woman is trying to seduce him away from Patsy."

Goodness! I wasn't accustomed to such plain-speaking from my clients. But what the heck, at least the woman was honest.

Thinking fast, I had the planchette circle the board slowly. Then I aimed it at the double rows of letters comprising the alphabet. I was so accustomed to performing my craft by this time that I could read upside down as well as I could right-side up.

Eventually—spelling everything out on the Ouija board takes time, even if you're not pretending to be a dead Scot who couldn't spell well —I had Rolly tell her that she was a good mother for being concerned about her children, but that they were adults and had to make their own choices.

"Should I talk to Dennis about my suspicions?"

Oh, dear. It was in situations like this when my job became kind of tricky. Being careful, I had Rolly spell out, "Only if you can be discreet and not accusatory."

"Oh, of course!" Mrs. B cried, as if she'd never thought to accuse her son of anything. "I don't think Dennis has any ulterior ideas. It's another woman I'm afraid might weasel her way into his affections."

Hmm. "You need to be careful how you speak to your son. You don't want him to think you're interfering in his life. And you don't want to make him think that you think he can't take care of himself. Is his wife worried about this other woman?"

"I...I don't know. I hope not. I...I don't think she suspects anything."

"Why do you suspect this other woman of going after your son?" asked Rolly, getting to the point.

"I've watched her." Mrs. Bissel's voice was grim. "She insinuates herself into every conversation I see Dennis having at parties, and she always tries to sit next to him. *Close* to him."

"And his wife hasn't noticed this?"

"I don't think so. Patsy is such a sweet girl, and she's so trusting."

Very well. Maybe Rolly should do some plain speaking here. Or plain writing. Well, you know what I mean. "Is Dennis worthy of her trust?"

"Yes!" exclaimed Mrs. Bissel as if she were offended by the question. Nuts.

"Then why are you worrying?" asked Rolly, and quite sensibly, too, I think.

"Because this woman has caused trouble in other people's marriages," said Mrs. Bissel. "Even marriages everyone thought were solid."

"She's some sort of a succubus, is she?"

"A what?"

"A devil in female form who seduces men." Never mind that succubae generally seduce men in their sleep. I liked the word, so I had Rolly use it, even though he was an uneducated ex-soldier, and they probably didn't have succubae in Scotland in the 1000s. And even they did, Rolly wouldn't be able to spell the word. But nobody ever called me on these inconsistencies for some reason unknown to me.

"I...I don't know." When I glanced from the board to Mrs. Bissel's face, she appeared thoughtful.

"You might have a friendly chat with your son and gently tell him your fears," suggested Rolly. "Is he easy for you to talk to?"

"Dennis? Oh, yes. He's a sweet young man. That's one of the reasons I'm so worried. He's not used to women like *that*."

"It might be appropriate to hint that this other woman is up to no good," Rolly suggested.

"Hmm. Yes. Yes, that might be a good thing to do. I don't think Dennis suspects a thing. In fact, he usually seems surprised when the harpy sidles up to him at parties and so forth."

"You probably shouldn't talk to his wife. That might just upset her," said Rolly.

"Oh, no! I'd never tell Patsy. She's so sweet and...and...well, sheltered, if you know what I mean."

I knew what she meant. So did Rolly.

Then I thought of another question Rolly could ask that might actually be pertinent, and had him ask it. "What is this other woman's name?"

After a disdainful sniff, Mrs. Bissel said, "Gloria. Gloria Lippincott."

I darned near dropped my spiritualist pose.

EIGHT

Gloria Lippincott! Only instead of being a damsel in distress, she was the one doing the distressing. At least she'd distressed Mrs. Bissel, who was worried about her son's marriage.

I'd met Dennis Bissel once or twice, and had met his wife slightly more often. They both had roles in *The Mikado*, and they were both as innocent as baby lambs, if I were any judge. Mrs. Bissel might well be right. If Mrs. Lippincott fixed her eyes upon Dennis and planned a seduction of him, he'd probably fall right into her snare.

Oh, dear. Oh, dear. What should a caring spiritualist do?

Well, for one thing, I could call Harold Kincaid. I'd have to wait until the evening, however, since he worked at a picture studio in Los Angeles during the day. So all I could do was drive the Chevrolet back down Lake Avenue to Colorado, turn right, drive to Marengo, turn left, and go home. And fret. I fretted all the way home.

Spike, naturally, awaited me with happiness and glee. And loud barking and a wagging tail. Spike was such a terrific companion. *Spike* never groused at me. *Spike* never had woman troubles. *Spike* never wailed at me or told me his problems or expected me to save his son's marriage.

Unfortunately, before I was finished thoroughly loving my dog, the blasted telephone rang.

"Bother, Spike. I'd better get that. It's probably for me, anyway."

Spike didn't object. I noticed he was alone in the house. My father had probably gone out to visit with a friend or six. My father is one of those people of whom it is said, "He never met a stranger." He loved everyone. I loved my dog. And my family. I wasn't so sure about the rest of the world.

Nevertheless, I went to the kitchen and to the telephone on the wall, took a deep breath in case it was an hysterical Mrs. Pinkerton, and began speaking. "Gumm-Majesty—"

That's as far as I got, because Harold Kincaid all but shouted into the receiver, "Gloria Lippincott's husband was murdered last night!"

It took me an instant to organize my thoughts. They didn't want to be organized. I guess Harold got tired of me trying to think, because he hollered, "Did you *hear* me?"

Well, I could at least answer that question. "Yes. I heard you. What was his name?"

"What do you mean, what was his name? It was Lippincott! I just told you that."

I sighed. "I mean his first name. What was his *first* name, Harold?"

"What difference does that make? For God's sake, stick to the matter at hand, will you?"

"You mean his murder?"

"Of *course*, I mean his murder!"

"Oh. All right."

"Well, what can you do?"

"What can *I* do? I can't do anything! It's up to the police now, for heaven's sake, Harold. Good Lord, what do you expect *me* to do?" My voice was sharp, but that's only because I was shocked and his question had been so stupid.

"Oh, God. Oh, God," said Harold, sounding a teensy bit like his addlebrained mother. "I know you can't do anything. Really, I do. But God, Daisy, do you know what this is going to do to the production?"

For a second or two, I didn't know what he was talking about. Then it hit me like a brick upside the head. "The *production*? Is that all you can think about at a time like this? For Pete's sake, Harold Kincaid, a man's been *murdered*!"

Just then a heavy knock came at the door, and Spike went into his "Oh, goody, a friend is coming to call" frenzy. Aw, shoot.

"You're right. I know you're right. I'm sorry, Daisy, I—"

"I can't talk to you any longer, Harold. I have a ghastly feeling my home is about to be invaded by the Pasadena Police Department."

"The Pa—"

But I hung the receiver on its cradle, sucked in a gallon or so of air in preparation for the unpleasantness to come, and walked to the front door. After I'd told my darling dog to sit and stay, which he did, thereby cementing him in my esteem as much superior to most of the human beings on earth. I opened the door.

"H'lo, Sam," said I even before I knew it was he.

"Let me in, dammit," said Sam, growling. He growled a lot. Especially at me.

I stepped aside, pulling the door with me, and told Spike he was free to lavish his affections upon Sam, who was unworthy of them. "No need to swear at me," I said. But I only said it out of…I don't know. Habit? Tradition? I guess one of those was it. I always told him not to swear at me, and he always swore at me, so nothing ever changed.

In spite of that kiss. Crumb.

Because I knew why he was there, I said, "Harold just called and told me."

Sam, who had been kneeling to pay homage to Spike, as was only right, stood and whirled around, making his heavy overcoat twirl out like a cape in a bad melodrama. "Harold called and told you what?"

"That Gloria Lippincott's husband was murdered last night."

"How the hell…?" His voice trailed off, and he pressed a hand to his forehead, dislodging his hat, which he caught with a deft movement. For such a large man, he could move quickly when necessity called for it.

"I don't know how he knows," I said in answer to his unasked question. "I suspect Gloria told him. She's been whining on his shoulder for weeks now. She probably did it. What was his name, anyway?"

"Michael. And why do you say she did it?"

"Come on in and sit down. Hang your coat and hat on the rack. I'll get us some…I don't know. Something to drink."

Sam did part of what I suggested and hung up his hat and coat on the rack by the door. He said, "Is your aunt home?"

I turned and squinted at him. "You know as well as I do that Vi works for the Pinkertons every day, Sam Rotondo. Of course, she's not home."

"In that case, I'll just have a glass of water, please."

I felt my lips press together. Very well. I know I'm a rotten cook. And Sam knows it, because he's tasted the results of some of my disasters in the kitchen. Still, if a man's going to kiss a woman one day, he shouldn't insult her the next, darn it.

But there was no way I was going to tell Sam I thought those things, especially about the kiss. "Milk might go better with the cookies Vi made the other day. She calls them sand tarts. They're made with ground pecans."

"Sounds good. I'll take a glass of milk and some cookies then."

"Sit at the table while I get them."

So Sam sat at the table, making it two males who'd followed my instructions in one day. Only I knew this obedience on Sam's part wouldn't last. Spike, I could depend on.

Nevertheless, I prepared a plate complete with a doily and a pile of Vi's scrumptious sand tarts, and poured two glasses of milk, one for Sam and one for me. I set his milk and the plate of cookies before him on the table. Spike sat at attention at his feet, hoping for a crumb or two.

I saw Sam break a cookie in half and said harshly, "Don't feed that to Spike!"

Sam glanced at me, frowning. No surprise there. "Why not?"

"Because dachshunds shouldn't eat cookies. They get fat easily, and the extra weight is bad for their backs."

"Oh." Sam shrugged and popped the half-cookie he had aimed to feed Spike into his mouth. "Sorry, Spike."

Spike took it like the man he was, and only sat there, alert and on guard. And cookieless. Poor Spike.

"Now, what about Mr. Lippincott?" I asked. "How'd he die?"

"First of all, why did you say Gloria Lippincott did it?"

I should have known he'd zero in on that. "A mere slip of the tongue," said I, and ate a cookie.

"Huh. He was hit by a car outside his club."

"That's odd. Just the other day, Mrs. Lippincott said *she'd* almost been run down outside Nash's."

"Yeah. I remember. But she didn't do it." Sam frowned at me some more. I was used to it.

"How do you know that? Have the police even bothered to question her?"

"She was taken in to the station and questioned for hours," said Sam.

"Well, how do you know for sure she didn't do it?" I asked, feeling outraged. Dagnabbit, Gloria Lippincott was a slithery snake in the grass who preyed on men. She *should* have done it!

"She was at a bridge game when the man was killed."

"Oh." Rats. There went my perfect theory. "Well, I'll bet she's in cahoots with whoever did it. Or should that be whomever?"

"How the hell should I know?" Sam thrust another sand tart into his mouth and chewed savagely.

I tried another tack. "Well, can you tell by what's left of him, or on him, what kind or color of automobile did him in?"

"The forensics people are working on that."

"Where's his club?" I asked for the heck of it.

"El Molino Avenue, a little north of Colorado."

"Oh." I tried to visualize the location in my mind. I kind of remembered a building on El Molino north of Colorado that might well have been a men's club.

"So why'd you say his wife did it?" Sam asked, after swallowing.

"I don't know," I told him. "I don't like the woman, and Mrs. Bissel told me just this morning that she's been trying to seduce Dennis. Dennis is her son. The woman's a she-devil."

"You know this how? That she's a she-devil, I mean."

He had me there. "Well, if Mrs. Bissel's right, Mrs. Lippincott is trying to break up her son's marriage. I think that qualifies her as a she-devil."

"If," Sam said. "If. It's a small word, but it carries a lot of weight."

"Yeah, yeah. I know." I was annoyed. Yes, I'd jumped the gun by naming Gloria Lippincott a murderess, but I didn't like her and figured better her than someone I *did* like. "So how do you know for sure she was at the bridge party? Where was it?"

"I know because the hostess of the bridge party was Mrs. Hastings, and she confirmed Mrs. Lippincott's presence at her home all evening."

"Drat. Mrs. Hastings wouldn't lie for that harpy." Mrs. Hastings was a lovely woman who grew orchids in her astonishingly large estate in the San Rafael hills of Pasadena. Her only son had been murdered several months prior.

"What do you know about this Lippincott dame?" By that time, Sam had demolished the cookies on the plate and finished his glass of milk.

"Not much. She has a beautiful soprano voice, which doesn't seem fair somehow, and she's playing Pitti-Sing in *The Mikado*. I don't think her husband, from whom she was estranged according to Harold, was cast in the play. She's…" I tried to think of a good word to describe what little I knew about Gloria Lippincott—and I came up with a good one, by gum! "She's sultry."

Sam wrinkled his nose and squinted at me. "Sultry? How so?"

I waved a hand, giving Spike hope, which was wrong of me. I'd give him a treat later to make up for it. "I don't know. She's slinky. Good looking. Elegant. Wears her eyes at half-mast in order to appear alluring, which, for all I know, she is, men being the foolish creatures they are. Older than I am by maybe ten years. Maybe more. Wears a lot of makeup. Flutters her eyelashes at the men and ignores the women. You know. She's that type."

"Great. That gives me a lot to go on."

"Darn it, Sam Rotondo, I don't know the woman!"

"You seem to have her pegged, even if you don't know her."

"I observed her at the rehearsal, and I've seen her at other people's houses. And Harold told me that she told him that her husband was trying to kill her." Drat. And I'd told Harold only days earlier than I never observed anything. Well, neither Sam nor Harold needed to know about my wishy-washiness. "Harold knows her heaps better than I do. Why don't you go and ask him?"

"I will. You say your next rehearsal is tomorrow night?"

I heaved a largish sigh. Thanks to Gloria Lippincott having someone murder her estranged husband—or maybe she didn't. What did I know?—Sam was going to see tomorrow's rehearsal whether I wanted him to or not. "Yes. Seven to nine. Sanctuary at the First Methodist-Episcopal Church on—"

"I know where it is," Sam barked at me.

"Good," I barked back. "If her husband just died, she might not be there," I reminded him.

He said, "Huh," which was typical.

"Well, Harold said they were estranged. Whatever that means. Maybe she doesn't care that he got murdered."

With a roll of his eyes, Sam rose from the table. "Thanks for the cookies and milk."

"You're welcome."

Because Spike had been so very patient and hadn't barked or begged, I said, "Before you go, I want to show you something."

"What?"

"Just a minute, and I'll show you."

I hurried to the kitchen and snatched an arrowroot biscuit from a tin in the cupboard. Arrowroot biscuits might not be dog food, but they were probably better for dachshunds than sand tarts. I broke the biscuit in half as I hurried back to the dining room.

Naturally, Sam hadn't waited for me there, but had gone to the living room, donned his hat and coat, and now stood impatiently before the front door, gazing at me crankily, as if I'd kept him waiting for hours and hours. Nuts to him.

"Watch this," I commanded Sam.

"Yeah. Go on."

I looked down upon my dog, who was in the process of frolicking at Sam's feet. I said, "Spike," and he stopped frolicking and looked up at me. I said, "Spike. Sit." He sat.

Sam grumbled something under his breath, but I ignored him.

"Spike, what's two plus two."

My faithful hound's tail started wagging up a storm. He knew this game. He barked four times and stopped.

I said, "Good boy!" and handed him half of the arrowroot biscuit.

Sam's eyebrows dipped over his eyes. They reminded me of a couple of fuzzy caterpillars having a conference right above his nose.

"Spike," I went on. "What's three times two?"

Spike barked six times and stopped, looking up at me with eyes aglow.

"What a special, good boy you are!" I cried at my amazing pooch, and I knelt and not only gave him the other half of the arrowroot biscuit, but petted him thoroughly.

"How'd you teach him math?" Sam asked. He wasn't even growling any longer, but sounded honestly curious.

Ha. Spike and I had managed to astonish the great detective. I peered up at him and grinned. "Spike is brilliant."

"No, really. How'd you teach him that?"

"Maybe, if you're good, I'll tell you. Some day."

"Cripes." Sam slammed the door on his way outside.

"Good boy, Spike!"

After I'd changed from my spiritualist clothes into a comfy old day dress, Spike and I retired to the sofa in the living room, and he sat on my lap while I read *The Triumph of the Scarlet Pimpernel*, by Baroness Orczy. I felt a little triumphant myself, for having flummoxed the great detective.

NINE

Rehearsal began promptly at seven p.m. that Thursday—choir practice had been rescheduled for six p.m. for the duration. I was pleased to see Dennis and Patsy Bissel holding hands. They were playing parts in the chorus. I guess Dennis hadn't succumbed to Gloria Lippincott's wiles. Yet, anyway. They were a sweet couple.

Lawrence and Sylvia Allen were there, too. They were a society couple, but they didn't seem as lovey-dovey as Dennis and Patsy. In fact, Sylvia appeared downright distressed. I cornered Harold, and he said that was because Lawrence and another woman were having a hot-and-heavy affair, and that Sylvia knew all about it, but that she loved Lawrence and didn't want to give him a divorce.

Hmm. People were sure wanting to divorce each other a lot in those loose days, weren't they? I'd never have divorced Billy. Never mind that our married life had been fraught with…well, it had been fraught, but that wasn't our fault. The fault lay with Kaiser Bill.

By the way, there were governmental talks underway about extracting some sort of retribution in monetary form from the land-grabbing, boy-killing Kaiser, but I doubted they'd do any good even if they could be enforced. Heck, Wilhelm II had abdicated, was in exile in

Holland, and the damage was already done. Anyway, how much money were several thousand dead people worth? Or the Belgian, French and British regions that had been bombed all to heck by the Germans? Mind you, if some Dutch citizen took it upon himself to kill the man, I doubt many tears would be shed.

Oh, don't let me get started.

Gloria Lippincott turned up at rehearsal on Thursday night. I'm not sure why I was surprised. After all, she had been estranged from her husband. I guess that meant they hadn't liked each other and weren't living together, although I wasn't positive about that last part.

So I asked Harold, "Why's the cat-woman here tonight? Isn't she in distress over her husband's demise?"

Harold said something like, "Tsch." Then he added, "They hadn't been living together for a couple of years. Anyway, she wants to be near her new prey."

"By that, I presume you mean other men, like Lawrence Allen and Dennis Bissel."

"Bingo."

"Well...still. Wouldn't you think she'd at least put on a show of being heartbroken or something?"

"Look at her," Harold advised. "If that's not heartbroken, I don't know what is."

I took his advice, not having wanted to make a spectacle of myself and stare at her when I first walked into the sanctuary. "Oh. I see."

"Indeed." Harold's voice was quite dry.

But, really. Somehow or other, Gloria Lippincott had managed to smudge her makeup around her eyes so that she appeared woebegone. She also had her hankie out and dabbed at her eyes whenever anyone passed her by—she sat in the front row of pews. That's something you don't see often, by the way. People in the front row of Methodist churches, I mean. I understand the Baptists aren't so shy, but we Methodists generally fill up the sanctuary from about the third row back.

Then there was Sam. Sam had driven me to rehearsal, over my objections. But he said he had a murder to investigate, and one of his suspects—who evidently hadn't done the deed herself, having been playing bridge at the time—had a part in *The Mikado*, so there wasn't much I could do about it.

So there he was. Not for Sam the front row. Not he. He stood on the right side of the chancel, his arms crossed over his chest, looking official, even though he wasn't wearing a uniform. But from the way he scowled as his gaze scanned everyone there, you'd have thought he was going to pounce upon all of us and arrest the whole cast. I tried not to stare at him, but kept my gaze on Gloria Lippincott.

"Hmm," said I. "Maybe I should go offer my sympathy."

Harold gawked at me. "You mean to Gloria?"

I shrugged. "Why not. Is anyone else you know bereaved? Maybe I can wrangle some information out of her."

"About what?"

"About whom she hired to murder her husband."

"What?"

People turned to stare at Harold and me, so I frowned and said, "Shh. No need to yell."

"But...do you really think she...?"

"I have no idea. But I'm going to go offer her my sympathy, which, I'm sure, is at least as genuine as her grief."

"The role of Katisha is beginning to affect you in adverse ways, Daisy Majesty."

I only grinned and walked down the chancel steps and up to Gloria Lippincott, composing my face into a mask of sympathetic understanding as I did so. She glanced up at me uneasily, as if she were hoping a male cast member would offer her comfort and was disappointed to find a female instead.

But I was a mistress of my art. I put on my most compassionate expression, and sank down onto the pew next to her. "I was so awfully sorry to learn of your husband's passing, Mrs. Lippincott. I know what it's like to lose a husband." Instantly my heart squished. Maybe Katisha *had* turned me sour. I'd loved my Billy. In fact, I loved him still. Yet here I was, using him as a prop for my snooping. I'd have been ashamed of myself if I weren't already in my role as consoler.

"Thank you, Mrs. Majesty. Yes." She paused to sniffle a couple of times. "Michael and I hadn't been getting along, but it was still such a shock."

"And so ironic that it happened so shortly after you were nearly run down, too."

Her eyes opened fully for the first time since I'd met her at Mrs. Pinkerton's party. "You know about that?"

I nodded, slathering on a sad face to go with my benevolent tone. "Yes. Harold told me. I'm so sorry. Do you have any idea who's doing these awful things?"

Another sniffle. "No. I don't have any idea. I...I originally thought Michael was trying to kill me, because he wouldn't give me a divorce, even though he was having an affair with another woman." She sniffed again, only this one sounded more irritated than tragic. "But strange things kept happening to me. And then a car almost hit me in front of Nash's the other day. I was *so* upset."

"I can imagine."

Suddenly, Gloria turned to face me and put a hand on my arm, as if she'd just thought of something pertinent. "Oh, Mrs. Majesty! You're the medium, aren't you?"

"Ah...yes, I'm a spiritualist-medium." So what? I wanted to add, but didn't.

"Could I hire you to do a séance? Perhaps Michael himself can tell us who tried to kill me and who *did* kill him!"

Well, pooh. This wasn't turning out the way I'd expected it to. I'd expected her to have been the evildoer in this melodrama, not an almost-murdered widow. But if she were asking me to perform a séance in order to get in touch with her late estranged husband, maybe I was wronging her. On the other hand, maybe she was just a good actress.

Putting on my spiritualist's cloak of mystery, I said, "I could, of course, perform a séance and attempt to get in touch with your late husband, Mrs. Lippincott. However, I must tell you that it often takes a spirit some time to settle into peace on the Other Side. This is especially true if a person has had his or her life cut short violently." I hauled out this excuse a lot, and it saved me a good deal of time and effort.

"Oh." She removed her hand from my arm, folded her hands in her lap, and recommenced looking heartbroken. "I see." Then she turned and faced me again, abruptly. I darned near jumped, but I'm better at my job than to allow folks to rattle me. "But could you *try*? Whoever killed Michael may still want to kill me, and I'm...I'm...I'm frightened." She brought her hankie to her eyes and pressed it to them, smudging more of her mascara.

Fiddlesticks. This was confusing. I said, "Of course, I can attempt to reach your late husband, if you'd like me to." If she'd pay me to, is what I meant, but she understood that, having already mentioned hiring me. "Where do you live?"

"I live in our home on California Boulevard. Michael's and mine, I mean."

California Boulevard, eh? Another street full of mansions and grand estates. "I see. Well, perhaps you can talk to Harold Kincaid about my services. His mother uses me all the time, and he can give you particulars." Especially about the money part.

"Mrs. Majesty!" came a stentorian voice from the chancel. I knew that voice and instantly hopped to my feet.

"Yes, Mr. Hostetter!"

"You're needed for this next scene."

"Coming!" And I trotted back onstage. Or on-chancel. Harold stood there, too, holding his fake Lord High Executioner's axe and looking fierce, in a Gilbert and Sullivan-ish sort of way.

"Sorry," I said, panting slightly. "Which scene are we doing?"

Mr. Hostetter frowned at me. I wasn't accustomed to being frowned at by my choir director. Generally he approved of me. Oh, well.

"We're blocking out the end of act one, in which Katisha appears for the first time," said Max Van der Linden. I think he took pity on me after Mr. Hostetter hollered.

"Very well. Where do you want me?" I asked, all attention in my effort to redeem myself.

"Stand off-stage, stage left."

I moved to my left.

Mr. Van der Linden said, "Other side. That's house left. You want stage left."

I stopped and stared at him for a moment. "Um…"

"Perhaps this would be a good time for an introduction to staging terms," said Max in a bright and friendly voice, probably trying not to make me sound like an idiot because I didn't know stage directions.

So he spent a few minutes with the cast and crew gathered around him, showing us on a piece of paper precisely where stage left, stage right, up-stage and down-stage were. To my mind, his directions were directly opposed to logic, but I wasn't an actor. Then I stood on the chancel, looked out upon the vast number of pews, and it suddenly clicked. From *that* position, stage left actually *was* to my left. I felt better after that.

Harold joined me back-stage. "Figure it out?"

"Yes. Finally. I feel stupid."

"No need to. Nobody else knew stage left from an elephant's hind leg, so it's good that you precipitated some instructions. I doubt many of these folks have done any more stage work than you have."

"And I haven't done any."

"Right."

"Harold? Are you ready with the Mikado's letter?" called Max to Harold.

"Right here," called Harold, and he waved a scroll-type thing at Max.

"Very well," said Floy Hostetter. "We'll begin at your entrance."

By the way, Max Van der Linden was the stage director. Floy Hostetter just usurped his duties from time to time, I presume because he was accustomed to ruling over the singers at the First Methodist-Episcopal Church.

"We'll begin after you and Nanki-Poo decide you'll execute him after a month of his being married to Yum-Yum," said Max.

When I turned to look at the piano, darned if Mrs. Fleming wasn't there in her accustomed place. She gave me a big smile, and I gave her one back. Things felt normal again. For a second or two. Then I had to disrupt the joy and gaiety going on in the town of Titipu by barging in on a love scene. Fortunately, in between walking Spike and performing my other duties, I'd been studying my lines, so I managed a pretty dramatic entrance, considering I'm only a little over five feet tall.

71

Rehearsal went well after that. We'd blocked the entirety of act one by the end of the evening, all of us making notes on our librettos. Or is that libretti? Oh, who cares? Sam had roamed around backstage and, as we went through the end of act one for the last time, had cornered Gloria Lippincott in the front pew after her "Three Little Maids from School" song was over. I kept slipping peeks at them, because—darn it! —she was trying out her seductress routine on *him*! I could tell.

But I didn't have time to dwell on Gloria's shenanigans. I had a part to sing. So I sang.

At one point during the scene, Lawrence Allen, who played the role of Go-To, a noble lord of Titipu, stopped singing and glared into the pews. We all stopped and stared at him.

"Mr. Allen?" said Max tentatively, as if he weren't sure what was going on.

"Detective!" roared Lawrence. "If you need to speak with Mrs. Lippincott, perhaps you can wait until rehearsal is over. Your conversation is distracting the cast."

I saw Sam's eyebrows lift over his dark eyes like larks ascending. Or maybe caterpillars ascending. They were dark and fuzzy, Sam's eyebrows. "I beg your pardon?" said he in his official detective's voice.

"You're interrupting the rehearsal," said Lawrence, not roaring. In truth, he appeared a little embarrassed about having made a scene.

"It's all right, Lawrence," said Gloria in her sultry tone. "We'll be still." She gazed at Sam with what looked awfully like significant adoration. "Won't we, Detective Rotondo?"

Lawrence squeaked.

Sam stood and gave her the same look he might have given a fly that had landed on his apple pie. "Yes. We're through here, although I'll probably need to speak with you again, Mrs. Lippincott."

"Of course, Detective Rotondo," she purred.

Sam drew back and peered at her as if he were looking at a specimen at a zoological garden somewhere.

Take that, you villainess, thought I. I felt better for the remainder of the rehearsal, though. So did Lawrence Allen. I could tell. I aimed to find out why he objected so strenuously to Gloria flirting with Sam, however. Could *he* be the man she was supposedly involved with? I knew he was married to Sylvia, and that Sylvia didn't appear very happy. But evidently Gloria didn't bother with trivialities like that. Anyhow, Harold had already told me he was having an affair with somebody besides his wife.

Shoot. Maybe I really *was* taking on Katisha's nastier characteristics.

I sure hoped so. Being a good girl all the time was darned boring.

TEN

Sam held the door to his Hudson open for me when we left the church. I could open my own car door, but I didn't argue. He was being polite.

After he was settled behind the wheel and had started the engine, I said, "So, what were you and Gloria Lippincott being so cozy about?"

He turned and squinted at me. "Huh?"

"Lawrence Allen sure objected to your tete-a-tete with Mrs. Lippincott," I reminded him.

"Yeah, I noticed that. What was he talking about? We weren't speaking very loudly."

Oh, brother! He couldn't possibly be *that* dim, could he? "She was plying her feminine wiles on you, Sam Rotondo! That's why Lawrence hollered at you. At least I think that's why."

"She was what?" Sam's eyes got squintier.

Shoot. Maybe he *was* that dim. "I think the two of them are having an affair," I told him. "Gloria and Lawrence. He's married to Sylvia, but Harold said he's been carrying on with another woman for several months. Bet it's Gloria."

"Yeah? I didn't know that."

"Yes. According to Mrs. Bissel, she's also trying to get her claws into Dennis Bissel, but Dennis seems firmly attached to his wife, Patsy."

"Where'd you learn all this?"

"Harold, of course. Well, and Mrs. Bissel told me about Dennis."

"Of course." Sam started motoring down the hill to our house, which was only a few blocks south of the church. "Well, you learned considerably more than I did tonight."

"Really?" That made me happy.

"Yeah. But you still don't know who killed her husband or why. Or do you?"

"Not a clue, but I bet she hired someone to knock him off."

"Of course you do." Sarcasm, thy name is Sam Rotondo.

I shrugged. "She wanted to get rid of her husband. He wouldn't give her a divorce, although I don't know why, since Harold told me he was involved with someone else. She's evidently involved with anyone she can get her hands on. Maybe she found better pickings and decided she didn't want to wait until her husband agreed to divorce her. Maybe she wanted to get it over with. Get *him* over with."

"Then why'd someone try to kill her?"

"*Did* someone try to kill her?"

"How the devil should I know? You're the one who told me that!"

"Don't yell at me. It's not my fault the woman called Harold with her wild story, and Harold called me. Either one of them would have been better off calling the police."

"Did you tell them that?"

"Yes, I did."

"Huh."

"I *did*!"

"We're here," said Sam, not bothering to argue with me any longer, I guess.

"You drive me nuts, Sam Rotondo!"

"Likewise, I'm sure."

He didn't get the opportunity to open my door for me, because I opened it myself. I also slammed it again once I was on the sidewalk—Sam had parked in the street in front of our house. I didn't get the chance to storm up the walkway to the door without him, though, because he was too quick for me and took my arm. Hard. I stopped walking, turned, and glared up at him.

"What?"

"I just want you to be careful, Daisy. I know you like to stick your nose in—"

"I don't either!"

Sam trod over my words as if I hadn't spoken, raising his voice as he did so. "Stick your nose into every mystery that comes your way, but a man was murdered a day or two ago, and his widow might just have a target on her back, too. Keep as far away from the mess as you can. That means Mr. Allen and Mr. Bissel and Mrs. Lippincott. I don't know if what you told me is true, but if it is, there are a whole lot of entanglements going on, and neither you nor I know who's doing what to—or with—whom."

Well…when he put it that way, I guess I couldn't object too much. "The only time I have anything to do with any of them is when we're rehearsing for *The Mikado*," I muttered, not wanting to yield the stage, but understanding his point.

"See that it stays that way," said Sam.

It was then I remembered Mrs. Lippincott had asked me to conduct a séance to see if I could find out who'd killed her husband. Bother. As Sam began walking to the front porch, I held him back.

"Um…Sam?"

He stopped and glared down at me some more. "What?"

I licked my lips and bit the bullet. "Mrs. Lippincott asked me to conduct a séance and try in that way to find out who killed her husband."

"Good God."

"Well?"

He shrugged. "Well, why the hell not? I don't suppose you can get into too much trouble if you conduct a séance, as long as Harold and maybe one of those old ladies you're always spewing nonsense to attend it, too."

"Thanks heaps. You have *such* a way with words, Sam."

"You don't believe in what you do any more than I do."

"That's true, but you don't have to be quite so brutal about it."

He smiled suddenly. It wasn't a friendly smile. "In fact, I'll sit in on the séance, too. That way I can keep an eye on everyone."

"You won't be able to *see* anyone, much less keep an eye on anyone. The room's dark."

"I have my ways."

"Oh, brother."

We continued up to the porch to the racket from an ecstatic Spike, who greeted us both as if he'd expected never to see either one of us again in this lifetime. Ma and Pa smiled at us as we entered the house.

The telephone began ringing. Ma, Pa, Sam and I all looked at each other. Spike didn't care. He merely kept greeting us.

"Good heavens, who could be calling at this time of night?" asked Ma.

"I don't know, but I expect it's for me," I said, and headed to the kitchen, where I picked up the receiver and said, "Gumm-Majesty residence, Mrs.—"

That's as far as I got, because Harold Kincaid hollered in my ear, "Daisy! Someone tried to drop a boulder on Gloria Lippincott right outside the church after rehearsal!"

My mouth opened, and nothing came out. Someone had tried to do *what* to Gloria Lippincott? "Um…Harold…"

"It's the truth! Is Sam there with you? Send him back. Gloria's all shaken up. God, Daisy, it was awful. That rock missed her by inches, and it was huge! It made a dent in the lawn when it landed."

"You're serious?"

"Dead serious. Please excuse the expression."

"I'll send Sam back."

"You come, too. Gloria wants you."

"Why?"

"I don't know, but she said she wants you."

"Sam's going to love that."

"I'm sure. But please come."

"I will." Even if I had to drive myself up there in the Chevrolet.

"Thanks." Harold ended the call.

I heard a bunch of clicks on the wire before I hung the receiver in the cradle, so I know our party-line neighbors had also heard the grim news. Oh, well. People like Harold—rich people, I mean—didn't have to suffer with party-line snoops. As soon as I turned away from the 'phone, I saw Ma, Pa, and Sam all staring at me. I heaved a sigh.

"Someone just tried to kill Gloria Lippincott again."

"What!" my mother cried.

"Someone did what?" said Pa.

Sam said, "Crap," and turned to go out to his automobile.

"Wait up, Sam," I hollered after him, hurrying to catch him and nearly tripping over Spike. "Gloria said she wants me there."

Sam stopped walking so suddenly, Spike bumped into his heel. He woofed. Spike, not Sam. Sam said, "Sorry, Spike." That was nice of him, although it was no more than Spike deserved. Sam turned to glare at me.

"It's not my fault!" I cried, peeved by his expression. "That was Harold on the wire. He said a huge boulder fell and nearly squashed Gloria flat. I guess she's upset, and she wants me there."

"What about her boyfriend? That Allen guy?"

"I don't know if he *is* her boyfriend! Look, if you don't want to drive me up there, I'll drive myself." I heeled around and started to depart the house via the side entrance. Our lovely, almost-new Chevrolet sat out there, waiting for me just down the porch steps.

"Wait!" Sam. "I'll take you. Hurry up."

I'd have rolled my eyes, but it wouldn't have been worth it.

"Be careful, sweetie," said Pa.

"Nobody's after me," I said, hoping to reassure him.

"Give them time," snarled Sam.

That wasn't very nice of him, but it's no more than I'd grown to expect. I said nothing, but trailed after him to the Hudson, where he opened the passenger-side door for me. I climbed in, wishing I could just go to bed. I was sick of Gloria Lippincott and her problems.

Sam turned into our driveway, backed out, and headed north on Marengo.

"When did this accident happen?"

"I don't know if it was an accident," I told him. "Harold said someone tried to throw a boulder on her. That sounds more like intent to commit murder than accident."

"Where'd this boulder come from? It's not like we're in the foothills or anything."

"I don't know. Harold was in a hurry. He just told me the bare facts." I thought about that call and frowned. "I should have told him to call the police."

"He *did* call the police," said Sam, not happy about it.

"Well, yes, I know that, but he should have called the station."

"Yeah, but what else is new?"

He had a point. People did seem inclined to burden me with their police problems rather than telephone the police department. I didn't bother to tell him that wasn't my fault, because we'd been over this ground before. Many, many times.

A crowd was gathered on Marengo Avenue near the side entrance of the First Methodist-Episcopal Church on the corner of Colorado and Marengo. Boy, you didn't see that very often in Pasadena, where they pretty much rolled up the streets after dark.

"Christ," said Sam irreverently.

"You're at the right place," said I, being a prig.

He pulled the Hudson to a stop at the edge of the crowd, which had gathered more on Marengo than Colorado, although the church sat on the corner. Harold emerged from the group of people and hurried over to my side of Sam's machine. "Daisy! Thank God you both came. Gloria's in a state."

"There sure are a lot of people here. Where'd they all come from?"

"The church. We were leaving rehearsal. You know that." Harold sounded grumpy.

Sam emerged from his side of the Hudson and scowled at Harold and me. "Can you tell me exactly what happened, Kincaid?"

For the record, we citizens of Pasadena were fortunate in that electrical street lighting had been installed several years earlier, so we could at least see each other after dark.

Harold passed a hand across his forehead. "I don't honestly know. A bunch of us, including Gloria and Lawrence and Sylvia and a few others, were walking to the street, and suddenly we heard a noise, I looked up, and I saw a huge stone falling right from the church roof."

Sam and I both looked up at the church roof. It was tall and pointy.

"How the heck did somebody toss a rock from up there?" I asked in honest curiosity.

"It wasn't a rock. It was a boulder, and I don't know."

"All right," said Sam, interrupting us in exasperation. "Where precisely did this happen. And what precisely *did* happen?"

"Come over here," said Harold, and he led the way.

ELEVEN

W hen we got to where the intended victim—at least, I suppose she was an intended victim—sat on a stone bench with Lawrence Allen's arms encircling her, I could see where someone might have stood in order to drop the stone. The door leading from the side of the sanctuary sat under a flat spot in the otherwise pointy roof. One of its points was the church's steeple, but the rest of it was plenty pointy, too. However, in that one flat spot, I could envision where someone might have stood or lain and shoved a boulder on top of a group of people.

"How'd whoever did it know the stone would hit Gloria?" I asked, thinking the question to be pertinent.

"How should I know?" asked Harold, irked.

"Be still, both of you," said Sam. He was also irked, but that was only natural for him. He raised his voice. "Be quiet, all of you!" He withdrew his wallet from his trouser pocket and held out his badge so everyone could see he was legitimate. "Now. I want to know precisely what happened here. Where's this rock that was supposedly shoved off the church's roof?"

He'd been so forceful that it took several seconds for the assembled cast and crew to react. Finally, Connie Van der Linden, whose face appeared white and pinched, walked over to the Marengo Avenue side of the church and pointed at a spot on the church lawn, right next to the walkway.

By gum, there was a rock, all right. And Harold was right; it was big. Only it looked to me as if it were more of a paving stone than a boulder. I strode over to it and took a squint.

"Stay back," Sam ordered.

I frowned, but took a step back. Sam joined me and stared down at the stone, which was squarish and flattish. Precisely like a paving stone, as I said.

"Huh," said Sam. "It's rough. Probably won't have held any fingerprints."

"But you're going to have your men dust it for prints, aren't you?" I said.

He frowned at me. Big surprise. "Yes."

"F-fingerprints?"

Connie Van der Linden took a step backward and then slithered into a heap on the ground.

"What the hell?" said Sam.

"I think she fainted," said Harold, heading toward Connie. Max beat him to his wife's fallen body.

"What the devil is going on here?" Max asked in a roar that could have rivaled one of Sam's best.

"Gloria was almost leveled by that boulder stuck in the lawn there." Harold pointed at the lawn and Sam and me.

"She *what?*"

Connie stirred and lifted a hand to touch her husband's cheek. "Don't-don't yell, Max. I have *such* a headache."

Max instantly turned his ministrations to her. "What happened, darling? Harold said something about Gloria and a boulder."

We all heard a siren and turned to watch as two police cars screeched to a stop on Colorado Boulevard right in front of the church. The machines held two uniformed officers each, and disgorged them at the same time. Their routine might have been choreographed. Kind of like the Keystone Kops.

I'm sorry. That was unkind of me. These fellows weren't humorous at all. They were efficient.

Sam instantly took over. "Everyone, stay exactly where you are. Doan and Ludlow, check out this stone here. That rock was evidently pushed from the roof of the church." He stepped aside so that the two men could see what he was talking about.

"Yes, sir," said Doan, whom I knew. Sort of.

"Perkins and Fowler, take statements. Start with her." He pointed at Gloria Lippincott, who was huddled on her bench, still being held by Lawrence Allen.

Sylvia Allen looked upon this display in patent disgust. Hmm. Wonder where she was when the stone hit the dirt. But that wouldn't work. She was too much of a lightweight to have carried that thing upstairs and heaved it off the church roof.

"How much does that stone weigh?" I asked of no one in particular.

"A lot," said Harold. "I suspect twenty or thirty pounds."

"And it could have killed anyone if it hit him or her on the head, right?"

"I think so."

"Then how do you know it was aimed at Gloria?"

"Because she was there on the walkway by herself."

"I thought there were a bunch of you walking together."

Harold passed a hand over his forehead again. He was still rattled, and I understood. Something like that was enough to rattle anyone. "We were sort of walking together, but Gloria was kind of by herself, standing and waiting for—" Harold looked around, as if to make sure no one except me would hear him. At last he whispered, "Waiting for Lawrence, if I were to guess."

"Hmm. Where was Sylvia?"

"Talking to Connie, I think. They were going over some costuming things. Sylvia's going to make most of the costumes."

"Thank God for that," I muttered, feeling reprieved. After all, Harold had introduced me as a good seamstress, and I felt abused enough at having been forced into playing Katisha.

With a quick grin, Harold said, "Yeah. Figured you'd appreciate that." He frowned. "Connie doesn't look well, does she?"

I squinted in Connie's direction. No, she didn't look well. On the other hand, she'd just fainted. Why'd she do that? I shook my head, which was already too full of odd goings-on to leave room to ponder Connie and her fainting spell. "She said she had a headache. Guess she fainted from the excitement."

Harold said, "Huh," reminding me of Sam.

"Hmm. So Gloria was essentially standing all alone on the path. Was there a big gap around her? I mean, if someone wanted to hurt her in particular, she'd made a good target of herself?"

"I'd say a practically perfect target. She was all alone with probably five or six feet of empty space around her."

"And she stood directly beneath the roof?" This was beginning to sound weird to me. Could Gloria have deliberately separated herself from the rest of the cast in order to make herself look like a target? I wouldn't put it past her.

Harold blinked a couple of times as if he, too, had begun to think upon similar lines. "Hmm. Yes. Yes, indeed. Do you think she did it on purpose and that she and someone else cooked up the scheme in order to make it look as though she were the object of a killer's missile?"

"Sounds right to me. Of course, we may be wronging the woman."

"Of course." Harold didn't believe it either.

"Where were the rest of the cast and crew?"

With a shrug, Harold said, "I really wasn't keeping track. I did see Connie and Sylvia chatting. I'm not sure where Max was, although he might have been going through the blocking with your choir director. I think they were both inside the church. Um…Dennis and his wife were holding hands and chatting with each other." Harold grimaced. I guess he didn't approve of public displays of affection.

"Anyone else you can think of whom you saw?"

"Um…All right. I'm pretty sure I saw the Mikado and Pish-Tush conferring over there by those hydrangeas. They were singing, so I guess they were trying to work something out."

The Mikado and Pish-Tush? "Oh, you mean George Finster and James Warden."

"Whatever their names are."

"All right, you two," said Sam, stamping up to us and making me jump with surprise, darn him. "I need to talk to you, Kincaid. Daisy, go away."

"No, I will not go away. This is my church, and something awfully strange happened here after rehearsal tonight."

As might be expected, Sam rolled his eyes. "Then stand out of the way. Come here, Kincaid." He led Harold off to another stone bench. There were several benches placed here and there on the church grounds, most of them bearing plaques honoring deceased church members and erected by said members' families.

I glanced about and saw that Gloria and Lawrence had separated, although he still stood close to her. Officer Perkins was questioning her now. I moseyed over closer and noted she was sobbing delicately. Huh. Sylvia had Lawrence by his arm, and it looked to me as if her grip were biting into his flesh. He didn't wince, so I might have been mistaken. I tried to make myself inconspicuous behind a gardenia bush and listened hard.

"Why do you think someone meant to drop the stone on you, Mrs. Lippincott?" asked Perkins.

"Because someone *did*!" she said, still sobbing. "I was standing right there. If Harold hadn't warned me, I'd be dead right this minute." She blubbered some more.

"But why do you think it was aimed at you and not someone else?" Perkins persisted stolidly, and I honored him for it. It couldn't be much fun to interrogate hysterical women. Or hysterical men, for that matter.

"Because I was standing all alone! I was the only one who could have been hit by the thing!" More piteous weeping.

"So you don't think it was an accident?"

Gloria's head lifted from her soggy handkerchief. "Accident? *Accident*! Someone tried to run me down on the street several days ago, someone murdered my husband three days ago, and now someone tried to smash me into a blob on the walkway! It was no accident!"

She had a way with words, I'll give her that.

Waving her arms in the air—which made her hankie flutter like a white flag—she went on. "How could it have been an accident? Did you *see* that thing? It couldn't have fallen by itself! Someone shoved it over the edge of the roof! Someone is trying to kill me!"

"Do you have any idea why anyone would want to do that? Or who it might be?" Perkins went on, persevering against heavy odds.

"No! I don't know who wants to kill me! Someone killed my husband. Maybe it's one of his enemies!"

He had enemies, eh? Interesting.

"He had enemies?" Perkins asked, echoing my thoughts. "Do you have any names?"

"Names? Names? What names?" Gloria blinked and appeared befuddled. "Oh. You mean names of Michael's enemies? Why…Why, I don't know. In particular."

"Did he have debts?" asked Perkins.

Gee, I'd never have thought to ask that, but it sounded pertinent. I saw Gloria's mouth pinch up, so I guess she thought it was, too.

"What do you mean by debts?" she asked, no longer weeping.

Stupid question. What did she *think* he meant?

"Did he owe people any money? Banks? Lawyers? Friends? Did he gamble? Did he owe any gambling debts?"

It looked for a moment as if Gloria were going to clam up. But finally, she heaved a huge sigh and said, "Yes. Yes, he owed people money. I'm not sure who they were, but I know he used to…gamble." She spoke the last word in a whisper. "Sometimes. And no, I don't know with whom he gambled or what he gambled on. He…he did not leave a large estate."

"Has his estate been settled already?" asked Perkins.

After another exhalation of breath, Gloria said, "No. Not yet. But I knew Michael." She said his name with a good deal of bitterness. "He was always broke. I…I'm afraid I'll have to sell our home."

She commenced crying again, and this time I didn't much blame her. It had been difficult for me to live with an invalid, and that was something Billy couldn't help being. It must drive a person flat crazy to live with someone who gambled away one's income. I almost felt sorry for Gloria, although the feeling didn't last long because she didn't bother to whisper her next words.

"I hated him for it! And he wouldn't give me a divorce! He just hung on like grim death, squandering his money and mine and causing me nothing but problems. I'm glad he's dead." She seemed to catch herself saying things she didn't mean to say, because she then wailed, "But *I* don't want to die because of him! And someone just tried to murder me!"

Interesting. If Michael Lippincott was an evil-minded gambler, what would it profit his creditors to kill his estranged wife? I hoped Perkins would ask that question, but I don't know if he did, because Sam Rotondo loomed over me at that instant, and I jumped.

"Eavesdropping, are we?" he snarled.

I slapped a hand over my heart and said, "Darn you, Sam Rotondo. Why do you have to sneak up on a person like that?"

"Why are you eavesdropping on a private conversation?"

"Pooh. It's not a private conversation. It's a policeman interrogating a witness. A witness and maybe even a target of murder, although I don't know why anybody'd want to kill her just because her estranged husband was a gambler and in debt up to his eyebrows."

Speaking of eyebrows, Sam's lifted nearly into his hairline. "He was a what?"

I shrugged. "That's what Gloria said. Her late husband was a gambler and owed a lot of people a lot of money. Why his creditors should want to kill her is something I'd like to know, but I won't now, because you sneaked up behind me, darn it."

"All right. Enough of this. Come on, and I'll take you home. Kincaid couldn't tell me much, and what he did tell me I'm sure you'll know soon enough. I'm through here. Perkins and the rest can finish taking statements."

"You're not going to stick around until everyone leaves?"

"I'll read the reports in the morning."

"Lucky you. Wish I could read the reports."

"Huh."

Sam had left his Hudson sitting in the middle of Marengo Avenue. Not that it mattered much. As I've already mentioned, very few people in Pasadena went out after dark. He opened the passenger door for me, and I climbed in, feeling as if my interesting evening had been cut short because of Sam. I *really* wanted to know why Gloria Lippincott thought someone was out to get her. Maybe she had lots of money.

But no. She said her husband had cleaned her out and she might have to sell her home. So that theory didn't hold water. If what she'd said was true.

Unless there was some kind of insurance policy on her life held by someone I didn't know about. "Say, Sam, do you know if anybody's taken out a life-insurance policy on Gloria Lippincott?"

Sam said, "No," in such a way that told me he didn't intend to entertain questions from me about the Gloria Lippincott problem. Blast.

He pulled the Hudson to a halt in front of my house, and I waited in the machine until he opened my door. This, in spite of his uncooperativeness.

Spike was overjoyed to see us again. So I sat down, smack, on the floor and let the sweet doggie crawl over me and give me kisses. Sam looked upon this with disfavor writ large on his features. I frowned up at him. "What's the matter? Don't you approve of people having fun with their dogs?"

"I don't care what people do with their dogs. I wouldn't want a dog licking my face, is all."

The telephone rang. Sam and I looked at each other.

"Maybe it's Kincaid," said Sam.

I groaned as I got to my feet, giving Spike one last pat. "Maybe it is. It's kind of late for anyone to be calling." Our party-line neighbors would be incensed. It was almost ten o'clock at night. Oh, well.

I answered the telephone as soon as I could get to it. "Gumm-Majesty residence. Mrs. Majesty speaking."

"Daisy!" shrieked a voice on the other end of the wire. The voice was so distraught, I couldn't tell who it belonged to at first.

"Yes?" I said, donning my purring, subdued spiritualist's voice. I was pretty sure this wasn't Mrs. Pinkerton calling, because I'd come to recognize her various squeals and wails years earlier.

"It's Griselda Bissel," sobbed the voice, surprising me. I was accustomed to wailing from Mrs. Pinkerton, but Mrs. Bissel was a sane and sober woman, even if she was rich as Croesus, whoever he was.

"Whatever is the matter, Mrs. Bissel?" I said, worried.

"They've arrested *Dennis!*"

I nearly dropped the receiver.

TWELVE

"They've *what?*" I confess to having been shocked out of my spiritualist role.

"They've arrested Dennis," Mrs. Bissel repeated. "They say he killed someone with his automobile! That woman's husband! The one who's after Dennis. Not the woman. Her husband. They say he killed him with his machine!"

"Good heavens. I can't believe Dennis would do any such thing."

"He didn't!"

"I'm sure he didn't." Her words had so rattled me, I didn't know what to say, but I was absolutely positive that sweet Dennis Bissel, whose sweet wife, Patsy, adored him, would never, in a million years, run over anybody with his automobile. Heck, hitting a body might dent the fender or something. Not that Dennis would think of anything like that. Oh, never mind.

"Oh, Daisy, I need you to do something!"

"Um...I'm not sure what I can do, Mrs. Bissel," I said, feeling as though I were letting my side down.

Then I nearly jumped out of my skin when a pair of big, warm hands settled on my shoulders. Sam. I was *so* tired and *so* sick of problems that I actually allowed myself to lean back against his big, warm chest for a minute.

"What is it, Daisy? What's going on?" he murmured in my ear.

To Mrs. Bissel, I said, "Can you hold the wire for a moment, Mrs. Bissel?" Putting my hand over the receiver, I told Sam about Dennis being arrested. He frowned, although this frown didn't seem to be aimed at me for once. With a gesture, he asked me to hand him the receiver. So I did, with fathomless relief. Sam would know what to do. Sam could take care of Dennis. Sam would sort it all out.

As for me, I more or less wilted onto a kitchen chair, and Spike put his paws in my lap. I petted him as I listened to Sam's side of the conversation.

His voice was surprisingly gentle when he said, "Mrs. Bissel, this is Detective Rotondo." Pause. "I drove Daisy home from the *Mikado* rehearsal tonight." Pause. "Yes, I saw your son and his wife there." Pause, and Sam's frown deepened. "No, I didn't realize that." Pause. "I'll be glad to look into the matter for you." Pause. "You're welcome." Pause, and Sam grimaced. "Yes. I'll give her back the receiver."

Glowering, he held out the receiver to me, so I had to get up and go to the telephone. I didn't want to. "Mrs. Bissel? Was Detective Rotondo of help to you?"

She seemed to have stopped crying, thank God. "He said he'll look into the problem for me. Oh, *thank* you, Daisy. I know Dennis would never have hurt anyone."

"I believe you, Mrs. Bissel. I can't imagine Dennis as a coldblooded murderer, either." I shot a glance at Sam, who rolled his eyes. Only to be expected from that source.

"Can you come over tomorrow, Daisy? Just to see if Rolly has anything to say about this mess?"

"Of course. I'll be happy to visit and consult Rolly with you." I lied quite nobly, if I do say so myself.

"Thank you, Daisy."

"You're welcome, Mrs. Bissel."

I hung the receiver in the cradle and went back to the kitchen table. Sam had taken a chair, and I sank into the one I'd recently vacated. "I really can't believe Dennis Bissel would murder anyone."

"I'll look into it," said Sam.

After thinking about and rejecting several pungent comments, I said only, "Thank you."

"You're welcome."

I walked him to the door with Spike trotting along at my side. At the door, I almost fell over when Sam bent and gave me a peck. On the lips. Lips that Spike had licked not long before.

Then he left, and I stood there gaping at the door until Spike nudged me. So I took the two of us off to bed.

I rolled out of bed about sevenish the following morning. I didn't want to rise. I wanted to curl up, pull the quilt over my head, and hide out for a year or so.

But I'd promised Mrs. Bissel I'd go to see her, and the poor woman was so upset, I couldn't in conscience break my word. Therefore, I forced myself to leave the nice, warm bed. Spike, I noticed, was long gone. He'd probably got down from the bed the minute Aunt Vi or Pa had walked into the kitchen. Spike was no fool. And I always made sure the hinges on my bedroom door were oiled so it wouldn't squeak when anyone opened it to allow Spike out.

After thinking about getting dressed for approximately thirty seconds, I decided I'd save big decisions until after breakfast, so I put my ratty old robe on over my ratty old nightgown, stuffed my feet into my ratty old slippers, and staggered out to the kitchen.

"Morning, sunshine," said Pa, grinning at me from the kitchen table.

"Uhhh. Morning, Pa." I shuffled over to the stove, where Vi had left a pot of coffee on the warming plate. I grabbed a mug from the cupboard and poured coffee into it. Then I went back to the table, where Pa was reading the morning *Star News*. Spike sat at his feet, looking up at him as if he expected a bite of food to appear miraculously, although he did turn his head and wag at me. I loved my dog. He was always happy to see me, even when I looked like the wrath of God.

"I see here where it says there was some excitement at church last night," said Pa, peering at me over the paper, which he'd crunched down.

I sipped the bitter brew. I really don't care for coffee, but it perks one up in the morning. Tea does, too, but you have to boil water and measure tea and heat the pot and so forth, and the coffee was already made, thanks to Aunt Vi.

After swallowing, I said, "You have no idea."

"It says here that a stone fell from the church roof and almost injured a member of the cast of *The Mikado*."

"It didn't fall. Someone threw—or maybe shoved—it from the roof. It almost hit Gloria Lippincott. She thinks somebody is trying to kill her."

"Lippincott? Isn't that the name of the man who was run down the other day?"

"Yes. She's his wife. Widow, I guess, at this point. They were estranged, whatever that means. I guess they'd lived apart for a couple of years. He wanted a divorce, but she wouldn't give him one. Or the other way around. I can't remember. Oh, and the police arrested Dennis Bissel, Mrs. Bissel's son, for murdering him. Gloria's husband. Late husband, I mean. Late estranged husband. Oh, bother. Anyhow, I don't believe for a single second that he did it. Dennis, I mean. He didn't kill Mr. Lippincott." I yawned and rubbed my gritty eyes. "What a mess."

Silence greeted my explanation. Opening my eyes wider, I saw Pa staring at me, an odd expression on his face.

"What?" I asked. "What's the matter?"

"Mrs. Bissel's son was arrested for murdering the husband of a woman who was almost killed last night at the church? *Our* church?"

Oh, dear. Perhaps I should have taken more care with my words. I sighed. "Yes. Our church. Bet the worship committee isn't going to like this one little bit."

"I'm on the worship committee, and I don't like it," said Pa, rather tartly for him. "Nor will Pastor Smith, I imagine." Pastor Merle Negley Smith had been the preacher in charge of the First Methodist-Episcopal Church for several years by that time.

Dismayed, I gazed at him for a couple of seconds, worried that he aimed to blame me for something. "It wasn't my idea to sing in *The Mikado*," I said, a plea in my voice. "And I had no idea Mr. Hostetter would agree to stage it at the church." I added lamely, "It's for a good cause."

Folding his newspaper and laying it on the table, Pa reached for the hand that wasn't clutching my coffee mug for dear life. "I know that, Daisy. None of that was your fault. But you do seem to get caught up in the most alarming circumstances sometimes."

"You sound like Sam," I told him bitterly.

He grinned. "Sorry, sweetheart. I just hate that such terrible things seem to happen around you." He shook his head.

I understood his concern. Things *did* seem to happen around me. I didn't like it, either. "Well, Sam was here when Mrs. Bissel telephoned last night, and he told her he'd look into the matter of Dennis running down Michael Lippincott. Which I'm sure he didn't." I groaned softly. "But I promised Mrs. Bissel I'd take Rolly up to her house and have him chat with her."

Pa squinted at me for a moment or two and then said, "Hmm. Maybe that's it."

"Maybe what's what?" I asked, not sure I wanted to know.

"Maybe your odd line of work attracts the strange things that seem to occur around you."

"You're not going to tell me you suddenly believe in ghosts, Pa!"

He chuckled. "No, no, no. But you have to admit that holding séances and pretending to talk to dead people isn't an average job for an average woman."

"Of course, it isn't. But I'm good at it, and I make a lot of money doing it."

"I know, sweetheart. But maybe...Oh, I don't know. I'm probably wrong, but you have an unusual profession, and unusual things seem to crop up in your vicinity. Quite often."

"I guess." But I didn't want to talk about it any longer. "Did Vi make anything for breakfast?" I grabbed an orange from the bowl on the table and began peeling it. It was of the navel variety and easy to peel.

"She fried up some cornmeal mush. I think she left a plate for you in the oven."

"Bless her heart." I grunted when I rose from my seat. I really had to get more exercise. I was turning into a marshmallow. However, that didn't prevent me from enjoying the fried mush and bacon my wonderful aunt had so thoughtfully left for me.

Speaking of my wonderful aunt, she appeared in the kitchen just then, along with my wonderful mother. Both of them were dressed for work. I felt like a slacker.

"Daisy, were you there when that stone fell on that woman?" Vi asked.

"That's terrible!" said my mother. "And at our church, too!"

Fudge. Why hadn't I just stayed in bed as I'd wanted to? Too late now. I smiled at the two most important women in my life and said, "Someone shoved a big paving stone off the roof of the church, but it didn't hit anyone. It sure rattled everybody, though. I wasn't there when it happened. Sam had just dropped me off at home, and we both drove back to the church after Harold called to tell me about it." I was pretty sure even my unimaginative mother could follow that speech.

Ma shook her head. "I'm not sure I approve of such goings-on at our church."

"I don't approve of such goings-on anywhere," I replied, meaning it sincerely. "That stone might have killed someone if it had hit him or her."

"Says here it was aimed at that lady whose husband was killed the other day," said Pa, pointing to the paper.

I sighed. "Well, it didn't hit her."

"I'm glad of that," said Ma. "But still..." She shook her head. "At our church."

"Pa's going to take it up with the worship committee," I told her.

"I expect Pastor Smith will have something to say about the matter, too," said Ma.

Oh, dear. I hated that my church was involved in an attempted crime. Well, the church itself wasn't, but...Oh, you know what I mean. Darn Mr. Floy Hostetter and Harold Kincaid both!

And, as if on cue, the telephone rang. I sagged slightly in my chair, but I knew where my duty lay, so I got up from the table and walked to the 'phone. It was early, dang it. Too early for people to be telephoning me. Not that the time of day had ever stopped anyone before.

I sucked in a gigantic breath and picked up the receiver. "Gumm-Majesty Res—"

"Dennis Bissel wasn't arrested."

Sam.

"He wasn't?"

"No. He was brought to the station for questioning last night. It's almost certain that Bissel's machine was used to run down Michael Lippincott. There's paint on Lippincott's body and a dent in Bissel's auto with what looks like a piece of Lippincott's coat stuck in it."

My comprehension skills weren't at their peak yet that morning. I stared at the cradle where the receiver had lately been and said, "Huh?"

"That's why Dennis Bissel was taken in to be questioned." Sam sounded annoyed. "Because his car was used to kill a man. And for all anyone knows at this point, Bissel was driving it at the time."

"But...But..."

"Don't ask me. I don't know any more than that."

"But did Dennis even *know* Michael Lippincott?"

"How the hell should I know? Bissel's car killed the man. That's all I know."

"Are they sure about this?"

"Of course, they're sure! We don't go around picking up people to question for the hell of it."

"Good Lord."

"Yeah, I guess so. An arrest may follow, depending on circumstances and if Bissel can prove where he was the night of the murder." And he hung up.

I stood there, staring at the receiver in my hand, for what seemed like infinity. I jumped when Pa said, "Daisy? Are you all right?" and gently put the receiver back into the cradle.

But I was far from all right. "That was Sam," I said. "He said it's been proved that Dennis Bissel's car was the one that ran down Michael Lippincott." I stared at my family, who all stared back at me, aghast. Except for Spike, of course, who was never aghast.

"Mrs. Bissel's son?" asked Ma, who liked to make sure everything was clear and precise before taking it as the truth.

"That's the one, all right," I said. "But I don't believe he did it. Someone must have borrowed his car, or stolen it. Or something like that. Dennis Bissel wouldn't hurt a fly. At least, I don't think he would."

Maybe I was wrong. What the heck did I know? At that point, nothing. Nuts.

"I've got to get dressed and go to Mrs. Bissel's house." I started for my bedroom, but Pa stopped me.

"You'd better telephone her first, to see if she's home. She might be down at the police station, trying to bail out her son or something."

I turned to stare at my father. "Oh, Lord. You're right." What a dismal thought.

Although, after I thought about the matter for a moment or two, it was better to have Mrs. Bissel mixed up in a mess than Mrs. Pinkerton. Mrs. Bissel was sure to be upset by these goings-on, but she didn't get irrational and wail at me.

Small comfort.

I decided to dress before using the telephone. After all, Sam had called me at an indecently early hour, but that didn't mean I had to be rude, too. So, after seeing my mother and aunt out the door with good wishes for them both, I went into our bathroom and took a bubble bath. What the heck. I needed soothing.

Then I approached my closet. I'd removed Billy's clothes from it, although they still sat in our basement, folded up in boxes, because I couldn't quite bear to get rid of them yet. Selfish, I guess. I should take his duds down to Johnny Buckingham, Captain in the Salvation Army, to use. He always had a bunch of down-and-out poor folks who could use them.

But I wasn't ready to lose of the last of my Billy yet.

The closet revealed a host of costumes, made by my own clever hands. I sneered at them all, then walked to the door of the outside deck Pa had built for Billy and me to use when we wanted to be private outdoors, to check the weather.

Nippy. Good. That gave me something to start with. I toddled back to the closet.

After some fumbling around—I *really* didn't want to go to Mrs. Bissel's house that day—I decided a sober brown suit would be appropriate. It wasn't a doleful dark brown, but a rusty-brown color that kind of matched my hair. The suit had a three-quarter length unfitted jacket with a wide collar, around which I'd cleverly sewn a dark brown edging. The straight skirt came to my mid-calf. With it I wore a white blouse and a man's tie with a brown-and-rust stripe. I wore my black low-heeled shoes, black gloves and plopped my brown cloche hat on my head. There. Serious but not despondent. Spike wagged at me, so I guess he approved.

I walked from my room to the kitchen, where Pa still sat at the table, cracking walnuts, probably for Aunt Vi to use when she baked something scrumptious. He liked to help around the house when he could, bless his heart. He looked up as I entered the room, and his eyebrows lifted in approval.

"You look swell," said he.

"Thanks," said I. "I'm trying to be serious but not dismal."

"I think you've pulled it off quite well."

"Thanks, Pa." Then I sighed and walked to the telephone, lifted the receiver, found none of our party-line neighbors on the wire, and dialed Mrs. Bissel's number.

She was home, darn it.

THIRTEEN

At least I knew I looked all right as I drove up Lake Avenue to Foothill Boulevard and turned right. Mrs. Bissel owned all the property from the corner of Maiden Lane on the east to Lake Avenue on the west. It was a huge estate, but I'd heard rumblings from her about how she might just sell some of her land now that her children had married and left the nest, and she only had her daughters' two horses to roam the vast acreage.

Must be nice to have property to sell off.

On the other hand, none of my kin owned automobiles that had been used to murder anyone. At least I hoped like mad they didn't.

I parked on the circular driveway in the back of the house and walked across the lovely paved courtyard to the back door. During the summer, the Daphne hedge lining the courtyard smelled heavenly. However, summer was gone and now everything was merely bleak and cold. I rang the bell, and Keiji Saito, who seemed to have been waiting for me, opened the door and let me in.

"Good morning, Keiji," I said, which was probably a stupid thing to say under the circumstances.

"You wouldn't know it from the mood around this place," said Keiji, confirming me in the notion that my comment had been inapt.

"Is Mrs. Bissel all right? I mean, I know she's worried and every-thing, but——"

"All things considered, she's doing okay. Dennis and Patsy are with her in the living room right now." Keiji's voice was soft, probably because we were in the sun room, and the living room was straight ahead of us.

I heaved a sigh, took a breath for courage, said, "Thanks, Keiji," and walked onto the field of battle—which was an almost-appropriate word when I saw that the room held only wounded people.

Very well; they weren't physically wounded, but I'd never seen a gloomier family gathering in my life…with the possible exception of the one at my house after Billy's funeral.

Dennis and Patsy sat together on a sofa, holding hands. Mrs. Bissel sat in a chair near the sofa, petting a couple of dachshunds. Everyone glanced at me as I entered the room. The dogs—I do believe they were Lucille and Lancelot, Spike's parents—bounded from Mrs. Bissel's lap in order to race over and say hello to me. They brightened my mood a bit as I stooped to pet them.

"Lucille!" cried Mrs. Bissel, confirming my suspicions about which of her billions of dachshunds had just vacated her lap. "Lancelot! Come here!"

Lucille and Lancelot, unlike their son, Spike, had never been to obedience school, I reckon, because they continued to frolic at my feet for several seconds until Mrs. Bissel clapped her hands. I could swear both dogs sighed as they trotted back to their mistress, jumped back onto the chair and snuggled their way onto her lap.

"Thank you so much for coming today, Daisy," said Mrs. Bissel.

"Yes," Patsy said in a voice thick with leftover tears. "Thank you, Mrs. Majesty."

Dennis stared at me with eyes that appeared to have sunk into his face. He wore an expression of befuddled misery. "I don't know how anyone used my machine to kill that man. I didn't even know him."

I walked over and took a chair near the family group. "Detective Rotondo is working on the case," I said, trying to sound as if Sam's interest in Dennis and his automobile were benign. For all I knew, Sam truly believed Dennis had deliberately set out to murder Mr. Lippincott.

"But who would have taken my machine to kill a man?" Dennis wailed softly.

I shook my head. "What kind of automobile do you own?"

"It's a Silver Ghost. 1922. Got it last year when Patsy and I were married."

Mercy sakes. He owned a Rolls Royce Silver Ghost. His mother had a Daimler and a chauffeur to drive it for her. I asked, "Do you have a chauffeur, or do you drive it yourself?" I considered my family fortunate to own a 1921 self-starting Chevrolet instead of the old 1909 Ford Model-T we'd had since...well, 1909. And we couldn't even have been able to afford that old Ford if not for one of Pa's old clients—he used to be a chauffeur for rich folks—who'd given it to us.

"No, I don't have a chauffeur. I drive it myself, although I didn't drive it that night. I was at the club, and took a cab there from work."

I perked up slightly. "Your club? Where's your club?"

"North El Molino, near Colorado," said Dennis.

Aha. The same club—perhaps—where Michael Lippincott held a membership. "I understand Mr. Lippincott was run down in front of his own club, which is on El Molino," I said.

Dennis's mouth fell open. "I-I-I...I don't know what to say. I didn't know the man."

"Do you know how many members belong to your club?"

Shaking his head, Dennis said, "A lot, I guess, although I don't know. There are many men I don't know who go there to play cards or pool or whatever. I just went there for a meal, because Patsy was attending a charity thing at church."

"A charity thing?" I asked, hoping for clarification.

"We sew and knit clothing for orphans of the Great War," Patsy said with another sniffle. "At St. Mark's."

"That's right across the street, isn't it?"

"Yes. Mother Bissel and I go every Wednesday evening. There were so many orphans left to fend for themselves after that awful conflict. We send at least one box of knitted or hand-sewn children's clothing every month to Belgium or France or Russia."

"I see. That's very good of you." Of course, there were orphans in the good old U.S. of A. thanks to that blasted war, too, but I didn't think it would be appropriate to say so. Both Mrs. Bissels meant their work kindly.

"Did you drive your automobile to St. Mark's?" I asked Patsy.

She looked at me as if she thought I was nuts. "Drive? Me? I don't drive. Henry picked me up with Mother Bissel, and drove us both to St. Mark's." Henry was Mrs. Bissel's chauffeur.

"So your machine was home alone," I said, musing, and sounding as if they'd abandoned a child to its fate that Wednesday night. I didn't mean to sound that way.

"Yes. It was parked in the drive. Well, you know where we live, don't you? Just down the street from Mother," said Dennis.

"A little east of here, right?"

"Yes. Next door to the Dearings."

"Ah. I see." Dr. Dearing and his family lived directly across Maiden Lane from Mrs. Bissel. They had a grand home, too, although it didn't have acres and acres of land around it. I was familiar with Foothill Boulevard, which ran east-west through Altadena until it took a dive south into Pasadena a little way past Allen Avenue. I couldn't quite visualize the home where Dennis and Patsy lived, but I knew for a rock-solid certainty that it was as huge an abode as Mrs. Bissel's. Probably without so much land circling it. "That's a large property for a young couple," I mentioned just for the heck of it.

Patsy's face bloomed red. "Well, we want to start a family soon."

"Of course." I thought for a second. "Is your property fenced off? I mean, do you have to open a gate or anything to get to the drive?"

"No," said Dennis.

"Out of curiosity, why didn't you take your automobile to work that day?" I asked him, feeling quite detective as I did so.

With a shrug, he said, "I knew Patsy wouldn't be home after I left work and that I'd dine at the club. There's not a lot of parking space available at the club, so I took a cab to work."

Sounded reasonable to me. But something else didn't. "Do you have any idea at all who would play such a trick on you? I mean, to steal your automobile in order to murder a man is terrible thing to do."

Dennis and Patsy looked at each other, and it appeared to me as if their handhold tightened. I couldn't see Gloria Lippincott prying a wedge between those two, although stranger things have happened, I suppose. After staring at each other for an appreciable time, they both turned to look at me.

Dennis said, "No."

So did Patsy.

I hadn't been paying attention to Mrs. Bissel during my inquisition of poor Dennis, but when she burst out with, "*I* do!" I jumped. I think Patsy and Dennis did, too. We turned as one to stare at her.

Dennis said, "You do?"

"Yes, I do! It's that awful woman who's been trying to get you away from Patsy! That's who did it!"

Both her son and his wife assumed blank expressions. Dennis said, "Um..."

Patsy said, "Er..."

I guess Mrs. Bissel was frustrated beyond bearing because she lifted a magazine—the latest *Saturday Evening Post*, from the looks of it, and slammed it on the table beside the sofa. Lancelot and Lucille both yipped and skedaddled out of the room as if someone had set fire to their tails.

"Oh, for heaven's sake! Don't tell me neither one of you have noticed that Lippincott creature has had her eye on you for months now, Dennis Bissel!"

An exchange of glances took place between Dennis and Patsy. Whatever Mrs. Bissel thought, it looked to me as if they not only hadn't noticed Mrs. Lippincott's intentions, but were at a loss to explain Mrs. Bissel's declaration.

"Mrs. Lippincott?" said Dennis, his eyebrows dipping above his nose. "Who's—? Oh. You mean that murdered man's wife. Widow, I guess I mean."

"Dennis Bissel, if you aren't the most innocent...Well, I just don't know what to say." Mrs. Bissel turned to Patsy. "And you! Don't tell me *you* never noticed that woman sidling up to your husband and insinuating herself into his company every time she has a chance."

Patsy opened her mouth, but it didn't seem to contain any words, because she shut it again.

"Mother," said Dennis, his dignity high. "I believe you must be mistaken."

"I'm *not* mistaken!" declared Mrs. Bissel. "I've seen her. Every time you enter a room, her claws come out, her whiskers twitch, and she tracks you like a cat stalking a mouse."

Impressed by her imaginative description, I still felt impelled to add my coin to the conversation. "Um...I'm not saying you're wrong about this, Mrs. Bissel, but at rehearsal last night, she seemed to have her claws firmly implanted in Lawrence Allen. I don't think she paid much attention to you, Dennis. Did she?"

"Lawrence Allen?" Dennis said. "But he's married!"

Dennis's mother rolled her eyes. I felt like doing the same thing.

Patsy frowned. "Sylvia Allen did look rather upset, if I recall correctly."

"I believe that was because Mrs. Lippincott had latched onto Mr. Allen after that rock was pushed off the church roof," I explained.

"Oh, now, I don't believe for one minute that—" Dennis stopped speaking abruptly and turned a sort of magenta color.

"Yes?" I asked, honey dripping from the word.

"I told you so," said Mrs. Bissel, sounding bitter.

"But..." Patsy evidently couldn't think of anything to follow the one word.

"I-I...Well, I think you're all maligning a perfectly decent woman. Gloria is—"

"You call her *Gloria?*" Patsy.

"That's her name, isn't it?" Dennis.

"I had no idea the two of you were on a first-name basis." Patsy.

"Oh, for heaven's sake. She's never given me any indication that she favors me particularly. In fact...In fact, she's been nothing but pleasant to me on the few occasions we've met at parties and so forth."

"Pleasant, my foot," said his mother.

Patsy tilted her head. "Hmm. Yes. Now that you mention it, Mother Bissel, I've noticed that she seems to...well, add herself to any group Dennis is a part of on social occasions. That is to say *Gloria* does."

"But..." Dennis appeared positively shocked.

"Told you so," said Mrs. Bissel. "You're too young and innocent to understand the wiles of a woman like that."

In order to forestall a family argument, I said, "She might be a seductress at heart, but it wasn't she who stole your Rolls and ran down her husband. The police have proved that she was playing bridge at Mrs. Hastings' house that night."

Silence fell over the room like a blanket.

"There. I told you she didn't have anything to do with it," said Dennis at last, seeming smug about it.

Patsy said, "Hmph."

"However," I went on, "she may well be in collaboration with someone, and that someone might have stolen—or borrowed—your automobile for the fell purpose of killing her estranged husband and implicating you."

"How…What do you mean?" Dennis demanded, sounding angry. "Why would she do that, anyway?"

"Why would anyone?" I asked back.

Dennis pursed his lips.

Mrs. Bissel said, "Good question."

I shrugged. "I don't know why your auto was chosen as the murder weapon, but Gloria Lippincott might well be in complicity with another person, although I don't know who, to do away with her husband."

"Not Lawrence Allen," said Patsy, clearly aghast and agog. "He's such a nice man!"

"He was snuggling with Mrs. Lippincott after the rock incident," I said, perhaps too acidly.

"But the woman had nearly been killed!" cried Dennis. "It was natural for a man to comfort her."

My cynical antennae began to buzz, but I didn't let on. Women need men to comfort them sort of like they need cobras with which to snuggle up at night.

"As long as it wasn't you," said Patsy with more spirit than I'd given her credit for up to this time.

"Of course, it wasn't me!" said Dennis, outraged, if I were to guess.

"Hmm. Well, say what you will about Mrs. Lippincott, I know

Sylvia Allen was upset by Lawrence's attentions to her last night," said Patsy. Then she sniffed.

Oh, dear. The two lovebirds' hands unclasped. I hadn't meant cause a rift between them. And I wasn't even a seductress.

"Stuff and nonsense!" said Mrs. Bissel, bringing the discussion to a close. "I've seen the woman in action, Dennis, and I *know* she's trying to get you away from Patsy. And *you*," she said, glaring at Patsy, "aren't doing yourself or Dennis any favors by hiding your head in the sand. Keep an eye on my boy, and don't let him stray."

"Mother!" Dennis's indignation was so high, it nearly hit the ceiling.

Patsy drew herself up straight and said, "Very well. I'll be observant and see that she doesn't...doesn't...take Dennis away from me." The young woman sounded more resolute than I'd have imagined she could sound, had I not heard her for myself.

"I can take care of myself!" cried Dennis.

"Stuff," said Mrs. Bissel.

"Come with me," said Patsy, and she grabbed her husband's hand and led him out of the room. He left under protest, but he left.

"I swear," said Mrs. Bissel. "I didn't realize I'd reared such a naïve son until this minute."

"Enlightening conversation. But would you like me to consult Rolly for you now, Mrs. Bissel?" I wasn't keen on more family drama.

"Thank you, dear. I'm sorry you have to be involved in this mess."

"I'm not involved," I told her, perhaps a shade too forcefully.

Mrs. Bissel, however, knew better. I could tell.

With a sigh, I withdrew my Ouija board from its cloth bag and placed it on the table in front of the sofa.

Rolly didn't have a whole lot to tell Mrs. Bissel, although she claimed our Ouija-board session helped calm her nerves.

"I'm so glad Rolly and I could help, Mrs. Bissel. I'm sure the police will discover the real culprit soon."

With a sniff, she said, "I don't know. Dennis's car was used to do the evil deed. Do you really think they'll look farther than Dennis?"

"I..." Oh, heck, I didn't know.

"But you *will* help, won't you, dear?" she said, giving me a speaking look. What that look said was, "You'll find the killer and make sure the police don't pin this ghastly crime on Dennis, won't you?"

I wanted to shriek at her that I was a phony spiritualist-medium, not a dratted detective, and to go away and leave me alone. Since I couldn't say that, I answered Mrs. Bissel's question to the best of my ability. "I don't know what I can do, Mrs. Bissel." It was the truth.

"But you can keep an eye on things, can't you?"

"Keep an eye on what things?"

"At rehearsals for *The Mikado*!" she said, as if I were a ninny for asking. "You can observe everyone, especially that Lippincott female, and make sure she doesn't snatch Dennis from Patsy."

"Um…"

"And don't forget that detective friend of yours."

I also wanted to scream at her that Sam Rotondo wasn't my friend, but a friend of my late husband's. But I knew that wasn't the truth any longer.

Oh, boy. But I needed my job, so I said without a whole lot of energy, "I suppose I can do that." As long as Sam Rotondo didn't catch me "observing". I didn't add that last part.

FOURTEEN

After I left Mrs. Bissel's house, I drove past the younger Bissels' home. There it was: huge and not particularly inviting; a giant of a house, waiting, if Patsy were to be believed, to be filled with happy, smiling children with rich parents and a proud grandma. Well, and I presume they'd have proud grandparents on their mother's side, too. Good luck to it, said I to myself. And to the Bissels.

I didn't see Dennis's Rolls-Royce in the drive. I suspected it was in police custody still. Depressing thought. How in the world could anyone prove that Dennis Bissel hadn't used his own automobile to run down Michael Lippincott? Evidently both Dennis and Michael had been at the self-same club at the time of the murder. Were there any witnesses to testify to the fact that Dennis and Michael didn't leave the club at the same time? Or that Dennis hadn't driven his machine to the club that day?

Fudge. Those were questions to which the police needed to find answers; I just hoped they'd bother to ask them.

I drove myself home after that, feeling drained. I felt sorry for Mrs. Bissel. I felt sorry for Patsy and Dennis Bissel, and I didn't for a second believe he'd had anything to do with the death of Michael Lippincott. But how to prove it?

Find the real murderer, of course. But how did one go about doing that? And if the one in question were me, did she even want to get involved in attempting to track down a vicious killer? The answer to *that* question was simple: heck, no.

For once, I found myself hoping Sam would come to dinner at our house that Friday night. I'd grill him like a leg of lamb over an open flame—I'd seen that done in Turkey, and the results had been truly delectable—and hope he wouldn't holler at me.

I was in luck, if you can call it that. Sam did come over for dinner that night. He showed up at about five o'clock, ostensibly to ask me questions about members of the *The Mikado's* cast. I suspected he only wanted a good meal cooked by Aunt Vi.

As I was in the process of setting the table for dinner, I roped Sam into helping me as I answered his questions.

"What do you know about Lawrence and Sylvia Allen?"

"Nothing. Only that they're married, not that you'd know it from the way Lawrence carried on with Gloria Lippincott last night."

"What about the Van der Lindens? What do you know about them?"

"You're supposed to put the fork on the left side of the plate, Sam. The knife and spoon go on the right." Before he could do more than frown at me, I said, "I don't know even more about the Van der Lindens than I don't know about the Allens. Why? Do you think Lawrence or Max shoved that paving stone off the roof?"

Changing the placement of the silverware, Sam said, "I'm the one asking questions here."

"Yeah, yeah, yeah. I know. But I still don't know anything about either couple. Harold Kincaid introduced me to the Van der Lindens. I'd met the Allens at other gatherings. At Mrs. Pinkerton's house, I think, although they may have been to a party at Mrs. Bissel's house. They aren't pals of mine, if that's what you mean."

"Huh."

I handed him some soup bowls.

"What do I do with these?"

"Put them on top of the dinner plates. Vi said we're having chicken stew for dinner, so we'll eat it out of bowls, and put our bread on the plates beside the bowls." I'm sure that wasn't how my wealthy clients dealt with chicken stew, but we weren't they. We were the Gumms and the one remaining Majesty. So phooey on them.

"Sounds good," said Sam.

"You know it'll be good. Aunt Vi's fixing it."

Vi, who had come home about an hour earlier, appeared at the door between the kitchen and the dining room. "Did I hear my name taken in vain?"

"Nope. I just told Sam I knew the chicken stew would be good because you're making it."

With a smile and a shake of her head, Vi said, "You're such a caution, Daisy."

Whatever that meant. Vi was full of odd expressions.

"Anything you cook is bound to be delicious, Mrs. Gumm," said Sam, slathering on the flattery. Not that he needed to. Everyone in the entire household loved Sam, with the possible exception of me, and I wasn't sure about me any longer. As soon as that thought hit me, I decided I'd best not think much for the rest of the evening.

However, my vow not to think didn't exclude the desire to learn the answers to several questions.

"I talked to Dennis Bissel today," I told Sam.

Naturally, he glowered at me. "Why the hell did you do that?"

"Don't swear at me. Especially in front of my aunt."

Sam's head snapped up and he glanced at the door to the kitchen. Vi was gone. I smirked. Not kind of me, but there you go.

"He was at his mother's house when I took my Ouija board up there. She asked me to come," I added before Sam could explode or anything. "Dennis and Patsy were there with Mrs. Bissel when we arrived. It was only natural that we discuss the murder of Michael Lippincott, since Dennis is a suspect in his death."

"Aw, cripes."

"Don't 'aw, cripes' me, Sam Rotondo. Dennis was at his club, which I think is the same one Michael Lippincott belonged to, the same evening that Mr. Lippincott was killed. Have you discussed both men with the club's members or management?"

"Yes," he said. "We know our job, Daisy."

"Just want to make sure. What did you find out?"

"What I found out is a police matter."

I darned nearly slammed the salt cellar onto the table. I'm glad I didn't, because I not only would probably have broken the salt cellar, which was a cute blue thing with curlicues around its top, but salt would have gone everywhere. "That's not fair! Here you come asking me all sorts of questions, to which I'm supposed to give honest answers, yet you won't tell me what's going on! I *know* Dennis Bissel didn't kill that harpy's husband! I want to know what you're doing to prove it, Sam Rotondo."

Sam's mouth opened, I'm sure in order to give me a piece of his mind, but I ran over anything he'd been going to say not unlike a freight train running over a cow. Erk. Don't know what made me think about a dead cow.

"For instance, I'll bet you anything that Gloria Lippincott is in cahoots with the man who stole Dennis's car and ran down Mr. Lippincott and then returned the machine to Dennis's driveway. I drove past the junior Bissels' house after I left Mrs. Bissel, and there's no fence or gate or anything. Naturally, the auto wasn't in the drive, because——"

"The forensics people still have it."

"Precisely. But it would be dead easy for someone to have taken it that Wednesday evening. Patsy and Mrs. B were at St. Mark's knitting or sewing stuff for orphans in Europe, and Dennis had taken a taxicab to work because he knew he'd be dining at his club that night."

"So he says."

"I believe him. He said parking is difficult to find near his club, so it's easier to take a cab."

From the frown on Sam's face, I concluded I'd introduced a salient point. Therefore, I pounded on it for a bit. "And that's something you can check in to without bestirring yourself. You can telephone the stupid club from your stupid office and find out if Dennis's story is true. And don't the men who belong to the club have to sign in and out or something? Betcha they have a record of who was there when on that fatal night."

"We're looking into——"

"And while you're at it, you can check with the taxicab company, can't you? Don't they have records of whom they take where?"

"We know our job, dammit."

"Pooh. And then there's Lawrence Allen, who was all over Gloria Lippincott last night after that stone thing fell. Sylvia Allen was livid. Have you checked Lawrence's alibi? And what about other men in Gloria Lippincott's life? According to gossip, she's after Dennis Bissel. Who else is she after? Could she have connived with one of her lovers to do away with her husband? And why? Did he have a big insurance policy on his life? There *has* to be a good reason for someone to murder someone else! It couldn't have been so she could marry Mr. Allen, because he's already married, and I can't see Sylvia giving him a divorce for Gloria's sake."

"Why?"

Drat. He would have to ask me that, wouldn't he? "I don't know! I don't know anything! But *you* should know! You should be finding out these things, instead of coming over here and harassing me!"

Sam put his big hands on the table and leaned over so that he was almost face-to-face with me, as I stood on the other side of the table. I kind of wanted to back up, but I wouldn't give him the satisfaction.

"I'm not here to harass you," he whispered savagely. "I'm here to ask you questions about various cast members of that operetta." He shot a peek at the kitchen door, and lowered his voice. "And to get a decent meal, dammit. Do you know what it's like to be a single man in the city? A home-cooked meal is like a Christmas present for a guy like me."

"Oh."

Sam straightened and fiddled with the silverware, which didn't need it.

"Um. Can *you* join a club? I guess they serve meals at clubs. At least they do at the one Dennis and Mr. L belonged to."

"A rich man's club, you mean? I don't think so, but thanks."

"Oh. Well, surely there are other single men on the police force. Can't you dine out with them from time to time?"

"Do you know how boring Chinese food gets after several days in a row? Anyhow, dining out all the time is expensive." The police department was within walking distance of the Crown Chop Suey Parlor on Fair Oaks Avenue, so I understood his reference to Chinese food.

"I know. I'm sorry, Sam. But you know you're welcome here any time, don't you?"

"Am I?" He gave me a searching look that made me want to squirm.

After several seconds, I told the truth, dropping my gaze to the table as I did so. "Yes. You are."

"Thanks."

"You're welcome."

Sam huffed out a sigh and then said, "Is the table set to your satisfaction? May we retire to the living room so I can ask more questions about members of the *Mikado* cast?"

After surveying the table and finding it set to a T, I said, "Sure."

So we took ourselves to the living room, where I sat on the piano bench and Sam sat on a chair near it. I purposely avoided the sofa, because I didn't want to sit next to him on a piece of furniture and be discovered there by my parents or aunt. They might get the wrong idea. Or maybe it was the right idea. Whatever it was, I didn't want to think about it.

Spike jumped up onto Sam's lap. Traitor. On the other hand, the piano bench wasn't even comfortable for me to sit on, and Spike had his priorities straight. He didn't give a yip what anyone thought about him.

After absently petting Spike for a moment, Sam pulled a small notebook and pencil from his inside coat pocket. "All right. Let me see if I have this right. Mr. and Mrs. Van der Linden are the producers of the play, right?"

"The producers? I'd never thought about them as producers, but I suppose they are. It was all their idea, anyway."

"Right. So they're responsible for getting the operetta staged in town."

"Right."

"And they also act the parts of the two lovers in the play, right?"

I nodded. "Yes. Mr. Van der Linden is Nanki-Poo and Connie is Yum-Yum."

Sam's nose wrinkled. I saw it. "Crazy names."

"It's a comic opera."

"I guess. So that takes care of the Van der Lindens. Insofar as their relationship goes, I mean. They're married."

"Correct."

"Good. Harold is the Lord High Whatever he is, right?"

"Yes. He's the Lord High Executioner."

"Right. Then there's the Mikado. Who plays him?"

"Mr. George Finster. He's also in the choir."

"Right. And Mr. Floy Hostetter is…" Sam squinted at his list.

"Besides being our choir director, he's Pooh-Bah, the Lord High Everything Else. Except executioner. Harold's in charge of executions."

"Criminy. These names are crazy."

"Gilbert and Sullivan were two crazy fellas. They were what the press at the time called the kings of topsy-turvydom."

"If you say so. So then this Lawrence Allen guy is a noble lord named…Go-To?"

"That's right."

"Sheesh. Who are the three little maids?"

"Connie Van der Linden is one of them. She's Yum-Yum, and Yum-Yum is not only the heroine of the piece, but she's also one of the three little maids. The other two are Lucille Spinks and Gloria Lippincott, who's about as little maidish as Lucrezia Borgia."

"I see."

Sam had been writing names on his pad as fast as he could. "Anyone else I should know about?"

"I don't know! How should I know? I don't know what you're looking for. For pity's sake, Sam Rotondo—"

Sam held up one of his big hands, and I stopped hollering at him. "I just needed to get the names straight. So Dennis Bissel isn't in one of the starring roles?"

"No, and neither is Patsy, his wife. They're both in the chorus, along with just about everyone else in the church choir."

"Got it. Thanks, Daisy."

"You're welcome."

Sam frowned at his notebook for a moment or two. "Um…You said Dennis and Patsy and people from the choir are in the chorus. Are Dennis and Patsy members of your church?"

"Lord, no. They're rich. They go to St. Mark's Episcopal Church in Altadena, right across the street from Mrs. Bissel's house. I think if you're rich, you have to be either Episcopalian or Presbyterian."

Sam squinted at me. "Are you serious?"

I thought about it. "Sort of. I don't suppose there's any rule or law about it or anything, but most of the rich folks I know are either Episcopalians or Presbyterians. There are a few wealthy families in our Methodist Church, I reckon, but you don't find too many rich Baptists in Pasadena."

Still squinting, Sam said, "What about Roman Catholics?"

That's right. Sam, of Italian extraction, was probably a Roman Catholic. I'd never asked him about his religious beliefs before, and he'd showed up at our Methodist-Episcopal Church a few times. "I don't think there are too many wealthy Catholics in Pasadena, either. What about New York?" I was honestly curious.

"How the hell should I know?"

Darn him! "Well, you're Catholic, aren't you?"

"I was. I'm not much of anything now. And my family isn't rich."

"I thought your family owned a jewelry store in New York City."

"Yeah. But it's just a family business. We aren't railroad magnates or millionaire industrialists or anything like that."

"And you no longer consider yourself a Catholic?"

With a shrug, Sam said, "I don't really consider myself much of anything. Margaret went to the Congregational Church, so I attended there with her."

Margaret was Sam's late wife, who'd died of tuberculosis shortly after they'd moved to Pasadena. They'd hoped the move to a warmer climate would be good for her health, but tuberculosis evidently doesn't care what the weather's like. It kills you, no matter where you live. Which was a melancholy thought. So I changed the subject. In a way. "Weren't the Congregationalists big supporters of abolition and women's suffrage?"

"Yeah. But I went there anyway."

Trust Sam. "I think there's a Congregational Church in Pasadena."

"West Side Church," said he. "Margaret and I attended there while she still could. They've started uniting themselves with the Universalists."

It was all too much for me. "Why does the Christian Church have so many different offshoots?"

With a shrug, Sam said, "Human beings have never been able to get along with each other. Even when we claim to hold a common belief, we're always arguing. And fighting each other and everyone else, especially people of other faiths. Look at the Crusades and the Christians versus the Saracens. Killing for Christ."

"Sam Rotondo! That sounds awful," I said; then I thought about his words. "But I suppose you're right." I heaved a sigh.

He shrugged, and I thought a little bit more. "But it's not just Christians. Remember when those Turkish Moslems slaughtered all those Armenians in nineteen fifteen?"

"No, I don't remember that far back." He eyed me slantways. "And frankly, I'm surprised you do."

"Well," I admitted, "I don't really *remember*, but I read an article about it recently."

"The Turks probably thought the Armenians would defect to Russia, since Russia was a supposedly Christian nation, too, and Armenians are Christians as a culture, aren't they?"

"I think so."

"I thought you liked Turkey when you were there with Harold," said Sam.

"I did. And you were there, too, don't forget."

"How could I ever forget?"

"Harold shot a man for you."

"Thanks for reminding me. But all those young Turks must have over-reacted to a perceived threat, don't you think? After all, Russia bowed out of the war a couple of years later, didn't they?"

"Yes. In nineteen seventeen, but that's because the Tsar abdicated and the citizens were revolting."

"Aw, they're probably not *that* bad."

"Sam!"

We stared at each other for a couple of seconds, and then we both burst out laughing. I had to grab a hankie from my pocket and wipe my eyes.

With a small gasp, Sam said, "But enough philosophy for one day." He gave himself a little shake, kind of like the way Spike would shake himself every now and then. "What time does rehearsal begin tomorrow morning?" He stuck his notebook back into his pocket.

"Ten. Why?" I peered narrowly at him, not liking the question a whole lot.

"Good. I'll pick you up at a quarter of and take you there."

"You don't need—"

"I'm *going* to the damned rehearsal. All of my suspects will be there. So I might as well pick you up, since you're right on the way."

"Oh." That made sense, even though I didn't want it to. "All right then."

"All right then."

The chicken stew Vi served for our dinner that night was as wonderful as all the rest of her meals. I know Sam enjoyed it. Then he and Pa played gin rummy while Ma and I washed up the dinner dishes.

For some reason, I kept thinking about church people killing each other. Not comforting, I have to admit.

FIFTEEN

$\mathbb{A}$mbivalent pretty well describes my mood the next morning when Sam picked me up to go to rehearsal.

For one thing, I kept thinking about Sam's revelations of the night before, if they could be called that. He hadn't sounded precisely bitter about religion, but he'd made it perfectly clear he didn't care one way or another about going to church. I guess I could understand that, although my church meant a lot to me. Not only was it a means for me to remain respectable in spite of my equivocal profession, but it was also a big part of my social life. I entertained the dismal thought that poor Sam didn't have a social life.

Then there was his bachelorhood, if it could be called that. He was, in fact, a widower. But until yesterday, I hadn't truly understood how lonely the poor guy must be. True, he had his co-workers, and I'm sure he had friends among them, but that's not the same as having a family to call one's own. His family lived in New York City. He'd brought his late wife to Pasadena in the feeble hope the weather would allow her to live a longer, happier life. That hadn't happened, and Sam was all by himself out west.

Except for us. Thanks to Billy, Sam was practically a member of our family now. I guess we were his social life.

Worse, I didn't want to lose him. But did I want to marry him? Not any time soon, I didn't. Besides, if he wanted a wife who would welcome him home from a hard day's work with a scrumptious meal, he'd be flat out of luck if he married me. Also, I didn't want to give up my business, at which I'd worked darned hard in order to succeed. If Sam and I married, would he still allow me to work as a spiritualist-medium?

Darn it! How come husbands could dictate to their wives? We were supposed to be equal to men. We even—finally—got the vote. But did we get treated as the equals of men? Of course not!

"Men are dictatorial pigs," I muttered as Sam steered his Hudson north on Marengo Avenue.

He shot me a mystified glance, accompanied by a largish frown. "What brought that on? All I did was pick you up for rehearsal. I don't recall being dictatorial about it."

Bother. "I didn't mean you."

"Who *did* you mean? Your father? Billy? Your brother? Harold Kincaid? Captain Buckingham?" I believe I've mentioned that Johnny Buckingham, an old friend of Billy's and mine, was a captain in the Salvation Army.

"No!"

"Well, then. Who did you mean?"

Fiddlesticks. I wished I'd kept my fat mouth shut. "No one in particular. But even though women got the vote in nineteen twenty, men still dictate what we can and can't do."

"I haven't noticed you doing much of anything even faintly resembling obedience to any man's dictate. Ever."

"I'm different." Because I didn't want to hear a snide rejoinder to that remark, I hurried on to say, "I've had to be different, because the men in my family couldn't support us, due to their ill health. It's the women who earn the dough in my family."

"And quite a bit of it, too. Correct?"

I frowned at him. "Maybe, but it's still a man's world. For example, if Ma were a man, she'd earn twice as much money at her job as she does now. For doing the very same thing! If Aunt Vi were a man, they'd call her a chef and pay her boocoo bucks. Of course, she'd have to wear one of those silly white chef's hats, too, but she'd be making mazuma by the bucketfuls."

"I don't think a male spiritualist-medium would make any more money than you do."

After thinking about that for almost as long as it took us to get to the church, I admitted, "Probably not. But it's a good thing I made up my job when I did, or my family might have been in the suds. We didn't know Pa would have a heart attack or that Billy would be so badly injured in the war."

As he pulled the Hudson to a stop on the Marengo side of the church, Sam said, "Are you a pinko, Daisy Gumm Majesty?"

"No! I'm not a Communist. I only think women ought to get paid the same as men for doing the same jobs men do."

With a sigh, Sam about shocked me to death when he said, "Yeah. I think you're right."

I didn't have time to register my astonishment aloud, because he left the car and walked around to my side and opened the door for me. As he did so, he said, "Well, life's not fair. If anyone should know that by this time, it's you."

"Too true."

We walked together to the door to the choir room. Which was locked. So we hoofed it around to the front of the church and discovered the sanctuary door unlocked.

"Daisy! So happy to see you. Good morning, Detective Rotondo."

"Hey, Harold," I said, delighted to see him. He'd stationed himself right inside the sanctuary door, so I think he was anticipating my arrival.

"Kincaid," said Sam, not nearly as delighted as I.

"Why's the door to the choir room locked, Harold? Do you know?"

"Everyone's worried that some loony got in and dumped that rock on Gloria, so they decided to have only one door to the outside unlocked."

"I guess that makes sense."

Gazing at the chancel, I saw Patsy and Dennis Bissel holding hands, Sylvia and Lawrence Allen not holding hands but standing together, and a few other cast members milling about and gabbing. Gloria Lippincott was actually talking to a female in the form of Lucille Spinks. Goodness gracious. I'd have expected her to collar a man by this time. Maybe she and Lucy were discussing their "Three Little Maids" song or something.

Then I noticed there seemed to be a serious conference taking place on the left side of chancel. That's house-left, not stage-left. Oh, never mind. "What's that about?" I asked Harold, nodding toward the chancel. I peered harder and saw Mr. Hostetter, Mr. Van der Linden and… "Heavens! Is that Pastor Smith up there with Mr. Hostetter and Max?"

"It is, indeed. Evidently, your minister doesn't appreciate his church being used as the site of an attempted murder. Hence the locked doors and serious conference."

"Huh. Don't much blame him," grumbled Sam.

"No. I don't, either. And I agree with him," I said.

"Maybe. But I hope we don't have to move the production," said Harold. "For one thing, I don't know where we could move it to. Plus, it would be a big hassle, and Connie doesn't feel well, poor thing."

"She didn't feel well on Thursday, either," I said, feeling sorry for Connie.

"True. She hasn't felt well a lot lately. Maybe there's something going around, because Mr. Finster has laryngitis, so we don't have a Mikado for this morning's rehearsal."

"That's too bad," I said, meaning it. After all, what was *The Mikado* without the Mikado? Actually, the Mikado doesn't show up much in the operetta, so we probably wouldn't miss him a whole lot, but…Then I bethought me of someone and turned slowly to Sam.

He knew what I was going to say before I said it. "Don't look at me like that. I'm here to investigate, not sing."

"But you'd be able to investigate more closely if you were part of the cast," I said, using my most ingenuous tone of voice.

"Don't give me that," said Sam, who was on to me, the rat.

"But the Mikado is in your voice range." I thought of something else that might actually persuade him. "Anyhow, you have a much better voice than Mr. Finster does."

"The hell—heck I do."

"You do," I told him. "I've heard you. Besides, you're one of the people who forced me to sing Katisha. This will be pay-back."

"Cripes," said Sam.

We were nearing the chancel via the center aisle by this time, and Harold spoke up. "Brilliant idea! Oh, Mr. Hostetter!" He raised his voice and darned near yodeled the last three words.

"Dammit," mumbled Sam.

"You're in church, you big galoot," I reminded him. "Don't swear."

"Nuts."

Mr. Hostetter didn't appear pleased to have been interrupted when he turned toward Harold. "Yes, Mr. Kincaid? We're having a serious conversation here."

"I understand that, but I do believe your Mikado problem is solved. At least for this morning's rehearsal."

Very well, I would never, ever, accuse Mr. Floy Hostetter of being more interested in a production of *The Mikado* than in the church for which he directs the choir. But I saw the smile beam forth from his countenance when Harold told him we had a substitute Mikado. He actually rubbed his hands together in glee when he said, "Is it? You have a substitute?"

"Sure do," said Harold, gesturing at Sam.

If I were Mr. Hostetter, I do believe Sam's glower might have put me off, but I'm not Mr. Hostetter. Anyhow, he didn't know Sam.

Squinting at us—the lighting in the sanctuary wasn't great—Mr. Hostetter said, "Do you mean you can sing, Detective Ro-Ro—"

"Rotondo," said Sam, still glowering. "And I'm not volunteering. I've been volunteered."

"But you *can* sing?"

Because Sam didn't look as though he were going to answer that question, I piped up. "Yes! He has a lovely bass voice. I'm sure he can follow the libretto, at least for this morning."

"What do you mean, *at least for this morning*?" Sam muttered at me.

"I'm so pleased!" said Mr. Hostetter, and I could tell he meant it.

However, Pastor Smith was a good deal less sanguine. "Floy, please. We need to get this issue settled." He gave me a brief smile, but I think it was only because I was a member of his congregation. It didn't look to me as if he meant it. Max didn't bother smiling at any of us, but seemed annoyed. The three men recommenced their consultation in low voices.

After several minutes of that, Pastor Smith said, "Very well, but if anything else of a like nature occurs, you'll have to move this production. I don't know why I gave my permission to begin with." He sounded grouchy.

"So many of your parishioners were delighted with the idea," said Mr. Hostetter. "That's the reason. And don't forget that it's for a very good cause."

"Perhaps. But none of the parishioners will be pleased if there are any more unsavory goings-on. I trust I make myself clear?" He looked at Max Van der Linden as he delivered the question.

"Yes, sir," said Max.

"There will be no more problems," Mr. Hostetter assured him.

Hmm. I don't know how he knew that, unless he'd pushed that paving stone from the church roof. Then I chastised myself as an idiot. Mr. Hostetter would no more try to kill a person than I would. And I wouldn't, so there you go.

Mr. Smith marched down the chancel steps, and aimed for the first pew. Guess he wanted to monitor rehearsal for himself.

"Thank you, Pastor Smith," I said as he marched past me.

"Hmph. You're welcome." He still didn't sound happy.

"All right, everyone!" Mr. Hostetter clapped his hands, and the echo in that huge sanctuary was a trifle uncanny. It worked, though. All buzzing and chatting stopped, and everyone started slightly and turned to look at him. "We have a substitute Mikado for today's rehearsal." He turned to Sam. "Thank you, Detective…uh…Detective." From which, I deduced he'd already forgot Sam's name. Again.

"You're welcome." I don't think Sam could sound too much more grudging. He, Harold, and I walked up the chancel steps and joined the rest of the cast.

"Aha. You *do* sing!" said Max, smiling broadly at Sam. When we'd first entered the church, Max had appeared annoyed. Not now.

"So these two say." Sam hooked a thumb at Harold and me.

"Wonderful." Max turned around, and his gaze lit on his wife. "Connie, darling, will you get one of the libretti for the detective to follow?"

Good heavens. I hadn't taken a good look at Connie yet that morning. She appeared gaunt and thin and…Well, the thought crossed my mind that she might have some wasting illness. Like, maybe, tuberculosis. I sure hoped not.

"I'll help you look!" I chirped, and ran across the chancel to join her. When I got to her, I said in a low voice, "You don't look as if you're feeling well, Connie. Is anything the matter?"

She took off backstage—which wasn't really backstage, since we were in a church. However, there were rooms on either side of the chancel and a back hallway, which Connie and Max said we'd use to hold the costumes. I followed her, concerned because she hadn't answered me. I found out why a second later.

Connie collapsed onto a bench in the room on stage-right (if you're looking at it from an actor's perspective) and began sobbing weakly. I sat next to her and put an arm around her shoulder. "Connie, what is it? Is there anything I can do to help you?"

"Oh, Daisy, I don't know what's *wrong* with me! I have such a headache all the time. And half the time, I don't know what I've been doing or anything. I lose track of time. My stomach is always upset, my insides hurt, my bones ache, and I'm exhausted all the time. I feel *awful*. Oh, Daisy, I'm afraid." She brought her hands to her face and wept miserably.

"Good heavens," said I. "That sounds terrible. Have you been to a doctor?"

She shook her head. "No. Max is a darling, and he's taking care of me. But I don't know what's wrong."

Nerts. If Max was such a darling and was taking such good care of her, why was she suffering so from headaches, pallor, a painful tummy, exhaustion and, if I understood her correctly, unstable thinking. "I still think you need to see a doctor. Your symptoms don't sound good to me. I'll be happy to accompany you to see Dr. Benjamin. He's our family physician and a great fellow."

"I don't think Max would like that," she said through sniffles. "He tends to believe in Mary Baker Eddy's Christian Science practices. He's sure I'll get better if I drink lots of orange juice and eat properly."

"Eating properly is important," I said because I couldn't think of anything else to say.

She took a deep breath and stood, withdrew a hankie from her skirt pocket, wiped her face, and said, "I'm sorry, Daisy. I didn't mean to burden you with my silly problems."

"They don't sound silly to me. They sound serious." I meant it.

She gave another weary shake of her head. "Oh, no. I'm sure Max is correct, and I just have a little bug or something that will go away if I rest and take my vitamins."

I'd heard of vitamins, but wasn't altogether sure what they were. "Vitamins?"

"Yes. Max gets vitamin pills at the vegetarian restaurant on Colorado. They're supposed to provide your body with the healthy benefits it needs when your body doesn't get the nutrients it requires from food—and I've had *such* problems with my digestive system lately. Therefore, I take a Vitamin C tablet every day and a spoonful of cod liver oil."

I shuddered involuntarily. "You take cod liver oil on purpose? My mother used to make me take it when I was sick."

"That's precisely right. I'm sick, so I take Vitamin C and cod liver oil," said Connie, sounding sure of herself.

"Isn't Vitamin C the stuff that comes from oranges?"

"Yes. It's supposed to be very good for you."

Hmm. I'd rather eat an orange than take a pill, but what did I know about vitamins? Clearly, nothing. "I can bring you some fresh oranges from our tree," I offered.

She gave me a shaky smile. In fact, her whole person appeared rather shaky that morning. "Thank you, Daisy. I'm really not awfully hungry these days, but that would be kind of you."

"Happy to do it." I sucked in a bushel full of stale church air. "Now. Where do we find a libretto for Sam?"

"Back here." And Connie led me to the hallway where the costumes would be kept. There, sure enough, we found a pile of extra libretti on a small table, so I snatched one for Sam.

As we walked back to the chancel, I said, "I really wish you'd see Dr. Benjamin, Connie. He might be able to give you more than…well, vitamins. Although I don't know what."

"No. Nobody knows what to give me," she said in a sad-sounding

124

voice. "But I do wish I'd perk up. My stomach hurts so badly, and I have all the energy of a wet noodle."

"I'm awfully sorry."

"Thank you."

Phooey.

SIXTEEN

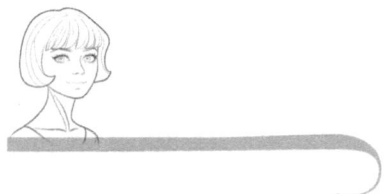

S am snatched the libretto from my hand as if he hated the very sight
of it and was only taking it because he had to. Gee, I wonder why
that was.

"Took you long enough," he snarled.

"Connie's ill. She won't see a doctor, because she says Max is
looking after her so well." I sniffed. "He's giving her cod liver oil and
vitamin pills."

Sam's nose wrinkled. "Huh. My mother used to force cod liver oil
down my throat when I was sick." Sam opened his libretto and flipped
through it. "Where the heck does my part start?"

"You don't show up until the second act."

"Huh." He glared at the libretto and shook it slightly. "Why do they
call the damned thing *The Mikado* if the Mikado doesn't even show up
until the second act?"

"I don't know. I guess because the Mikado's dictates are what moti-
vate everyone in the play to do what they do."

"Huh. Well, when will they do that part?"

"I don't know. Mr. Hostetter—or maybe Max—will tell us in a
minute."

It didn't even take a minute. All at once, Mr. Hostetter clapped again. This clap received every bit as much attention as his first one had. All chitchat stopped, we leaped slightly, and turned to pay attention to him. I hadn't realized until that day how many echoes a large congregation sitting in a church sanctuary can soak up. Without the congregants to muffle the noise, Mr. Hostetter's claps sounded like thunder and bounced around the room like India rubber balls.

"Ladies and gentlemen, we need to go over the part in act one where Ko-Ko receives word that the Mikado plans to eliminate the post of Lord High Executioner unless an execution takes place soon." He squinted at the paper in his hand. "All right. We'll begin when Mr. Van der Linden brings the rope onstage and tries to kill himself."

"That means they won't need you or me for a while." I tugged on Sam's coat sleeve. "Come and sit with me in the pew. I have something to talk to you about."

Sam scowled at me. Big surprise. "I'm supposed to be investigating a murder at this minute, you know, not chatting with you."

"But I'm worried about Connie."

"Huh. I'm going to talk to Gloria Lippincott. That woman must know more than she's told the police so far."

I didn't doubt it for a second. "But, Sam, what if someone is trying to poison Connie?"

He'd started to stomp off to the other side of the sanctuary, but stopped when he realized Gloria, as one of the three little maids, had to be onstage during part of this scene. I heard him utter a low growl, but he turned and came back to sit beside me.

"What the devil are you talking about? Poison? Where'd you get that crazy idea?"

"Well..." This was difficult, mainly because I hadn't thought it out before tackling Sam. I regret to say this was typical of me. "It's her symptoms." Maybe he was right, and I was crazy.

"Her symptoms?" He didn't believe me for a second; I could tell.

"Well...Yes. Her symptoms. She has a headache all the time, and digestive troubles, fatigue, and she forgets stuff. Isn't there a poison that creates those same exact symptoms?"

"Probably," Sam said with a grumpy huff. "So what? Lots of other stuff makes people feel bad, including influenza, malaria, and tuberculosis. The woman's sick. Did she tell you she thinks she's being poisoned?"

"No. She said Max is taking care of her."

"Well? What makes you think he isn't?"

I thought about it and then gave a huff of my own. "Nothing."

"He's not involved with the Lippincott dame, is he?" He shook his head. "How does she fit them all in?"

"I don't think he's involved with Gloria. In fact, he seems devoted to Connie."

"Well, then, if he's not poisoning her, who the hell is?"

Crumb. "I don't know. It doesn't make any sense, does it?"

"No. It doesn't."

So much for that. I gazed at the stage, where Harold and Max were having a comical heyday with their scene. They were both very good at their parts, and even Sam chuckled a time or two as Harold tried to persuade Max to allow him to execute him rather than let him take his own life. After they'd decided Max (Nanki-Poo) could marry Connie (Yum-Yum) and experience a month of wedded bliss, Sam actually laughed out loud. Of course, then Nanki-Poo would have his head chopped off and Yum-Yum would have to be buried alive, but they could be happy as a couple of larks for a whole month.

The townspeople entered on-cue, and my gaze got stuck on Connie. She really did appear haggard, poor thing. But Sam was doubtless right; my notion about poison was ridiculous. Just then she pressed a hand to her stomach, and I started thinking again, which was probably stupid, too. I narrowed my gaze and peered from Max to Gloria, just to see if the two of them were scrutinizing Connie.

But they were both singing and acting and paying no attention to—

"Mrs. Majesty!" Mr. Hostetter bellowed.

Egad! I forgot I had to appear in this scene. I scrambled up from my pew and dashed to the choir room, from which I'd have to appear in a couple of seconds. Luckily for me, I'd memorized my part, so I came on at the right time, and was pleased when everyone onstage drew away from me as if I were a wicked witch.

It was almost frightening how much I enjoyed playing Katisha.

"Very well. Stop!" Mr. Hostetter called out.

So I stopped singing and hoped he wasn't going to scold me for allowing my mind to wander.

"Mrs. Van der Linden, are you feeling quite well?" Mr. Hostetter asked Connie. "You don't seem to be singing with your usual vigor today." He didn't frown or anything, but I sensed he was a trifle annoyed with Connie.

Because I couldn't seem to help myself, I butted in. "She's a little under the weather today, Mr. Hostetter. She'll be back to singing with her usual vigor when…well, when she's feeling better." Then I felt like a dimwit.

"Connie! What's the matter?" Max rushed to his wife, who sort of melted into him and began weeping softly.

"I'm sorry, Max. I felt all right this morning, but now I feel just awful."

"Oh, dear. Oh, dear." Patently worried, Max drew Connie aside and sat her in one of the choir chairs. He took the one next to her and kept hold of her hands. They chatted softly as we all looked on, Mr. Hostetter with a frown, most of the rest of us with compassion.

It occurred to me that perhaps Gloria had some reason to do away with Connie. So I searched for her, only to find her with her talons firmly attached to Dennis Bissel. Fortunately, Patsy had hold of his other arm and didn't seem inclined to give him up any time soon. Dennis appeared merely embarrassed.

Bother. So far, my detectival skills really stank.

But Mr. Hostetter spoke up again, so I had to stop berating myself and concentrate.

"Very well, let's see what we can do with the Mikado's first scene." He peered into the sanctuary, evidently searching for Sam. "Detective? We'll need you for this next scene."

"Right here," rumbled Sam, making me jump because I'd expected him still to be perched on the first pew. But there he was, looming behind Max and Connie amid the choir's chairs.

"Very good. Let me see here…" Mr. Hostetter peered at his stage directions. "You follow the procession in from stage-right."

"Who else is in the procession?" asked Sam, frowning hideously.

"Everybody. I'll show you," chirped Harold. He grabbed Sam by one arm and James Warden (who played Pish-Tush) by the other, nodded to the folks who made up the chorus of townsfolk and said, "Come on, everyone. You coming, Mr. Hostetter, or do you want to watch?"

"I'll watch until it's my turn to show up." Mr. Hostetter quickly set his stage diagram on top of the piano, behind which sat a delighted Mrs. Fleming. She was doing a masterful job of playing the piano for this operetta. In fact, if I were to guess, she was happy to be playing something other than church music for once. I didn't quite dare ask her, but I don't think I'd ever seen her so cheerful. Anyway, Mr. Hostetter trotted down the chancel steps and stood before the front pew in order to observe the action onstage with a critical eye.

I was pondering critical eyes—I don't think I have one—church music, operettas and so forth when Harold's peered at me through the open door to stage-right. "Daisy! You're in this scene, too."

Whoops. I'd completely forgotten that Katisha arrives on the scene with the Mikado, and makes quite a pest of herself, calling herself the Mikado's "daughter-in-law elect." I cast one last glance at poor Connie, who was still being comforted by Max, and scooted over to join in the royal procession.

Let me say right here and now that Sam Rotondo is a lousy actor. But, boy, does he have a voice! I swear, if he ever gets tired of police work, he could sing in any chorus known to man. If he ever learned how to act, he could probably be in grand opera. He didn't know the Mikado's part so he had to keep his gaze glued to the libretto, but his voice was deep and rich and precisely on-pitch. In fact, when I, as Katisha, performed my role, I noticed Mr. Hostetter gazing at Sam as if he wanted to chuck George Finster and install Sam as the permanent Mikado. Of course, Sam would have to learn his part and act as if he were enjoying himself, and I doubted that would ever happen, so it was idle speculation on my part.

The chorus sounded good, although I did notice several creaks and groans as the townsfolk fell to their knees and then bowed before Sam. But heck, we were a pack of amateurs, many of us members of the congregation, and some of us definitely not youngsters. I noticed that Dennis, or perhaps Patsy, had managed to disengage Gloria Lippincott's claws from his arm, because he was right down there in the chorus, kneeling and bowing like a champion Japanese person from the town of Titipu.

After I sat on the stool set out for me by Katisha's minions, I observed that Sylvia Allen also knelt and bowed, as befitted a commoner. She had an eagle eye on Lawrence, however, who had moseyed over to kneel beside Gloria Lippincott. As Sam regaled us with the Mikado's version of making punishments fit various crimes, I noticed Sylvia scowling up a storm as Gloria rubbed Lawrence's arm; she reminded me of a cat. I began to wonder, as Sam had, how she managed to juggle so many men.

Oh, well. I couldn't do much from Katisha's official stool, but, nose in the air as befitted Katisha, I watched. In fact, I watched Max tenderly escort Connie out the door on stage-left, and wished I knew what was wrong with her. Why wouldn't she see a doctor? Just because her husband didn't approve of doctors? Piffle.

I also watched as Lawrence seemed to have to wrench himself away from Gloria in order to participate in the next scene, in which the Lord High Executioner describes how he dispatched Nanki-Poo with his snickersnee. I don't know if you're familiar with the plot, but the Lord High Executioner bribes the Poo-Bah (Floy Hostetter) to provide an affidavit attesting to his execution of Nanki-Poo. In order to do so, he has to bribe all the people in all the jobs the Poo-Bah holds, even though they're the same person.

Gee, that sounds complicated. It works in the operetta, though.

Right before Harold was set to begin his recitation of Nanki-Poo's execution, Mr. Hostetter brought the action to a stop with another clap of his hands, and a loud, "All right, people. Let's go over a few blocking errors." He turned to Sam. "You have a wonderful voice, Detective. With a little more animation, you'd make a delightful Mikado."

Sam muttered something that sounded to me like, "Not in this lifetime," but I'm not sure about that.

Mr. Hostetter proceeded to tell us what we'd done wrong in the scene, and various townspeople scurried around to place themselves where the director wanted them to be. As he was in the middle of things, Max Van der Linden came on-stage and whispered something to Harold. He appeared worried, and he hurried off again.

Because I didn't have anything particular to do at the moment, I scuttled over to Harold and asked what Max had said to him.

"He's taking Connie home. She doesn't feel well."

"No, she doesn't." After thinking about Connie's symptoms for a moment, I decided not to ask Harold if he thought she could be suffering from some kind of poisoning, but I did resolve to visit the Pasadena Public Library on Monday, to look up the effects of various poisons. I know, I know. I have a suspicious mind.

But I might just be right.

Rehearsal came to a close shortly after that. It was a little past noon, and we were all tired and hungry. Sam handed his libretto to Mr. Hostetter, who didn't want to take it, but Sam insisted. "I'm not doing this again," he declared.

Mr. Hostetter sighed, and Sam stomped up to Harold and me. "Get your coat, and let's get out of here," he growled at me.

"You were wonderful as the Mikado," said Harold, ignoring Sam's foul mood.

"You really were," I said, doing likewise.

"Huh."

"Why don't we all go out to luncheon?" Harold asked us brightly. "My treat. We can go to the Tea Cup Inn. That's close to your house, isn't it, Daisy?"

"Yes. That would be nice, Harold."

"I don't think it's a good idea," said Sam, grumpy as all get-out.

"Well, then, I can take Daisy in my machine, and you can go home, Detective Rotondo," said Harold with a wicked smile.

We ended up going to the Tea Cup Inn, which sat on North Marengo Avenue, near Washington Boulevard. I knew the two ladies who owned the place, Mrs. McKenna and Mrs. Fincher, and they served soups and sandwiches and pies and things like that. Nothing fancy, but all of it tasty. It was a genteel sort of place, most often frequented by women, and Sam looked big and bulky and out of place. He knew it too, and frowned heavily as Mrs. McKenna led us to a table.

"This isn't the kind of place I'm used to," he said as he sat on the delicate little chair Mrs. McKenna had indicated he should take.

"Mine either," said Harold. "But I figured Daisy would like it."

"I do like it." In fact, I vividly recalled the day I'd taken Flossie Buckingham, then Flossie Mossar and in thrall to a brute of a gangster named Jinx, to lunch there. Poor Flossie had just had the stuffing beaten out of her by Jinx, and she didn't think it was her kind of place, either. But I made it my job to make her feel at home there. Thinking about poor Flossie, who was now happily married and a mother, to boot, made me sigh.

"What's the matter now?" said Sam, frowning at me as usual.

"Nothing. I was just thinking about Flossie Buckingham."

Both Harold and Sam tilted their heads and squinted at me. I said, "It's nothing. We just had lunch here once, Flossie and me."

Sam said, "Huh."

Harold said, "Oh."

Mrs. McKenna had delivered flowery menus to us as we sat at our table, so we concentrated on the foodstuffs available. Sam turned his menu over as if hoping there would be more selections on the other side.

"The food's good," I told him. "You can order soup and a sandwich and even a salad if you want. And they make good pies."

"Huh."

With a huge grin, Harold said, "I'm going to have the potato soup, ham on rye, and a piece of huckleberry pie."

"Sounds good to me," said Sam, slapping his menu on the table.

"Me, too," said I, only I laid my menu gently beside my plate.

He didn't want to, but at the end of our meal, Sam said, "That was tasty."

"I agree," said I. "And if you're good, you can probably wrangle another good meal out of Aunt Vi for supper tonight."

"Lucky you," said Harold.

"Huh," said Sam.

SEVENTEEN

S am couldn't stay for dinner that night because he was called to the police station to investigate some kind of emergency. He wouldn't say what it was, which was typical. Nuts to him.

The next day at church, I was amazed that the chancel again looked precisely like a chancel. The day before, a bunch of fake Japanese singers had taken it over and the chairs had all been shoved hither and thither. Now they resided in their accustomed neat little rows, and a sense of security enveloped me. Don't ask me why. I guess it was comforting to be doing something normal instead of pretending to be something I'm not. Of course, pretending to be something I'm not is how I earn my living, but never mind. I'm only confusing myself here.

Lucille Spinks was excited as we donned our choir robes. "Isn't the operetta fun, Daisy? Albert is going to attend the rehearsal on Tuesday evening."

Albert Zollinger, Lucy's intended, was a member of our church. Which made me think of something. "Why didn't Mr. Zollinger try out for a part in the operetta?"

Giggling like a girl half her age—she was a year or two older than I —she said, "He can't sing. Can't hold a note to save himself."

"Oh." I thought about Albert Zollinger's inability to sing as I hooked up my robe. "That's kind of too bad, isn't it? I mean, you love to sing so much, and music is such a big part of your life."

With a toss of her shingled head, Lucy said, "I don't mind. He's such a wonderful man. And we both enjoy music, so it will still be a part of my life. Anyhow, I don't consider his inability to hold a note a serious flaw."

"I don't suppose it is." Plus, even though he was a widower and a good deal older than Lucy, he was alive. The Great War had wiped out more than my darling Billy, and marriageable young men were thin on the ground in those days. I understand the problem was worse in Europe. Can you imagine losing half of your country's young men to that ghastly war? Belgium, France, and England did. And maybe Russia, too, although the atmosphere surrounding Russia was so murky in those days, nobody who didn't live there knew what went on.

Probably Germany had lost a lot of boys to war, too, but since Kaiser Bill, in his grab to rule the world, had started the whole thing, I wasn't always eager to feel sorry for Germans. Which I know is unfair of me. Just because their former leader was a power-hungry fiend didn't mean the rest of the people in Germany were.

Although German scientists had created poisoned gas and submarines and German leaders had allowed submarines to torpedo ships without warning. Like, for example, *Lusitania*. Hmm. Maybe something in the German air turned people into bestial beings.

"You're doing a wonderful job playing Katisha," said Lucy, drawing my mind out of the muddy, bloody trenches of the late war. "I didn't think you could act so mean and nasty."

With a genuine smile, I said, "I didn't, either. But it's fun. I've never been able to act like such a witch before."

Lucy peered at me oddly. "You mean, you *want* to be unpleasant?"

As I made sure my hooks were hooked, I said, "Well...Yes. I mean, I don't want to be unpleasant to people I like or anything. But I have to be nice for my job all the time, when sometimes I'd like to conk the people I work for over the head. Do you know what I mean?"

After thinking about it for a second or two, Lucy said, "Um...No. I don't."

Heaving a sigh, I picked up my hymnal and my little black book containing the music for that day's anthem, and said, "Do you have a job, Lucy?"

"No. I live with Mother and Father. I thought you knew that."

"I guess I forgot. But let me tell you, when you work for a living and have to be nice to the people who pay you, even when they're pills, it gets downright tiresome."

"Oh. Do you have many…What do you call them? Clients? Like that?"

"Fortunately, no, I don't." I marched over to line up behind the tenors so that we could process into the church in an orderly line. Lucy, being a soprano, got to lead the way. I swear, not only do sopranos always get the melody, but they always get to sit up front, too. Mind you, because I was kind of short, I sat in the front row as well, but if I'd been taller, I'd have been relegated to a back row.

At that very moment, Mrs. Fleming began playing the prelude, Beethoven's "Ode to Joy," on the organ, and Lucy had to hurry to the front of the line so we could enter the church.

And, as I stood next to my fellow altos in the front row—I was separated from the sopranos by one other alto—the first person I saw in the congregation, seated next to Ma, Pa, and Aunt Vi, was Sam Rotondo. Joy, my foot. Sorry, Beethoven.

But we sang out little hearts out, and our anthem went well. Before I could join my family in Fellowship Hall for tea and cookies, I had to hoof it back into the choir room and remove my robe. Lucy stood beside me, doing the same thing, and it occurred to me I might actually do a little sleuthing.

"How do you like being one of the three little maids from school, Lucy?" I asked as I unhooked my robe.

"It's fun," she said. Then her brow wrinkled. "Although…" Her voice petered out. Perhaps that was because she was in the process of pulling her robe over her head, but I thought not. Well, I thought *maybe* not.

"Although what?" I grabbed a coat hanger and carefully hung up my robe. I tried to be precise when I stored my robe, because the silly things wrinkled easily.

Lucy did likewise. Her robe was a good deal longer than mine, since

Lucy was a good deal taller than I. "Well, poor Connie Van der Linden seems so unwell. I wonder if she's seriously ill. I'm a little worried about her. She's *such* a nice person, I'd hate for anything bad to happen to her."

"Yes. I wondered the same thing. What about Gloria Lippincott? Is she easy to work with?"

Lucy sniffed, which answered that question, although she went on to elaborate. "I know it's not nice of me to say this," said she, "especially in church. But I really don't like that woman."

"How come? I mean, I don't like her, either, but why don't you?"

"She's coy and sneaky. She makes cutting remarks about those of us who don't have her singing experience. To be fair, she does have a beautiful voice, but I don't think that's any excuse to be nasty to the rest of us. And she goes after every man she sees. Why, she was all cuddled up with James Warden at rehearsal yesterday."

"She *was*?" Boy, I hadn't seen any cuddling going on between Mr. Warden and Gloria. Shoot, she *did* get around, didn't she? Mr. Warden was another married man, and his wife's name was Faith, which evidently wasn't applicable when it came to their marriage.

Another sniff. "They don't know I saw them. But I had to go back to the choir room to get my fan"—fans played a major role in *The Mikado* —"and...Well, let's just say if I saw Albert being that cozy with another woman, I'd be extremely annoyed."

"Goodness. I had no idea."

"And while I was picking up my fan, Mr. Allen came in, Mrs. Lippincott looked up from Mr. Warden's embrace, and...Oh, Daisy, they *winked* at each other."

What? "I don't...Oh. Do you mean Mrs. Lippincott and Mr. Allen winked at each other? While she was cuddling with Mr. Warden?" What the heck, I thought she was having an affair with Lawrence Allen. Was she having affairs with both men?

"Yes. None of them pay any attention to each other onstage. Maybe I was mistaken, but they appeared a little *too* cozy for my taste, what with her being a recent widow and him being married to dear Faith and all. And I'll never understand that wink Mrs. Lippincott and Mr. Allen gave each other."

"I see."

I didn't see a darned thing. Did this observation of Lucy's mean anything? Had Mr. Warden and Gloria really been cuddling during rehearsal the day before? Or had they merely been conferring about some aspect of the operetta? Or perhaps he was helping her get an eyelash out of her eye. And what did that wink between Gloria and Lawrence Allen mean? I sniffed. Some men thought it was funny when other men had their way with females other than their wives. But I'd never pegged Lawrence Allen as one of those brutes, even if he did seem to have an unhealthy interest in Gloria Lippincott. Blast! Wish I'd observed the scene myself.

But my contemplation came to an abrupt end when I left the sanctity (so to speak) of the choir room and joined my family and Sam in Fellowship Hall. We didn't generally stay long to socialize with friends after church, mainly because Aunt Vi always had something spectacularly delicious cooking at home, just waiting for us to gobble it down. No number of cookies can compete with one of Vi's meals.

"You sounded good up there," said Sam, eyeing my hair. I patted it, wishing I'd taken time to comb it in the choir room.

"Thanks."

"That's one of my favorite hymns," said Ma, smiling at me.

"Mine, too," I said. "Next week we'll be singing 'For All the Saints,' because it'll be November fourth."

"You always sing 'For All the Saints' on November fourth?" asked Sam.

Feeling superior, I said, "November first is All Saints' Day. In our church, we honor all of the members of our congregation who passed away during the year prior to the current year's All Saints' Day."

"Oh. That makes sense." He gave me a grave look (so to speak). "Last year's All Saints' Day must have been rough on you."

Even thinking about that day, the first All Saints' Day since my Billy passed, made my eyes tear up. "It was." I choked a little, and was surprised when Sam put one of his arms around my shoulder.

"I'm sorry," he said. "Didn't mean to bring up a sad memory."

His arm felt warm and comforting. "That's all right. Nothing anyone can do about it now." I had to lift a gloved hand to wipe away a tear, and I felt kind of silly.

"Best not to dwell on past tragedies," said my mother briskly. Always practical, my mother. "We should get home so Vi can put our dinner on the table. Do join us, Sam."

"Thank you." He gazed down at me, and I could tell he felt bad for having brought up a sad subject. "That all right with you, Daisy?"

"Of course, it is," I told him, wiping away another tear. "Glad to have you."

"Really?"

"Really." I thought about what Lucy had revealed about Mr. Warden and Gloria, perked up some, and added, "Besides, I have something to talk to you about."

"Uh-oh." He removed his arm from my shoulder, leaving a cold patch across my back. "I don't like the sound of that."

"Nonsense. I just want to tell you something Lucy Spinks noticed at rehearsal yesterday."

I could almost hear the man roll his eyes. I'll admit here and now that Sam has some good qualities, but he could still drive me crazy faster than anyone else I knew.

In spite of Sam, Spike was overjoyed to have his family and his good friend home from church. Vi's roasted pork, mashed potatoes, gravy, green beans (that I'd helped my aunt and mother preserve when our bean crop was at its peak), and flaky dinner rolls were all delicious. So was the devil's food cake she'd baked for dessert. I tell you, it was a wonder we weren't a family of dumplings with Aunt Vi doing the cooking for us.

After we were all stuffed to the gills and sitting back in our chairs contemplating rising from the table, which didn't sound like a good idea, Sam said, "That was the best meal I've had since...Well, since the last time I ate here, Mrs. Gumm." The smile he gave Aunt Vi was almost as delightful as the meal he'd just consumed.

"Go along with you, Sam Rotondo," said my aunt, making Sam the recipient of one of Vi's mysterious sayings. She was always saying that to me, too.

"He's right, Vi. I don't know how we'd eat if you didn't live with us," said Pa.

"Fiddlesticks," said my aunt. "You did fine before my Paul died and I moved in with you."

Pa and I both looked at my mother, whose cheeks had taken on a pinkish hue. But the truth was that, while I adore my mother, I sort of inherited her cooking skills, which was unfortunate, since she had none. Neither Pa nor I said so.

"You know that's not true, Vi. I'm a terrible cook," said Ma, sparing Pa and me from telling the truth. "I'm surprised George, Daphne and Daisy survived to grow up, and that Joe didn't get sick when I was cooking for the family."

"You're not *that* bad, Ma," I said, sticking up for my mother, who deserved being stuck up for, even though I was lying through my teeth. My satisfied teeth.

"Oh, I am, too. You know that as well as I do, Daisy Gumm Majesty."

"Well..." I didn't want to lie anymore.

"But that doesn't matter," said Pa. "We just partook of a delicious meal, and now I want to go to the living room and relax."

That meant it was time for me to clean off the table and wash the dishes. Never mind that I wanted to vegetate in that chair until some of my recent meal sank in and I could comfortably move again. With a heavy sigh, I rose to my feet.

"I'll help," said Sam.

"You will not!" said my mother.

"Why not?" I asked her.

"Sam is a guest, and guests don't have to clean up after themselves."

Aw, nuts. Sam was about as much of a guest in that house by that time as I was. And I wasn't. "If you say so, Ma."

Sam grinned at me and rose from his place.

"I'll help," said Ma.

"I'd probably better get going," said Sam.

"No you don't!" Very well, my voice was a trifle loud. But I didn't want him getting away from me before I'd told him what Lucy'd seen. "I have to talk to you," I said in a more moderate tone.

I wondered if Gloria Lippincott kept a score card on the men she seduced, and if she chalked up another check mark every time a male succumbed to her wiles.

With a huff, Sam said, "All right. I'll sit in the living room with your father. But I have paperwork to catch up on, so don't be long."

Well, I liked that! He'd helped create the mess Ma and I were getting ready to clean up, but he wanted me to hurry so he could do paperwork. Huh.

"A policeman's lot is not a happy one," I quoted from (I think) *The Pirates of Penzance*.

"If you say so," muttered Sam. "I don't mind investigating. It's the paperwork that bogs me down."

At any rate, Ma and I cleaned up the dinner dishes. I washed and she dried, so I could leave the kitchen sooner than she. After I'd scrubbed the last pot, I all but ran out to the living room. Where Sam was nowhere to be seen.

I whirled on my father. "You let him get away!"

Poor Pa jumped in his chair, and I only then realized he'd been snoozing. "Wh-what?"

"Where's Sam?"

"Sam? I think he took Spike for a walk."

"Oh." Very well, so that had been a nice thing for Sam to do. "I think I'll try to find them. I have to tell Sam something I learned today."

"About that man's murder?"

"That's just it. I don't know if it's important or not."

"I swear, Daisy, you get into more pickles than anyone else I know."

I didn't point out to him that his assessment was not merely unfair, but outrageous. I love my father, and I'd never holler at him. Sam was another kettle of fish entirely.

Therefore, I dashed to my room, pulled on a warm woolen cloche and gloves, grabbed my coat from the closet, and raced to the door. As soon as I stepped out onto the porch, I saw Spike and Sam returning to the house.

Good. I could corner him on the front porch.

Sam, not Spike.

EIGHTEEN

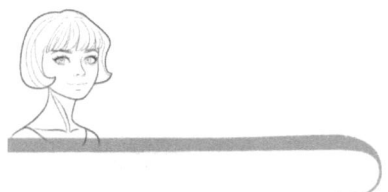

I t was darned cold outside as we settled onto the porch steps, and the sky was darkening fast. During the Great War, the government had implemented what it called Daylight Saving Time, mainly so that people who farmed would have more daylight hours in which to work. Daylight Saving Time had ended the prior week, so even though it was actually only around four o'clock by the time we sat on the steps, the clocks all said it was five. Wars create more problems than they're worth, if you ask me.

I took the leash off Spike and allowed him to chase leaves around the yard. We folks who live in Pasadena don't have gorgeously colored fall leaves that folks back east have, but some leaves on some trees do turn brown and fall off. Fortunately for Spike, the Wilsons' cat, Samson, put in an appearance, so he got to chase the cat. I swear, everything Spike did, he did with vigor and enthusiasm. Wish I were more like him.

"All right," said Sam, sounding resigned to his fate. "What is this momentous thing that lady saw yesterday at rehearsal."

That lady. I swear. I'd introduced Sam to Lucille Spinks about a dozen times by that evening, and he still couldn't remember her name.

"Lucy Spinks," I reminded him. "Engaged to Albert Zollinger."

"Whatever you say."

I wanted to whack him on the arm, but I resisted the impulse. "Lucy saw James Warden and Gloria Lippincott in a compromising situation yesterday during rehearsal."

"A 'compromising situation'? What does that mean?"

Bother the man. "She said they were cuddled up together."

It was dark out there, and I couldn't really see Sam well, but I felt him shrug. "She's a man-eater, isn't she? Isn't that what she does?"

Nerts. "But don't you see? Gloria has her claws into Dennis Bissel, Lawrence Allen and now James Warden. According to Lucy, Lawrence Allen and Gloria exchanged a wink while she was getting cozy with Mr. Warden."

"A wink? Anyway, so what? What difference would that make?"

"Darn you, Sam Rotondo! I don't know! But that wink bothered me more than knowing she was getting chummy with Mr. Warden. Maybe she and Lawrence are actually in cahoots together, and she's grabbing all the men in sight to throw the police off the track. What if she's got her heart set on Max Van der Linden next?"

"What if she does?"

"Well...*I* don't know! But don't you think it's odd that she and Lawrence Allen exchanged a wink when she was cuddled up with James Warden? I do. And it worries me to think that she might have her sights set on Max Van der Linden, and is using all the others as a ruse."

"A ruse?"

"Yes, darn it. A ruse."

"Why?"

Bother. He asked the most annoying questions. After thinking about it for about a second and a half, I said slowly, "It occurred to me that perhaps Max and Gloria are involved in a love affair, but they don't want anyone to know about it. If that were so, and if one of them is actually poisoning Connie, they could get together after they succeed in bumping off Connie!"

After a significant pause, Sam said, "Let me get this straight. Mrs. Lippincott was getting cozy with yet another man at yesterday's rehearsal. Mr. Allen strolled by and winked at her."

"They *exchanged* winks!" I said, trying to straighten out his thought processes.

"I see. They exchanged winks while she was cuddling with another man. And Max Van der Linden was nowhere in sight as this took place. That doesn't sound much like a recipe for murder to me."

Put that way, it didn't to me, either. "Well, I still think someone is making Connie sick, and whoever it is might be using poison to accomplish her end. Connie's definitely sick, and Gloria's a man-crazy vamp. She might have her sights set on Max Van der Linden, even if he doesn't want Connie dead. It's *possible!*"

"Vaguely possible, I suppose, if highly unlikely."

Oh, bother the man. "I'm going to the library tomorrow, and I'm going to look up poisons and see if I can find one that creates the symptoms Connie has."

Sam huffed a breath that even in the semi-darkness came out frosty and white. "What are her symptoms?"

"She said she has a headache all the time, she's exhausted all the time, and her stomach hurts all the time."

"Huh. Is her hair falling out?"

I squinted at him. Didn't do any good; still couldn't see him well enough to determine if he was teasing me. "I don't think so. She'd probably have mentioned it. Why?"

He shrugged again. "Classic symptoms of arsenical poisoning."

"Good Lord! Are you serious?"

"Well, I doubt the woman's being poisoned, but yes, those are symptoms of arsenical poisoning. They're also symptoms of influenza, tuberculosis, and malaria. Has she ever been anyplace where she might have contracted malaria? Once you get it, it doesn't ever go away entirely, but comes and goes, you know. If it's malaria, quinine will fix her up until the next time it rears its ugly head."

"How should I know if she's ever been to a place where there's malaria?"

"Don't know. It's pretty much endemic in the southern states where there are swamps and bayous and mires of muddy water. Malaria's spread by mosquitoes in those areas."

"Oh. I didn't know that. I'll ask her."

"Good idea. And let me know if her symptoms continue. Do you have any idea why her husband might want to poison her?"

"Money. Harold said Connie's got heaps of money."

Sam pondered that silently too long for my comfort.

Therefore, I added, "And Gloria Lippincott," although I decided to give malaria some more thought.

"Couldn't he just divorce her?"

"Probably. Oh, *I* don't know! There's just so much stupid stuff going on. Someone stole Dennis Bissel's automobile in order to kill Mr. Lippincott, and now Mrs. Van der Linden is sick. Maybe Mr. V will inherit a bunch of money if she dies. He wouldn't get anything if they divorced, would he?"

"I have no idea what arrangements the Van der Lindens might have made in case either of them dies or they get divorced."

"Hmph. Might be worth looking in to. If Harold's right and Connie has a lot of money, Max will probably inherit it if she dies."

"He won't get anything if we pin her murder on him."

"Hmm. I suppose you're right about that. You can at least look into their assorted backgrounds, can't you?"

"We're already doing that. We actually know how to do our job, Daisy. We don't need you to solve our cases for us."

"Huh." Maybe he was right about that, too, but I still thought he ought to pay more attention to my suggestions.

"We're still trying to figure out who could have borrowed Bissel's machine in order to run down Lippincott."

"Aha! So you *don't* think Dennis Bissel is a coldblooded murderer."

"Never did. But we need to find out who is."

Spike set up a racket just then, and I jumped to my feet. "Bet he's chased Samson up a tree. I hate when he does that, because he'll sit under the tree and bark until the cows come home if I don't go fetch him."

"I thought you'd taken him to obedience school."

"You know I did. He came in first in his class."

"Well, then, why don't you call him?"

"His obedience training didn't cover cats."

I hurried to the yard next door and, sure enough, there was Spike, gleefully wagging his tail, staring up into the Wilsons' pepper tree— Marengo Avenue was lined on both sides with huge pepper trees—and barking his fool head off. "Spike!" I said in my sternest master's voice. "Stop that."

Spike gave one last bark, looked at me as though I'd just deprived him of his greatest joy in life, and agreed to walk with me back to the house. Poor dog.

Sam left shortly after that. He gave me a big hug before he got into his Hudson and tootled on down the road. I have to admit that I was beginning to enjoy Sam's hugs and kisses, which sounds terrible, but there you go.

By the time I got Spike into the house, the telephone had begun to ring.

"Who the heck is that?" I grumbled as I headed for the telephone. Whoever was on the other end of the wire, I was pretty sure the intended party on this end was me. I snatched the receiver from the cradle and forced myself to sound pleasant when I gave my traditional greeting. "Gumm-Majesty residence. Mrs. Majesty speaking."

"M-Mrs. Majesty?" a shaky voice on the other end of the wire said.

"Yes. This is she." Hadn't I just said so? I didn't recognize the voice.

"It's Gloria Lippincott," the wobbly voice said.

Well, goodness gracious sakes alive, as some of the old ladies at church are fond of saying. "Good evening, Mrs. Lippincott," I said, still sounding spiritual. "May I help you with anything?"

"Yes. Yes, you can. Oh, please say you can hold a séance and get in touch with Michael. *Please*! I need to know who killed him, because I think whoever it was is trying to kill me!"

She'd told me that before. Anyhow, she'd done it herself, hadn't she? Or at least hired someone to do it? Oh, well. I didn't believe I should say so to the woman. She did seem upset. "I can certainly conduct a séance for you, Mrs. Lippincott, but you sound...rattled. Has something happened?"

"Yes, yes, yes! I'm sick."

"You're sick?"

"Deathly ill."

What the heck did she want *me* to do about it? Conduct a séance? Why? Could Michael Lippincott, who had evidently not cared a whole lot for his wife in life, tell her from his grave why she was sick? But I couldn't say that, either. "Um…What are your symptoms?"

"I'm *sick*!" she repeated.

Oh, brother. "I understand that. What are your specific symptoms?"

"I have a terrible headache. And my stomach hurts so much, I can hardly stand it." She began to cry softly. Shoot.

"I'm very sorry, Mrs. Lippincott, but I'm not a doctor. I think you need to see a doctor."

"But I think I know what's the matter! That's why I need you!"

Huh? "If you know what's the matter, what do you need me for?" I tried not to sound sarcastic. "Do you expect your late husband to be able to cure you?" After the words left my mouth, I hoped she wouldn't take them amiss.

"Yes! No. Oh, I don't know."

I hated having to drag information out of people. Holding on to my patience with great effort, I said, "You don't sound too sure of yourself. With regard to the séance, I mean."

"But…But Michael would *know*!"

See what I mean? If the woman wanted me to do something for her, don't you think it would have been wise of her to be specific? However, human beings are often irrational. I know it for a certified fact, because I made my living taking advantage of the trait. People being irrational, I mean.

"He'd know what?" I asked sweetly.

"What I should *do*."

God give me patience. Quickly, please. "Do about what?"

"About what's happening to me!"

"You're sick, you said. Perhaps you have what Connie Van der Linden has," I said, attempting to sound practical and not as though I wanted to wring her neck.

"But that's just *it*!" she cried, further muddying the conversational waters.

"What's just it?"

"I know why I'm sick, and I think it's a criminal matter." By golly, she got out that whole sentence without once breaking down or chopping it into little pieces for me to drag out by asking various questions.

"Well, then, you should call the police."

"The…the police?"

"Yes."

"But I can't do that." Her voice had sunk to a whisper.

"Why not? The police are investigating your husband's death. If you think someone killed him and has now deliberately…What? Poisoned you?" Hmm. Maybe my poisoning idea wasn't so daft after all. "You should call the police."

"No! I can't! It's…It's too complicated to explain."

All right. That was it for me. "I see. Well, I'll be happy to arrange a séance for you, but you really need to telephone the police if you suspect criminal activity."

She whimpered. "But what should I *do*?"

I'd just told her what to do, for Pete's sake! "Call a doctor and then call the police," I repeated. And my voice was still sweet and spiritualistic, too.

"But…But I don't think the police like me."

I prayed for patience again but, again, my prayer was not granted. So I sucked in a deep breath and used it to say, "The police are there to protect and serve all the citizens of Pasadena. They investigate crimes, no matter against whom they're perpetrated. And if you truly believe someone is out to get you, you *need* to call the police. I'm sure they don't dislike you in particular."

"What about that detective friend of yours?"

Aha. Perhaps this was the real reason of this idiotic telephone call. She wanted to seduce Sam. Huh. "Detective Rotondo? He works primarily on murder investigations, and I don't believe he's at the station at the moment. If someone really *is* trying to kill you, he won't be of any help until after you're dead."

"What? *No!* That's a terrible thing to say!"

I kind of liked it myself. I didn't say so. "What you need to do is telephone the police department and report what happened to the officer who answers the telephone. The appropriate people will be sent to your residence to collect evidence and…do whatever needs to be done."

"Oh, but…Oh, Mrs. Majesty, can you come here and be with me when they come? I'm so *afraid!*"

"Of the police?"

"No. Not the police, exactly. It's just that so many horrible things are happening to me and the people around me, and I'm frightened."

If I didn't think she had collaborated with someone to do away with her husband and was now perhaps collaborating with that same person to kill Connie Van der Linden, I probably wouldn't have faulted her for being afraid. It occurred to me to tell her Harold Kincaid had a gun and knew how to use it and suggest she call him, but I didn't. I'd be sure to tell Harold about my restraint, because he'd appreciate my thoughtfulness. Maybe he'd even treat me to another luncheon.

After contemplating Gloria's bizarre request for several seconds, I said, "I'm sorry. I can't come to your house right now. I have family matters to attend to." Very well, I'd just lied to a frightened woman. A perhaps-frightened woman. Please scold me later.

"You can't?" she said pleadingly. "Then what should I *do*?"

Back to that, were we? "Um, well, don't you have any other women friends who can come over and stay with you until the police leave?"

"W-women friends?" She sounded as if she didn't know what a woman friend was, which was probably true for her.

"Yes." An idea struck me then, kind of like a baseball to the head. "What about Mrs. Warden? Or Mrs. Van der Linden? You and Connie are close, aren't you? And you both seem to have the same symptoms. Maybe you can come up with a solution between you."

"Faith? *Connie*?" she squealed. "I-I don't know. Yes, I've known Faith and James and Connie and Max for a long time, but…" Her voice trailed off.

"Well, isn't one of them a good-enough friend that you could call her?" Was I a sleuth, or was I not a sleuth? It's probably better if you don't answer that question.

"But Connie's been sick lately."

"Yes," I said, purring a bit. "She has been sick, hasn't she? And now you claim you're sick, too. Do you have any idea what's the matter with the two of you?"

"I? How should I know?"

"I thought you just said you *did* know."

"Well…I don't. Really. It was just a…a thought."

149

"Then why not ask Connie to visit? You're friends with the Van der Lindens. You said so yourself." Then, greatly daring, I added, "Or perhaps you should call Sylvia Allen. You and Lawrence were pretty cozy at rehearsal yesterday." They'd winked at each other, according to Lucy. Oh, well.

"*Lawrence* and me? Whatever are you talking about? Lawrence and Sylvia are dear friends. I don't know what you mean about Lawrence and me being *cozy* together. In fact, that sounds like slander."

I gathered she no longer wanted me to visit her and hold her hand through the police investigation of her symptoms. "It wasn't meant to be slanderous. I only reported what was told to me."

"Well, for your information, whoever told you that was misinformed."

"Or she didn't see what she said she saw?"

"*What?*"

"I didn't see what the person who told me about it saw, so this is second-hand information." Did that sentence even make sense? Oh, who cares?

"It's also incorrect. Now what am I supposed to do about being so damned sick?"

"Your symptoms, you mean?"

"Yes! What else do you suppose I'm talking about?"

"I already told you what to do. If you're sick, call a doctor. If you suspect you're being poisoned or something like that, call the police and report your suspicions to them. I'm only a spiritualist-medium. I can't do police work, and I can't cure the ill. However, I can set up a séance for you, if you still want to do that."

"What?" she asked again, not screaming this time. "Oh. Oh, yes, the séance. Yes, yes. I want to do that."

"Very well. Let me look at my calendar." I already knew my schedule, but I figured it was best to let people think I was going out of my way for them. It made them want me more. Maybe. Therefore I let the receiver dangle for a moment or two so she could think I was trying to make room for her séance in my incredibly crowded schedule—I'm joking. When I put the receiver to my ear again, it sounded as if Gloria were talking to someone. A man, if I were to judge by the background grumbles. "Mrs. Lippincott?" I said.

"Thanks. But I'll get back to you later about that. Right now, I guess I'd better—" She stopped speaking so suddenly, I thought we'd been disconnected.

I said tentatively, "Mrs. Lippincott?"

She sounded scared to death when she whispered, "I can't talk right now."

And I guess she hung up on me. Well!

NINETEEN

I hadn't even made it out of the kitchen when the telephone rang again. I paused and listened and, sure enough, it was our ring. With a sigh, I walked back to the telephone and plucked the receiver from the cradle.

"Gumm-Majesty residence. Mrs. Majesty speaking."

"Mrs. Majesty?" a nasal New-York voice said.

"Mrs. Barrow?" I asked, astonished. The very nosiest of our party-line neighbors, Mrs. Barrow was the last person on the face of the earth from whom I'd expect to receive a telephone call.

"Yes, this is Mrs. Barrow," she said, not in her usual scolding tone.

At a loss to account for this call from the party-line neighbor who complained the most about my use of the telephone, I stammered slightly. "Um…May I help you?"

"No. But I might be able to help you. That lady who just called you?"

She'd been listening, the meddlesome old bat! Ah, well. My fault for not shooing her off the line before I conversed with Gloria. "Mrs. Lippincott. Yes?"

"Well, I think something's wrong with her."

I already knew there was something wrong with Gloria Lippincott.

She was man-stealing seductress and, I believed, as near as she could come to being a murderess. However, I sensed that's not why Mrs. Barrow had telephoned.

"You do?"

"Yeah. Right before she said to you that she couldn't talk right now? You remember that?"

"Yes. I remember." I didn't holler at her for remaining on the line and listening in on other people's telephone calls, for which instance of self-control I believe I should be applauded.

"Well, right before then, I heard a door open on her end of the wire, and a guy, he says, 'Who're you talking to?' Real nasty-like, if you know what I mean. And then she says, 'Oh, it's just...' Well, I can't remember what name she said, but it wasn't yours."

"Oh. How odd."

"Yeah, I thought so, too. But she sounded scared. And the guy, he sounded mean."

Interesting. Was Gloria Lippincott's partner in crime turning against her? Who could it be? "Did you hear any names?"

"Only the one I don't remember that she called you, but it wasn't your name."

"So you didn't hear Mrs. Lippincott and the man call each other by name?"

"No, but I thought you might could do something. If she's that scared of the guy, maybe he's gonna do something bad to her."

"Yes. Maybe so. Thank you, Mrs. Barrow. Please let me know if you remember anything else."

"Yeah. Will do."

And she hung up on me, too. I didn't mind this time.

But what should I do with this sketchy bit of information relayed to me by our intrusive party-line neighbor? Call Sam? I didn't have much to tell him.

On the other hand, Gloria *had* sounded frightened. Even Mrs. Barrow thought so. And she'd also described the same symptoms Connie had relayed to me only the day before yesterday. Was someone poisoning the both of them? And Mrs. Barrow had heard a man speak in a mean manner to Gloria, and Gloria had sounded afraid, even to me, who believed her to be a villainess. It was possible, I supposed, that if Sam or some other police person drove immediately to her home, he or they might catch whoever was threatening Gloria. *If* she were being threatened.

Bother! I didn't know what to do.

Therefore, feeling as though I were taking my life in my hands, I got the Pasadena telephone directory and looked up Sam's home number. He was probably napping at the moment—I didn't buy the paperwork excuse for a minute—but Gloria's call and Mrs. Barrow's information might be important.

Picking up the receiver for the third time in a half-hour, I pressed the cradle several times. A voice I remembered well answered.

"Medora? This is Daisy." Medora Cox and I had gone to school together.

"Hey, Daisy. What can I do you for?"

"You can connect me to Colorado five-two-five-six, if you don't mind."

"Sure thing."

Clicking sounds commenced, and after a few seconds, I heard a telephone ring on the other end of the wire. It rang for so long, I despaired of Sam being home. Maybe he'd been called out on another case. Maybe he was in the bath. Maybe—

"Rotondo," he growled.

"Sam! I'm so glad you're there." Very well, I'm not usually so enthusiastic when I telephone the grouchy Gus.

"Daisy?"

"Yes."

"What the devil do you want?"

Oh, boy. The man was *such* a cheerful specimen. "I don't want anything. But Gloria Lippincott just called me, and she claims she sick with the same symptoms as Connie Van der Linden, and—"

"What the hell am I supposed to do about it?" he snarled.

"Will you just *listen* for a minute?" I exclaimed, irked.

"Go on."

"Well, Gloria sounded shaky when she first called, and she hemmed and hawed and wouldn't get to the point, until at last she said she wanted me to schedule a séance so she could find out who killed her husband because she thought whoever it was is now trying to kill her, but I didn't believe that for a second."

"Go *on*," Sam said again, even more gruffly.

"I'm telling you! She blathered on about her symptoms, which are just like Connie's, and I said she should go to the doctor, and she said she thinks she knows what's wrong, and that somebody's doing something to harm her. So then I said she should call the police, and she hemmed and hawed some more. Then I offered to schedule a séance for her and let the receiver dangle for a minute so she'd think I was so busy that I had to look at a calendar. Then, when I got back on the wire, she sounded strange. Sort of like she wasn't talking to me anymore, but to someone else. Then she said she couldn't talk, and hung up. I guess. I didn't hear the receiver plop into the cradle."

"So what the hell—"

"Stop swearing at me! I'm not through! After I hung up, Mrs. Barrow, our snoopy party-line neighbor 'phoned me. She said that while my receiver was hanging there, some guy entered Gloria's house, and he sounded menacing."

"Menacing?"

I could almost hear Sam rolling his eyes.

"That's what Mrs. Barrow said. And Gloria seemed awfully scared when she called, and especially when she hung up. If she hung up."

"What do you mean, *if* she hung up?"

"Well, maybe someone killed her and let the receiver dangle."

I heard Sam suck in a truckload of air. "If she didn't hang up, that other lady wouldn't have been able to get through to you."

"Oh. I hadn't thought of that."

"Surprise, surprise."

"Don't be unpleasant, Sam Rotondo. What if someone is at Gloria's house right now, trying to murder her?"

"I thought she was the one doing the murdering."

I huffed. "I thought so, too, but now she claims to be sick. Maybe whoever's poisoning Connie is poisoning her, too."

"Back to poison again, are you?"

"Oh, bother you, Sam Rotondo! Gloria asked me to go to her

house, and I'm going to do it right this minute! If you don't want to know what's going on, *I* do!"

"Oh, no you don't!"

"Oh, yes I will!"

"Damnation, Daisy Majesty, stay right where you are. I'll pick you up, and we'll *both* drive to the Lippincott place."

How sweet! I'd never in a million years tell him so. With barely a sniff, I said, "Thank you, Sam. That's kind of you."

"Huh."

And, for the third time that day, someone hung up on me. This time I didn't mind even more than I didn't mind when Mrs. Barrow hung up on me. Bless Sam's crabby little heart, he was going to take me to Gloria's! It crossed my mind to wonder if he knew where she lived, but then I recalled he'd questioned the woman before with regard to the police investigation of her husband's death, so he must know her address.

"What's going on out here?" My mother appeared in the kitchen, rubbing her eyes. Guess she'd taken a nap after that gigantic meal Vi had fed us.

"Sam's going to pick me up in a minute or two," I told her. "We're going to be visiting one of the *Mikado* cast members."

"Didn't I hear the telephone ring a couple of times?"

"Yes. The first time it was Gloria Lippincott calling, and the second time it was Mrs. Barrow."

Ma stared at me. "Mrs. *Barrow*? Did she call to yell at you or something?"

I grinned as I headed to my bedroom to get my hat, gloves and coat. "Oddly enough, no. She called because she'd listened in on my conversation with Mrs. Lippincott—"

"The nosy old thing!" cried my mother, bless her.

"Yes, she is. But she might have overheard something important, and she telephoned to tell me about it. That was nice of her."

"If you say so," Ma said. She headed toward the refrigerator, so I guess her nap had helped her digest that mammoth meal. But she only reached for the milk and poured herself a glass. "Why is Sam taking you to that woman's house?"

Hmm. How should I explain this excursion to my mother without worrying her? "Mrs. Barrow said she thought she heard someone threatening Gloria." That wasn't much of a fib. "And I called Sam to tell him about it, and he said he'd pick me up, and we could go over to Mrs. Lippincott's house together. She asked me to visit her, but I didn't want to go alone. I'm not sure I trust her."

Shaking her head, Ma said, "I don't know about those theater people, Daisy. I've always heard they're a rum lot. Maybe the rumors are true."

"Maybe. But Harold works in the pictures, and he's a great guy."

"But he's not an actor."

"He is in *The Mikado*. He's got a huge role."

"But he's not an actor by trade. I think most of them—the actors, I mean—are crazy. Well, they must be if they want to parade themselves all over the screen for the whole world to see. And you're forever reading about them killing themselves with drugs and alcohol and things like that. And then there's' that awful Fatty Arbuckle who killed that woman."

"He was found not guilty," I said for the heck of it. "In fact, in three trials, two voted primarily for acquittal, and the last one actually wrote him an apology."

"Hmph. He was guilty of lewd behavior at the very least. And that poor murdered William Desmond Taylor. You don't hear about people in our circle getting murdered. It's always those picture people. Most unsavory." Ma frowned.

Interesting perspective, and one I'd heard before. Or at least read about. "You may well be right. Connie and Max Van der Linden seem nice, but Gloria Lippincott is another kettle of fish entirely. A kind of stinky one."

"Daisy!"

"You started it."

"Don't be childish," advised my mother.

"You're right. Sorry, Ma."

Ma said no more, but drank her milk, rinsed out her glass, and retired to the living room. After I'd put on my coat, hat and gloves, I walked to the living room, too, and saw she was all snug on the sofa,

Spike reclining beside her, and she was reading *The Man Who Knew Too Much*, by Mr. G. K. Chesterton. I still hadn't figured out why so many British authors only used their initials. Not that it matters.

Because I didn't want to upset Spike by exciting him with Sam's arrival and then making him miserable because of Sam's departure, I decided to wait for Sam on the front porch. It was *cold* out there. I pulled my cloche down to cover my ears, crossed my arms over my chest, and stamped back and forth on the front porch in order to keep from freezing to the spot. I guess people get soft from living in California. I expect my Eastern relations would scoff at me for being a sissy as they shoveled snow off their sidewalks. Oh, well. It all boils down to what one is accustomed to when it comes to weather.

Sam didn't keep me waiting long. I saw his headlamps as he drove up Marengo Avenue, and I walked out to the street so he wouldn't have to park or anything. He parked anyway, and opened my door for me.

I said, "Thanks, Sam."

He said, "Huh."

"Do you know Gloria's address?"

"Yes."

"I hope she's all right."

"I bet you do."

"I *do*," I said, stung, although not a whole lot.

"Thought you hated the woman."

"I don't hate anybody. I don't much like her, but I don't want anyone to murder her, either."

"Right."

Very well. So much for conversation with the granite slab that was Detective Sam Rotondo when he was being difficult.

Gloria Lippincott's lavish California Boulevard home wasn't awfully far away from our more modest abode on Marengo Avenue. We passed groves and groves of orange trees on our way south to California, but since it was the beginning of autumn, no sweet-smelling orange-blossom scent kissed our nostrils. In truth, it was dark as pitch out there, and I couldn't see anything beyond the strip of road Sam's head lamps illuminated. It was kind of eerie.

After several silent minutes, Sam said, "Here it is. Eight forty-eight

East California Boulevard." I guess he squinted into the darkness because he said, "Big place."

"All the houses down here are big."

"Yeah."

He pulled to a stop in front of a dense hedge of something or other. Couldn't tell what it was in the dark. "Don't park so close that I can't open my door," I told Sam.

"I didn't. You can get out."

"All right."

"Wait until I get my flashlight, so you don't fall and break your neck."

How kind and considerate of him. But he was in copper mode, so I guess he didn't feel particularly sentimental about being out with me after dark. This was especially true since I'd more or less forced him to take this trip with me.

By the light of Sam's big, policemanly flashlight, I discovered he was right about not being too close to the hedge. I opened my own door, and, thanks to Sam's light, recognized the hedge as a bunch of gardenia bushes. "Boy, I bet these smell swell during the summer months." We had a couple of gardenia bushes at home, but there must have been twenty or thirty of them in the Lippincotts' hedge.

"Yeah. You'll have to visit during the summer since you're such pals with Mrs. Lippincott."

"Why are you being so hateful tonight, Sam Rotondo?"

"No reason. I love being interrupted in the middle of doing paper-work in order to go on nutty errands with you."

"You didn't have to come. I said I'd come by myself," I reminded him.

"Right. Sure as anything, if you did that, something *would* be wrong here, and I'd have to come rescue you."

"I don't need rescuing!"

However, I truly was grateful that I hadn't made this trip by myself. Except for Sam's flashlight, there wasn't a single other light around at first. Once we found the drive, I could see that light emanated from the stately home, which sat a hundred yards or so from the street. "Hmm. She must still be awake, anyhow," I murmured.

"It's only around seven or seven-thirty," said Sam.

"Seems later than that."

"Because of the time change."

"I guess."

Sam took my arm, I guess so I wouldn't trip and fall over my own feet, since nothing else seemed to be in the way, and we walked up the drive together. About seventy-five yards of not much of anything but lawn and cement driveway, I saw a long white porch to the right of us. Lights blazed all over the place, and the door to the mansion stood slightly ajar. I squinted to make sure of that. I was definitely ajar.

"That doesn't seem right," I said.

"What doesn't seem right?"

"The door being left open like that."

"Well, let's go and see if the lady's been poisoned to death."

"Sam Rotondo—"

I didn't get any father into my lecture than that, because as soon as Sam pushed the already-slightly-open door a little bit more open, we saw a woman lying on the floor.

TWENTY

"Oh, my Lord!" I cried from the doorway, my hands at my frozen cheeks. "Is she dead?"

"I don't know. Stay there," Sam ordered.

I didn't stay there. I followed him to the figure on the floor. Gloria Lippincott. I could tell it was she by the white-blond waves of hair, although she was lying on her side facing away from us.

Sam leaned over Gloria, and felt for a pulse in her neck.

"Is she dead?" I asked again.

"No. She's alive, but her pulse feels weak."

"Does she have any injuries that you can see?"

"I don't *know*. Dammit, let me do my job, will you?"

"Sorry," I muttered, irked.

"See if you can find a telephone. Call an ambulance. I'll see what I can do for her here."

Familiar as I was with homes of rich people, I headed for the staircase straight ahead. Most of the rich folks I knew had a telephone closet underneath the staircase.

Gloria didn't. Nuts. I searched some more and eventually found that she had an entire room given over to the telephone, which I imagine she used a lot, because it wasn't a mere wall 'phone like the ones we middle-class people use, but was rather an elaborate, enameled candlestick number perched on a desk. I rushed over, picked up the receiver and clicked the cradle several times. When the operator answered—it wasn't Medora Cox this time—I couldn't remember the number of Gloria's house. Nuts again.

"I need an ambulance," I told the operator. She asked for the address, which is when I realized I didn't recall what Sam had said on our way here. "Um…Just a minute." I set the receiver on the desk and ran to the huge hallway, which was where Gloria lay.

Sam had sort of sat her up, but her head lolled to one side. She looked dead to me. Ugh. "Sam, what's the number of this house."

"How the hell should I know?" he barked.

"The *address*, darn you!"

"Eight forty-eight."

"Thank you."

I raced back to the telephone room. "Eight forty-eight East California Boulevard," I panted at the operator. "And please hurry. I think a woman is dead here."

Which didn't make any sense. If Gloria were dead, she wouldn't need an ambulance. Oh, well. The operator agreed to get an ambulance to eight forty-eight East California Boulevard. My heart was hammering like thunder when I walked back to where Sam cradled Gloria.

Actually, he'd laid her on a sofa and was patting her cheeks. I'd wanted to do that myself a few times, only much harder than he was doing.

"Is she going to be all right?" I asked, knowing even as I did so that Sam couldn't answer that question.

"Depends on what's wrong with her. She has no visible wounds, so I don't think she's been shot or knifed. And there are no marks of strangulation. As much as I hate to say this, she might have taken or been given some kind of drug or poison. If I knew she'd taken morphine or chloral, I'd have her throw it up, but whatever it was might be corrosive."

Ew. "Oh, dear. I didn't like her, but I didn't want her dead, either."

"She's not dead yet," said Sam grimly. "Call the station, will you? Tell whoever answers to send two uniforms to eight forty-eight East

California. Can you remember the number, or shall I write it down for you?"

"Darn you, Sam! I'm...rattled. Frightened. I don't stumble over bodies every day, you know."

"You didn't stumble over this one, either."

He would have to say that. I stomped to the telephone room again and did as he'd commanded. If Sam ever asked me to marry him, we were going to have to have a serious discussion about how he spoke to me. The policeman who answered at the station was nice, however. I told him Sam Rotondo wanted two uniforms at Gloria's house and why, and he said he'd get two coppers there right away.

About five or ten minutes later—it seemed like eons—lights and sirens rent the formerly quiet air around the Lippincott home, and uniformed attendants scurried in through the front door, carrying a stretcher. They lifted Gloria's limp self onto the stretcher and headed to the front door again.

"Castleton?" asked Sam of one of the attendants.

"Yes, sir," said the attendant.

From that brief exchange, I understood that Gloria was going to be rushed to the Castleton Memorial Hospital, which was also on California Boulevard, only west of Fair Oaks Avenue, and quite close to her home. I wanted to go there, too, but didn't know if Sam would let me.

A cop car screeched to a halt outside on the drive, and a couple of seconds later, two uniforms rushed into the house. They had to leap aside to make room for the ambulance attendants with the stretcher.

When they finally reached Sam, he said, "You two go over this place as carefully as you can. Dust for prints and be on the lookout for anything that might suggest what the woman took that knocked her out. I don't know if it's a liquid or pills or what. Just be thorough. I'm going to the hospital. If they can do a gastric lavage, we might have some idea what she took."

"Or was given," I said.

All three members of the Pasadena Police Department turned blank stares upon me. I shrugged. "Just a thought," I said in a tiny voice.

After taking a huge breath and exhaling slowly, Sam said, "Yes. It's possible someone gave her something. Just be as thorough as you can be." He turned to me. "I guess you'll have to come with me."

Goody! I didn't say that aloud, but rather donned a somber expression. "Yes. All right."

So, by the beam of Sam's flashlight and the flashing lights atop the police vehicle, we again made our way to his big Hudson, and climbed in. Sam drove rather fast, considering it was dark as an ebony slab out there and the only illumination came from his two head lamps, but we arrived at the hospital in one piece. Sam parked directly in front of the hospital's big front doors, reached into the back seat, pulled out a cardboard sign that read "Pasadena Police Department. Official Business," and propped it against the front windshield. He'd lent me one of those signs once to prevent me from getting shot, but that's another story entirely.

We hurried into the hospital lobby, and Sam was accosted by a uniformed officer. I guess one of the officers at Gloria's house had radioed in a call that we were headed to the hospital and why. "Detective Rotondo?" the man said.

"Yes. That's me."

"The woman's in an operating room right now. The doctor is doing a lavage on her stomach in order to find out what she's taken."

I wondered what a lavage was, but didn't believe it would be prudent of me to ask at that precise moment.

"Good. Where can I wait for the doctor?"

"I'll take you." The officer glanced at me, then back at Sam. "The two of you together?"

With a huff, Sam said, "Yes. Take us both there. I didn't have time to get rid of her before I drove here."

Well, I liked that!

"Right," said the officer, not flinching at Sam's horrid words.

I did more than flinch. I told Sam Rotondo precisely what I thought. "That was flat nasty, Sam Rotondo. You wouldn't even have known about Gloria having been drugged if it weren't for me."

"Yeah. I'm so much better off now, huh?"

"Oh, bother you!"

I heard a funny noise from the officer who was leading us down a long hallway. It took me a second to realize the man was trying to muffle a laugh. Of all the nerve! Of course, I should have been used to it by this time. It seemed that everyone in the Pasadena Police Department knew Sam and I were acquainted, if not more than that. A year or so earlier, I'd made a spectacle of myself by rushing from a crime scene and straight into Sam's arms. In the lobby of the police department. It was very embarrassing. But I was running away from a vicious murderer and scared witless at the time, darn it!

We were all as serious as judges when the officer, whose name tag revealed him as Patrol Officer William Griggs, opened the door to a small waiting room. The room had a window in it, so that we could see what the doctor was doing to Gloria. After an initial peek, I decided I didn't want to see anymore. During that peek, I viewed a doctor in a white coat feeding a long tube into Gloria's throat, presumably directing it to her stomach. Next to him stood a nurse in a white uniform and cap holding a pump-like device connected to the long tube. I assumed that, after the doctor got the tubing into Gloria's stomach, he and/or the nurse would use the pump device to withdraw her stomach's contents. Ugh.

"That's what a gastric lavage is?" I asked Sam, deeming it safe to speak.

"Yeah. They pump whatever's in the stomach out."

"I see." Ick.

I sat in an uncomfortable straight-backed wooden chair and looked around to see if the hospital had provided any reading material to keep its visitors entertained. It hadn't. So I sat there, bored and feeling a little sick—that tube-and-pump device looked as though it would be awfully uncomfortable for the person upon whom it was used—crossed my arms over my chest and waited. After a few minutes, I removed my gloves and hat, although I kept my coat on.

It was I don't even know how much later when the doctor I'd seen in the operating room opened the door and approached Sam. He had disgusting-looking stains on his white coat. I figured they'd come from Gloria's stomach but didn't ask.

"Are you Detective Rotondo?" he said. He glanced at me, but evidently I wasn't important enough for him to talk to.

"Yes. Do you have any idea what the woman took, or do you have to run tests?"

"We'll run tests," said the doctor. "But right offhand, I'd say she took or was given a pretty big dose of chloral hydrate. There may be something else in her stomach contents, but we won't know until the lab tests them. I suspect she might also have taken Veronal, although we can't be sure until the tests come back. The chloral and the barbital taken together are generally lethal."

My nose wrinkled, and I was glad the two men were ignoring me. But...ew.

"Is she going to live?"

The doctor heaved a big sigh. "I can't honestly tell you one way or another at this point if she'll live. If she wakes up—and she may not—she's going to have a really sore throat from the lavage tube, and she'll be too groggy to question for quite a while."

"What constitutes 'quite a while'?" Sam wanted to know.

"Hours. Days. It's hard to say, especially since I don't know if there's anything besides chloral in her system. Do you have any idea when she might have taken or been given the drug?"

I was surprised when Sam turned around and stared at me. I blinked up at him, and he began to frown.

Understanding—at last—what he wanted to know, I said, "Uh...I'm not sure. I think it wasn't more than an hour or so ago when I talked to her. When did I call you, Sam?"

Shaking his head, Sam said, "About seven. So you think you talked to her around six or six-thirty?"

"I guess. I'm sorry. I didn't look at a clock or anything."

"Well, if that's the time we're looking at, her chances are better than if she'd been lying around for several hours. In fact, if she'd taken the stuff much earlier than that, she'd already be dead," said the doctor.

Good heavens, I might have saved a woman's life! Not that I much liked the woman, but still. I'd taken the initiative, braved Sam Rotondo's native surliness, and forced him to go to Gloria Lippincott's house. Perhaps *forced* isn't the correct word. Maybe *coerced* might be more accurate. But he'd picked me up, we'd gone to Gloria's, and I'd followed Sam's directions regarding telephoning the ambulance and the police.

Since I knew very well that Sam would never thank me, perhaps I could look forward to some gratitude from Gloria. If she survived this ordeal. I shuddered involuntarily. Gloria wasn't a nice person; she stole other women's men; she might have collaborated with the person who killed her husband; she might be in cahoots with someone who may or may not be poisoning Connie Van der Linden. Those were a lot of mights and mays. I hoped she survived, mainly because I wanted to get to the bottom of the various mysteries surrounding *The Mikado* and its cast members.

The doctor left us then, and Sam said, "I'll take you home. I'll have to come back here and wait around until she either dies or wakes up."

"I'd like to talk to her when she's able to talk. I might be able to convince her to confess to involvement with her husband's death."

"Leave the police alone to do their jobs, Daisy. We'll get everything out of her. Well, everything the doc left." He grinned.

I didn't. "That's disgusting, Sam."

"Yeah. It is, kind of." He chuckled.

Deciding there was no use arguing with the man, I donned my hat and gloves again, and we walked out to the Hudson. I was home in no time, and Sam was on his way back to the hospital. I didn't know what impact Gloria's...accident? Whatever it was, I didn't know what impact it would have on *The Mikado*. I'd begun to think the production was cursed.

Ma, Pa, Aunt Vi, and Spike were all in the living room when Sam dropped me off. He didn't see me to the door, which was all right with me. Spike danced around my legs as if he hadn't seen me for a decade or three. I bent and scooped him up. Ugh. He was getting heavier and heavier. Pansy Hanratty, who'd taught Spike's obedience class, would never forgive me if I let my dachshund get fat.

Nevertheless, I carried him to the sofa and plopped us both down thereon. As Spike licked my face, I removed my hat and gloves once more.

"What happened to that woman?" Ma demanded.

"Who was it?" asked Vi.

"Your mother said you think someone was trying to kill her," said Pa. "I don't know why these things always happen around you, Daisy."

With a sigh, I said, "I don't, either, Pa. But the woman is Gloria Lippincott."

"Isn't that the one whose husband was run down and killed the other day?" asked Vi.

"She's the one, all right. And now it looks as if either someone's trying to do her in, or she tried to commit suicide. The doctor said her chances of surviving whatever it was she took—or was given—are iffy."

"Good heavens," said Ma. "I really don't think you should be around those acting people, Daisy. They're nothing but trouble."

"Most of the cast are members of our church, Ma. It's only a few of them who aren't."

Ma's lips pinched, and she said, "I don't think Pastor Smith should have allowed that production to take place in a house of worship. I don't care if it *is* for a good cause."

With a sigh, I gently shoved Spike aside and struggled out of my coat. The house was quite toasty. "I think there are only one or two bad apples in the cast, Ma."

"It only takes one bad apple to ruin a whole bushel, you know," said Ma, spouting an adage from the wisdom of ages.

"I know."

"Want a sandwich?" asked Vi. "We each had a roast pork sandwich, and I can make one for you. I'll even slice an apple for you to eat with it."

Boy, it seemed like we'd barely finished dinner, but when I glanced at the clock on the mantel, darned if it wasn't almost ten o'clock. I hadn't realized how long it had taken Sam and me to get to Gloria's, get Gloria to the hospital, and wait for the doctor to finish his repulsive operation and come out to chat with Sam.

My stomach took that opportunity to grumble slightly, surprising me. "Thanks, Vi. I'd like that."

So, bless my darling aunt, she made me a sandwich and sliced an apple for me. After I'd finished my supper, I washed up after myself, and Spike and I went to bed.

TWENTY-ONE

On Monday morning, before I was fully awake, I got a telephone call from Sam, who was ringing from the Castleton Hospital.

"Can you come down here?" he asked. "Mrs. Lippincott is asking for you."

To say I was surprised, both by Sam's call, during which he didn't even sound grumpy, and by Gloria's request, would be a vast understatement. I was, in fact, so thunderstruck—or should that be thunderstricken? Oh, who cares?—that I stared at the instrument hanging on the kitchen wall for some seconds, unable to find words in my mouth. The fact that the hour was early and that I'd only minutes earlier crawled from beneath my comfy quilt might have had something to do with my muteness. I'd aimed to go to the library that day and look up poisons. Was Sam going to spoil my day?

"Daisy?" Sam's voice was a trifle louder and harsher.

"Oh! Oh, yes. Yes, I can do that. Um…So I guess she didn't die." I shook my head hard and spoke before Sam could pounce on my words and shred them to tatters. "I mean, she's awake and coherent?" That was more than could be said for me at the moment.

"She can't talk very well, but she's been asking for you. She won't talk to anyone else."

"My word. How odd. I wonder what she wants with me."

"If you'd drive down here, you could find out."

"You're getting snappish, Sam. Stop it. I just got up and am not quite awake yet, and your call and request are two things I didn't anticipate first thing on a Monday morning."

"I've been here all night long. If I'm snappish, that might be one reason. Another reason is that the idiotic woman won't talk to the coppers. She wants you."

"Very well. I'll have breakfast—"

"Which is more than I've had."

"And after I have breakfast, I'll get dressed and drive down to the Castleton. Will you still be there?"

"Yes, I'll still be here," he said peevishly.

"Um…does the hospital have a canteen or something? Maybe you can get a bite to eat there."

"Yeah. I'll do that. Just get here as soon as you can, all right?"

"Yes. Of course. I'll be there in a jiffy."

"Good." He hung up.

Blasted man! But I guess he had a reason to be surly, given the circumstances. When I turned away from the telephone, my mother, Aunt Vi, and Pa were all looking at me. Well, and so was Spike, but he was wagging and happy. It didn't seem to me as if any of my kin were happy at all.

"That was Sam," I said.

"We figured that out for ourselves," said Ma in an uncharacteristically caustic tone. "Where is it he wants you to go? To that woman's room at the hospital?"

"Yes." I shrugged and my shabby robe slithered down my right arm. I hoisted it back up with my left hand and said, "He said she's awake, wants to talk to me, and refuses to talk to anyone else."

"Why?" asked Pa.

This time when I shrugged, my robe slithered down my left arm. I determined then and there to make new robes for everyone in the family. I thought I'd seen in the newspaper that Maxime's Fabrics was holding a sale on flannel.

"I don't know," I said. "I don't really even know the woman. I can't imagine why she wants to talk to me."

"Do you suppose she's afraid of the police for some reason?" asked Ma, who is sensible under almost all circumstances.

"Good question. She might well be." I yawned. "But I have to eat breakfast now and get down there before Sam blows a gasket."

Ma's brow wrinkled. "What is a gasket, anyway?"

Trust my mother.

Pa said, "It's a seal in an automobile's engine. If you blow a gasket in a machine, it gets hot and steamy and doesn't run anymore."

"That's Sam, all right," I mumbled, heading for the stove, hoping Vi had fixed something for breakfast.

"I left some ham for you in the warming oven, Daisy," said Vi, answering my unasked question.

"Thanks, Vi. You're forever saving my life."

"Pooh," said Vi, although I could see she was pleased.

"So are you going to the hospital to talk to that woman?" asked Ma, pulling on her gloves in preparation for walking to her job as head bookkeeper at the Hotel Marengo.

"I guess I will," said I, grabbing a dishtowel and hauling the plate holding the ham out of the oven. Toast and ham would make a good breakfast. I'd try to fry an egg, but I wasn't very good at frying eggs.

Vi, who knew all about my cooking skills—or lack thereof—nudged me out of the way. "You fix your toast. I'll fry you an egg."

With a deep and heartfelt sigh, I said, "Thanks, Vi. I really wish I weren't so clumsy in the kitchen."

"It's just that you don't pay attention, is all," said Vi.

She'd said that before, but I think my culinary failures went deeper than lack of attention. I think, by then, that I had developed some kind of complex about cooking. And don't ask me what a complex is, because I don't know. I only know that the rich people I consorted with back then were tossing the word around like confetti on New Year's Day, because the latest fad amongst the socialites for whom I worked was being "analyzed" by psychiatrists because of their various complexes. We plain folks couldn't afford to be analyzed. We had to struggle along as well as we could on our own, complexes or no complexes. That was all right by me.

Anyhow, thanks to Vi, I ate a good breakfast, then washed and dried the dishes, washed and dried myself, then studied the clothes in my closet for a minute or two. I didn't have to dress up in particular, since Gloria Lippincott probably wasn't going to judge me by my wardrobe that day. Nevertheless, I selected a nice dark green woolen suit I'd made a year or so earlier. The weather remained cold, so the wool would be welcome, mainly because I'd lined the suit with *faux* silk. I couldn't afford real silk, but used the fake stuff anyway because wool against my skin made me itch. Anyhow, nobody would see the lining.

When I emerged from my bedroom, it was to find Spike staring at me with a doleful expression on his doggy face. He knew, when I dressed up, it wasn't to take him for a walk. Instantly I felt guilty.

"Oh, Spike, I'm so sorry." I knelt in front of my pooch and held my arms out for him to leap into. He did, and I smothered him with affection for several moments. I know he'd rather have gone for a walk. So would I. I didn't want to talk to Gloria Lippincott. Or maybe I did. I sure wanted to know what had happened to her. Still, I liked Spike considerably better than I liked Gloria, so I'd rather have walked him than talk to her.

Fortunately for the both of us, Pa was on hand. "I'll take him out this morning, Daisy, and maybe you can go with us for another walk this afternoon."

Bless my father's soft heart! "Thanks, Pa. I really appreciate this."

"That's all right. I want to know what that woman has to tell you." He winked at me.

"If I can tell you, I will. If whatever she says involves the police..." My words trailed off, and I felt guilty again. Here I was, tempting my family with snippets of information only to tell them I might not be able to complete the puzzle. "I'll tell you," I said firmly. "If the police are involved or not." There. Sam could lump it if he didn't like it.

"Don't tell us if it'll annoy the police," said Pa with a grin.

"Phooey on the police. If Mrs. Lippincott wanted to talk to the police, she could do so. She wants to talk to me. And then I'll talk to you."

And with that and another quick Spike-pat, I sailed out the side door and into our zippy Chevrolet. I had to stop at a filling station along the way, but that was all right. My old school pal, Frank Bowers, filled my tank, washed my windows, and chatted with me as he did so. He even complimented me on how fancy I was looking. Maybe it was more like a tease. Whatever it was, I could tell he approved of my looks, which brightened a dull day a trifle.

The sky had actually begun to drip a little by the time I got to the Castleton Hospital. Fiddlesticks. And me with no umbrella. One didn't generally need an umbrella in Pasadena, but every now and then the weather could surprise one. I held my handbag over my head as I hurried to the hospital's doors.

When I stopped in the lobby to shake water droplets from my handbag and suit coat, a gruff voice greeted me.

"It's about time you got here."

Sam. Of course.

Frowning, I looked up to see him looming at the bottom of the staircase to the second floor.

Rather than blowing up at him, I said, "I got here as quickly as I could." Peering at him more closely, I said, "You look kind of like the wrath of God, Sam. Did you ever get anything to eat?"

"A sinker and a cup of Joe," he growled.

"That's not very nutritious," I said, and then felt stupid. "But I guess your choices were limited."

"You can say that again. Better hurry up now. They still don't know if the lady's going to make it. She's in and out of consciousness, but every time she has a lucid moment, she asks for you."

"I wonder why."

"Who the hell knows?" And Sam turned on his heel and lumbered up the staircase. I went after him, much more daintily.

A policeman stood guard at Gloria's door, I guess because no one was sure if she'd poisoned herself or been poisoned by someone else, and if she had been poisoned, they didn't want whoever'd poisoned her to come in and finish her off. I nodded to the officer, a dour specimen named Doan whom I'd met before, and quietly entered Gloria's room.

Sam followed me in. I guess he was hoping she wouldn't notice him. Fat chance. He was big as a house.

I probably should say here that Sam Rotondo wasn't fat. He was big. He was tall and wide and built rather like one of those giant redwood trees they have in Northern California. He sure as anything couldn't hide behind me, if that's what he'd planned.

Gloria looked horrible. Her hair was matted, her skin was blotchy, and she seemed to be asleep. Unsure of what to do, I glanced at Sam.

He whispered, "Talk to her."

So I talked to her. "Gloria?" I whispered. "Mrs. Lippincott?"

Nothing. I again glanced over my shoulder at Sam.

He muttered a soft, "Damn," and went to the bedside. There he lifted Gloria's hand, which was lying limply on the white hospital sheet covering her. "She's got a pulse," he said. "Try again."

So I tried again. A bit louder than before, I said, "Gloria? Mrs. Lippincott?"

Gloria stirred a bit and muttered something incomprehensible. Encouraged—although I'm not sure why—I picked up her hand, which Sam had lowered to the bed covers once more. "Gloria? It's Mrs. Majesty. I understand you want to speak with me."

Her eyelids fluttered and her eyes opened slightly. "Mrs. Majesty?"

Merciful heavens, her voice was as hoarse as a frog's. I guess the doctor wasn't kidding when he'd said she'd have a sore throat after last night's procedure.

"Yes. It's Mrs. Majesty. Did you wish to speak with me?"

"No cops," she said, her eyes opening a bit wider. She scanned the room, and her attention landed on Sam. She repeated, "No cops."

"I'll wait outside," said Sam, sounding disgruntled.

I sat on the chair next to Gloria's bed, still holding her hand. When the door closed behind Sam, I told her, "We're alone. What did you wish to say to me?"

"Stop him," said Gloria.

If I was supposed to understand her meaning, I failed miserably. "Stop who? Whom? Whoever." Darn the English language, anyhow! "Stop him from doing what?"

She seemed to relapse into unconsciousness. I didn't know what to do, although I sure wished she hadn't sent Sam away. I let go of her hand, which was damp and clammy.

After sitting in that chair for what seemed like eternity, I rose to my feet and headed softly to the door. Maybe she needed a doctor. Heck, maybe she was dead! That thought made me hurry, and I guess I made a noise, because Gloria's voice stopped me before I reached for the doorknob.

"Don't go. Please. Don't go."

Well, at least she hadn't died on me. I turned and stepped toward the chair again. "I was told you wanted to talk to me."

"Yes. I want you. Need to tell you something."

So why didn't she spit it out? So to speak. Recalling her telephone call to me the evening before, I wondered if she were playing some kind of game, making me draw the words out of her mouth one by one. Another glance at her, looking as close to being dead as made no matter, softened my opinion. Slightly. With a smallish huff, I went back to the chair and sat.

"Yes? What is it you wish to tell me?" I asked, attempting to sound mystical and spiritualistic, while, at the same time, disliking this woman a good deal.

"Poison," she whispered, somehow endowing the word with mystery.

"What about poison?" I regret to say my spiritualist's voice contained a trace of tartness.

"Poison. He poisoned me."

'Round and 'round she goes; where she stops, nobody knows, flitted through my brain. Don't ask me why, because I don't know, except that I sensed something amiss here.

Then I chided myself for being a mean-spirited cow. The poor woman had almost died. I supposed I should give her the benefit of the doubt. Perhaps she really *was* confused and unable to form coherent sentences.

That being the case, I stood again. "Perhaps I should come back later, Gloria, when you're better able to express yourself. I fear I don't know what you're trying to tell me."

Darned if she didn't grab my hand! Her grip wasn't strong, but it

175

surprised me into a tiny squeak.

"No! Need to tell you something," she croaked in her frog-voice. She sure didn't sound like one of the three little maids from school any longer.

Well, then do *it,* I wanted to scream at her. Instead, I said gently, "Yes? Please tell me what you need to tell me, then." *And quit beating around the bush.* I didn't add that last part.

"He did it."

"Who did what?"

"He poisoned me."

"Who poisoned you?"

"Jack."

"Jack?" Who the heck was Jack?

"Yes. Jack."

"I…don't know anyone named Jack, Mrs. Lippincott."

She shook her head in what looked to me like frustration. I knew how she felt.

"Jack," she repeated. "He poisoned me. He's poisoning Connie."

"Who is Jack?" I asked rather more sharply than I'd intended.

"Jack. He calls himself Max," she said, nearly startling the socks off me. "Max poisoned me. He's poisoning Connie. It's Max. Arrest him."

TWENTY-TWO

Y ou could have knocked me over with a dust mote when Gloria finally told me who Jack was. Max. Max? I sat, plump, onto the chair beside her bed again.

"He is? I mean, Jack is Max? Max is Jack? I mean...*Max*? Max Van der Linden? He's going around poisoning people?" I didn't believe it.

Or maybe I did.

But...*Max*? He seemed like such a nice, gentle man. And he had a spectacular voice.

Not, of course, that the quality of his voice mattered. I didn't like Gloria, and she had a spectacular voice, too.

"Max. Save Connie," Gloria whispered. "Arrest him."

"I can't arrest anyone. You need to be a policeman to arrest someone. You need to tell this to the police."

"No!" For a croak, the one small word came out with remarkable firmness.

"Why not? You're not making sense, Gloria. If Max is actually someone named Jack and he's going around poisoning people, you need to file a report against him. The police need to stop him. I can't do it. You certainly can't do it, lying in this hospital bed. And Connie seems to think he's the cat's pajamas, even if he does only want to feed her vitamin pills." Instead of taking her to a doctor, who might actually be able to diagnose whatever was wrong with her.

"No. Need you. Séance."

Oh, boy, we were back to the séance, were we? "What good will a séance do?" I asked more bluntly than was usual for me when dealing with nutty women.

"Michael will know."

I heaved a big sigh. "Michael will know what?"

"Who killed him."

"I thought you said Max did it."

She shook her head, which evidently hurt, because she groaned a little. "No. Another person. Max hired. Killed Michael. Michael will know."

Good old Michael. A fount of information from the grave. If I believed in this sort of thing, I might have had an ounce or two of sympathy to spare for Gloria. "Listen, Gloria, I will gladly set up a séance for you any time you want me to. But you need to get well and get out of the hospital. And if Max did this to you, you need to tell the police."

"No!"

Ow. That exclamation must have hurt, because it hurtled from her damaged throat almost as a yell. Then she pressed a hand to her neck and moaned some more.

"Gloria. I can set up a séance for you. Would you like that?"

She nodded, and I noticed a couple of tears had leaked out from her tightly closed eyelids. Either she was the world's best actress, or she was in distress. Maybe both.

"When would you like me to hold this séance?"

"Soon."

"At your house?"

"No." She shuddered, although I wasn't sure why.

"Perhaps Mrs. Bissel will allow me to hold a séance at her house. Would that do?"

"Yes."

"Very well. I'll telephone Mrs. Bissel and see if we can arrange a séance for…next Saturday night? Will you be well by then?"

"Yes."

"Very well."

"Thank you."

"You're welcome."

I rose from the chair once more, but Gloria again caught my hand. What now?

"Daisy?"

Who did she think I was? Sweetly, I said, "Yes?"

"Don't tell cops."

"Nobody but the cops can arrest Max," I reminded her.

"Don't let Max know."

"Don't let him know what?" Darn the woman anyhow! Was I supposed to read her mind?

"Don't let him know we talked."

Well, that was easy enough to promise. "I won't."

"Don't tell cops."

"I can't promise you that," I said firmly but still sweetly.

"No. No, don't tell. Max will hurt Connie if you tell."

From what I'd gathered of this idiotic conversation so far, Max was already hurting Connie. I refused to lie to the woman. "We'll see," I said.

"Séance," she said. "Wait for séance."

Like heck I would. I only said, "I'll let you get some rest now, Gloria. Save your strength, and get well. We need you in *The Mikado*."

She smiled faintly, and I got the heck out of there.

Sam stood in the hall, his arms crossed over his chest, frowning as I exited Gloria's room. I held my finger to my lips so he wouldn't roar before we got out of hearing distance of the patient. Still frowning, Sam allowed me to lead him down the hall.

"What did she want?"

"She still wants me to hold a séance. And don't roll your eyes at me!" I told him as he rolled his eyes at me. "It's not my fault she's an idiot. She claims Max Van der Linden is actually somebody named Jack, and he poisoned her and is poisoning Connie, which I guess is why Connie's been so sick. If Gloria's telling the truth."

179

"Max Van der Linden is actually a man named Jack, and he's poisoning his wife and Mrs. Lippincott?"

"Yeah, I don't know if I believe her, but you'd better check the backgrounds on all these people. According to Gloria Lippincott, her husband lost all his money gambling. Have you checked into the Van der Lindens' backgrounds yet?"

"We're working on it."

"You're always working on it," I said bitterly. "And you want me to help, but you won't tell me what you've learned. For all you know, *I'm* in danger from Max. Jack. Whoever he is."

"You might be," Sam said, frowning, his brow beetling. He even appeared slightly worried. "When's the next rehearsal?"

"Tomorrow night at the church."

"Don't go there alone. I'll take you."

"I don't think anyone will do anything to anyone at the church, Sam," I said. I saw his ironic expression and backtracked. "Oh, yeah. That paving stone."

"Yeah. That paving stone. Where was Van der Linden when that thing was pushed from the roof?"

"How should I know? I wasn't there. I was with you, remember?"

"Yeah. I'd better go over my notes."

Eyeing him critically, I said, "You'd better eat something and catch a nap. Come over for dinner tonight, and I'll let you know what I've set up as far as a séance goes."

"What do you need a séance for?"

"*I* don't need a séance for anything! Gloria Lippincott maintains I'll be able to get in touch with her late husband—her late *estranged* husband—and he'll be able to tell us who stole Dennis Bissel's Rolls and ran him down."

"Oh, brother."

"Right."

We both stood there in the hospital corridor, studying the dingy carpeting at our feet, for a moment or two. Then Sam looked up, narrowed his eyes, and said in a musing tone of voice, "Hmm. Maybe that's not a bad idea."

I squinted up at him. "Maybe what's not a bad idea?"

"Holding a séance. Maybe we can get some answers there."

"From whom? The late Michael Lippincott?"

"No. But I just thought of something."

"What did you just think of?"

"I'll tell you later. Let me walk you to your machine. I've got to get something to eat and take a nap."

"You're actually going to take a suggestion from *me*?" I asked in feigned astonishment.

"No. I'd already planned to do both of those things."

"You're a beast, Sam Rotondo."

"Yeah, I know." He grinned, the beast.

Then he walked me out to the family's Chevrolet, and I tootled home so I could telephone Mrs. Bissel and ask her if we could hold a séance in her breakfast room in order to get to the bottom of Michael Lippincott's death. I wouldn't tell her about the possible poisoning of Connie Van der Linden and Gloria Lippincott, since I couldn't make heads or tails out of that mystery. If there was one. I also wouldn't tell her that Max Van der Linden, according to Gloria Lippincott, was actually a fellow named Jack, and that he was a vicious poisoner and perhaps paving stone-thrower.

My job sounds so complicated sometimes. I think it's actually more idiotic than complicated. Still, Sam wanted me to hold the séance Gloria'd been begging me to hold. But why? He generally denigrated my job and everything to do with it. What did this mean? I wasn't sure, but I figured it boded ill for my own personal self.

I decided mine was not to question why…And I don't think I'll finish that famous quotation since it ends badly. I feared my séance might, too. However, as soon as I got home, I called Mrs. Bissel.

"A séance?" Mrs. Bissel asked, sounding pleased. "Oh, my, yes! You really think this will help to absolve my Dennis from any blame for that man's death?"

"Um…Actually, I'm not sure, but Detective Rotondo thinks it's a good idea."

"Detective Rotondo?" The two words held a universe of astonishment.

"Yes. He thinks if I hold the séance, the…uh, the spirits might be

able to tell us something that could point him in the right direction."
Claptrap, Daisy Majesty. Pure claptrap.

"Aha. So he's coming around, is he?"

Coming around? "Um…I'm not sure what you mean, Mrs. Bissel."

"I could tell he was a skeptic, Daisy. But if he's calling on you to help the police via a séance, he's clearly begun to realize what an asset you can be to his work."

Little did she know. However, I wasn't going to burst her happy bubble. "Yes. It is nice to know he's…beginning to take my skills seriously."

"This will be grand! It will be thrilling to be part of the solution of a crime. Detective Rotondo has always struck me as an intelligent man. I'm so glad he's discovered a good use for your superb talents." I could almost hear Mrs. Bissel rubbing her hands together in delight.

"Yes, indeed."

"Do you suppose the detective wants me to invite certain people?"

Good question. "Yes, he probably does. May I get back to you on the invitation list?"

"Of course. I can hardly wait for Saturday night," cooed Mrs. B.

"Yes. Me, too." Oh, boy. What a fibber I could be!

On the other hand, why *did* Sam want me to conduct a séance for Gloria's sake? Could he actually have been working on the murder of Michael Lippincott?

Silly me! Of *course* he'd been working on the case! Just because he withheld all the interesting information he'd discovered from me didn't mean he hadn't been a busy bee. Darn the man! Had he come up with some angle that still eluded me? Had he discovered that Max Van der Linden really *was* a guy named Jack? If he had, so what? Max might want to kill Connie because she had a lot of money? Why would he want to kill Gloria and her husband? Bother.

It was all too much for me, so I decided to take Spike for a walk.

Pa joined us, and we had quite a nice time, considering the weather was nippy and my brain was in a muddle.

TWENTY-THREE

R ehearsal Tuesday evening was sparsely populated. Sam wouldn't
tell me if Gloria remained in the hospital, but if she'd been
released, I guess either she or her voice wasn't up to the rigors of
rehearsal. Perhaps both. Whatever the problem, if there was one, she
wasn't at rehearsal.

"I think you're being mean, Sam Rotondo. It's not as though I'd tell
anyone if you let on how your investigation is going. I think I deserve to
know if you expect me to help you by holding a séance. I know darned
good and well you don't believe I can talk to spirits."

"Nuts. I'm doing my job. You can do your job by singing tonight,
Thursday and Saturday, and holding that séance on Saturday night."

During this conversation we were walking from his Hudson to the
door to the church sanctuary. When I glanced at him, I noticed a
distinctly smug expression on his face. Darn it all! He was up to something! If he expected me to help him with it, he really *should* let me in on
the details. After all, I'd helped him before a good deal. I'd never blab.
He should have known that by then.

When we entered the sanctuary, the lights were on for once, so we
could see the entire large room. I was amazed and delighted to look at
the chancel and spy Flossie Buckingham, a dear friend whom I'd met

during a...Hmm. Well, I'd met Flossie during a raid on a speakeasy, but I hadn't been there to carouse. I'd gone there as a favor to Mrs. Pinkerton. Flossie had been there because she was attached in an illicit manner to a vicious gangster named Jinx Jenkins. But Johnny Buckingham, a captain in the Salvation Army, and I had saved both her life and, I guess, her soul, because they'd been married for a couple of years by that time and were, as far as I knew, blissfully happy.

Therefore, I called out, "Flossie! How good to see you here!" I ran the last few yards down the center aisle of the church and bounded up onto the chancel. Not precisely churchlike behavior on my part, but the church was being used as an opera house at the moment, so I don't believe I should be censured for my exuberance, even though Mr. Hostetter did frown at me. He was such a stuffy person!

"Daisy! I'm so happy you're here. Detective Rotondo asked if I could come here and help out this evening, since I guess one of the three little maids is sick."

"Sam? *Sam* asked you to come?" I whirled around and tried to find Sam in the sanctuary. Aha. There he was. Smiling like the Cheshire cat from a front pew. Puzzled, I turned back to Flossie.

"Yes. He came to our church yesterday, and he and Johnny talked for the longest time. Then it was actually Johnny who asked me to sing tonight. And Thursday, if that poor woman is still under the weather."

I dearly loved both Johnny, whom I'd known from childhood, and Flossie, who used to be a gangster's moll but who wasn't any longer. She also used to have a perfectly hideous New York accent, but she'd taken her release from the gangsters seriously, and now she spoke as though she might have visited New York once upon a time, but was really just one of our native Pasadenans. Sort of.

Her physical appearance had undergone even more of a change than her accent. To look at her, you'd never have guessed her background. She had a charming brown bob, as opposed to the violent blond locks of three years prior, and she wore demure, tasteful clothing, most of which she made herself. I tell you, until I met Flossie, I didn't know a person could change so much.

Except, of course, for my Billy, but the Kaiser had done him in. Flossie had perpetrated her redemption via her own efforts. Well, and those of Johnny, who loved her deeply. Flossie has always credited me with her salvation, but truth to tell, I'd been trying to get rid of her when I palmed her off onto Johnny.

That sounds terrible, and it isn't entirely true, but there's enough truth in the statement to make me feel guilty a whole lot. But I felt guilty all the time anyway, so I guess it doesn't matter.

"Well, I'm so glad you're here. I didn't know you could sing!"

"Oh, yeah. I used to sing in clubs when I was a kid."

I didn't ask her what kinds of clubs, since I thought I knew, and I shuddered inside. The poor woman had been born in one of New York's roughest, meanest neighborhoods, and had been on her own since she was a young adolescent. Small wonder she'd fallen into shady ways with shady characters. But not any longer. She made the perfect Salvation Army Captain's wife. What's more, she and Johnny had a little boy whom they named William, after my Billy.

"If you ladies don't mind," said Mr. Hostetter coldly. "We need to get this rehearsal under way. Mrs. Buckingham, thank you very much for filling in for Mrs. Lippincott, who is under the weather. Let me introduce you to the rest of the cast."

So he did, and I watched. I took particular notice of Max and Connie Van der Linden. Connie didn't look quite as sick today as she had on Saturday. Max still seemed to hover over her solicitously. I didn't know whether to brand him as a murdering maniac or applaud him for the tender care he extended to his wife. They were both nice to Flossie, so I decided to await events before making any judgments.

How kind of me, huh?

"And you read music, Mrs. Buckingham?" Max asked her.

"Sort of. I know the music to *The Mikado*, because I sang one of the three little maids back in New York."

"Wonderful." Mr. Hostetter unbent enough to give her a warm smile.

"Thank you so much for helping us out," said Max, shaking Flossie's hand.

"Yes. Thank you, Mrs. Buckingham," said Connie, smiling her sweet smile at Flossie.

The schedule for that day was to go over the entire operetta scene by scene. The ultimate performances were scheduled for Friday and Saturday, December seventh and eighth; and Friday and Saturday, December fourteenth and fifteenth. That was cutting our Advent and Christmas schedules mighty short, but, as everyone kept telling everyone else, it was for a good cause.

Flossie had a lovely, rich soprano voice. Maybe it wasn't quite as great as Gloria's, but I suspect Gloria'd had vocal training. Poor Flossie had just struggled along on her own all her life until she met Johnny. It was sure more fun for me to be in the cast with Flossie than with Gloria. I do believe others felt the same way. Maybe not. Perhaps my own views on Gloria were coloring my perception.

George Finster, while not entirely recovered from his bout of laryngitis, was back and whispering his part as the Mikado. This left Sam free to peruse the cast, take notes and...talk to Johnny Buckingham.

Johnny Buckingham? I squinted into the sanctuary, where the lights had been dimmed. I guess Flossie saw me, because she moseyed over and said, "Johnny brought me. One of our dear ladies at the Salvation Army is taking care of Billy." She giggled. "It's kind of fun for the two of us to get away without the baby for once."

I think I goggled at Flossie, although I'm not sure. But...They'd left their baby alone with a congregant so they could come to a rehearsal of *The Mikado*? What kind of holiday was that?

On the other hand, what did I know about rearing children? Perhaps even an evening at a rehearsal was like a holiday for the fairly new parents.

"Do you know why Sam and Johnny are talking? They look mighty serious to me."

"Yes," said Flossie. "But you'll have to get Detective Rotondo to tell you about it. I've been sworn to secrecy."

"You've *what?*"

Another giggle. "Sorry, Daisy. I have to run now. The three little maids have their song coming up."

"But—"

But nothing. Flossie was off, joining Connie Van der Linden and Lucy Spinks. The trio sounded good together; at least as good as the trio featuring Gloria Lippincott. I had the no-doubt sinful wish that Gloria would be too sick to continue in her role as Pitti-Sing.

I was going to have a serious talk with Sam, however, as soon as ever I could, which wouldn't be until after rehearsal.

Immediately after rehearsal, however, I didn't get to interrogate the big brute because Flossie, Johnny, Sam, and I went to the soda fountain at the Rexall Drug Store on Colorado to get an ice-cream soda. On a freezing Tuesday evening in November. But never mind that.

"This is fun," said Flossie, her cheeks pink with pleasure and her hand in that of her husband, who was also cheerful as all get-out.

"It is," agreed Johnny. "We don't get to dine out often."

"I don't know if you can call this dining, exactly," I said, aching to get Sam to myself so I could pester him until he told me what he had planned. This was especially true since what he had planned clearly—at least it seemed clear to me—involved my own personal self and my own personal séance. Perhaps even my own personal safety.

"Our standards aren't as high as yours," said Johnny with a laugh. "We never get to have a meal—or even a dessert—out. Besides, this is where we met."

The loving glance he shared with Flossie would have made me blush if it hadn't made my eyes fill with tears instead. How silly of me. But I remembered being in love like that. It seemed like a long time ago now. But once upon a time Billy and I had been just as starry-eyed as Johnny and Flossie.

I glanced at Sam in the glare of the drug-store lights. He had declared his love for me a year or so earlier. We hadn't talked about it much since, although we'd grown closer in the ensuing months. Could I ever feel that same amazing love for Sam that I'd felt for Billy?

Actually, probably not. I wasn't a romantic seventeen-year-old girl any longer. I was a widow of twenty-three, and Sam was a widower of nearly thirty. We'd both been through the rapture of what we'd presumed would be deathless love. But both of our loves had died anyway, and in both cases, slowly and painfully.

Oh, well.

We had an enjoyable treat, I selecting hot chocolate over ice cream, and then Flossie and Johnny headed back to the Salvation Army, where they lived in a little house behind the church, and Sam and I got into his Hudson and headed north on Marengo to my house.

Sam had just got into the machine and shut his door when I started in on him. "Very well, Sam Rotondo, you'd better tell me what's going on and what it has to do with the séance on Saturday. And why have you involved Johnny and Flossie? It's not fair of you to keep secrets from me, especially since I'm involved. Heck, we're talking about a cold-blooded murderer—or maybe even two of them—and I might be in danger!"

"Keep your socks on," he told me, sounding snarly. No surprise there.

"I'm not wearing socks."

"Keep your stockings on, then. I'll tell you all about it when we get to your house."

"Promise?"

He eyed me as if I were a crawly worm, which I don't think was fair. "Promise."

"Thank you." I sat back, if not satisfied, at least glad about Sam's promise of satisfaction to come.

Pa and Spike greeted us, Pa with the news that Ma and Vi had gone to bed. Spike was only glad to see the two of us. I love dogs. They don't allow themselves to become confused the way people do. They're loving and loyal, and they're always happy to greet their humans, even when their humans are grumpy or annoyed. In this case, Sam was grumpy and I was annoyed.

"How'd rehearsal go?" asked Pa as if he really wanted to know.

"It was swell," I said. "Flossie Buckingham is filling in for Gloria Lippincott while she's sick. Actually, I hope she fills in for her for the entire show."

"She probably will," said Sam, with something of a smirk.

"All right, Sam Rotondo," said I, taking off my warm woolen coat and tossing it on the piano bench in the living room. Then I sat on the bench, too, and crossed my arms over my chest. "Tell me right this minute what's going on."

Pa's eyebrows lifted. "Something's going on?"

"Yes. And Sam's using me to do it, but I swear to heaven, I won't perform that dratted séance until you tell me why I'm doing it, Detective." I gave Sam as steely a glare as I could come up with.

"All right, all right. I'll tell you."

"May I listen in?" asked Pa mildly. "Sounds interesting so far."

"As long as you don't tell anyone else," said Sam, making my short temper spike once more.

"My father, for your information, is not a blabbermouth!"

"Never said he was," said Sam, hanging his heavy overcoat on the coat tree beside the front door. He plopped his hat on another hook. "Just want to be clear. Nobody is to know about our machinations until the time comes."

"Machinations, eh? Now I'm really interested," said Pa, grinning and sitting in a chair next to the piano bench.

Sam came over and plunked himself on the sofa so that he was facing Pa and me. "Very well," said he. "It's like this."

And he told us everything.

Or so I thought.

TWENTY-FOUR

"Are you kidding me?" I asked, shocked out of my temper fit. "Nope," said Sam, looking smug. "We did the background checks, and that's what we came up with. Michael Lippincott is the third of Gloria's husbands to come to a sticky end. We know she's behind whatever it is that's going on."

"She's been married three times?" Heck, one marriage had about done me in, although that wasn't my fault. Or Billy's. I still blame the Kaiser for our marital troubles.

"She has, indeed. And, as I said, all three of her husbands have died in mysterious automobile accidents. They've all had money, too. Michael Lippincott left her a small fortune."

"I'm pretty sure she told me he was in debt to gamblers."

"She lied." Sam shrugged.

I let that sit for a moment as I tried to digest it. "But if she's already got a fortune—"

"As of a week or so ago, she's got three of them," said Sam, interrupting me.

"Then if she doesn't need money, why does she keep marrying and bumping off her spouses?"

"Greedy, I reckon," said Sam.

"Extremely greedy, I'd say," said Pa.

"I guess so," I muttered, trying to imagine what kind of person would marry and then murder his or her spouses. Well, I guess all I had to do was look at Gloria to see what kind of person would do that. Still...It was difficult to imagine a *woman* committing those awful murders.

Sam went on, "She's worked her way from New York through Kansas City, and she ended up in Pasadena two and a half years ago. She married Michael Lippincott three years ago in KC, and then she wanted to move to California, so he brought her here."

"Goodness gracious. She told me she and her husband had been estranged. Was that a lie?"

"I doubt it," said Sam. "They weren't living together for some time. I think he wanted a divorce. I think she decided she'd make more money if she killed him than if she divorced him."

"But she couldn't have run him down," I pointed out. "You yourself told me she was at a blameless bridge party at the Hastings' mansion when the deed was done."

"She must have an accomplice," said Pa.

"That's what I've been saying all along," I agreed. "But who is it? Do you know that part yet, Sam?"

"Nope. That's what we're using the séance for."

Mouth agape, I stared at him, unable to find words in my brain that would string themselves together into a coherent sentence.

That was all right. Sam understood. "This is where your buddy, Captain Buckingham, comes in," he told Pa and me. "He's going to be the ghost of Michael Lippincott, and he'll appear at your séance. We figure whoever is aiding the Lippincott dame will cave when they see a real—well, a fake, but you know what I mean—ghost. Not too many people are as coldblooded as she is."

"I hope you're right. What if no one confesses?"

"Gloria will fold eventually."

"You hope," I said dryly.

"We hope," admitted Sam. "We think it might be Max Van der Linden, since he's got the best access to the extremely wealthy Connie, and she's evidently being poisoned."

"Oh. I hope it isn't Max. I like him. And Connie."

"Huh," said Sam.

"But wait a minute. Gloria ended up in the hospital after taking or being given some kind of drug. Is her accomplice trying to do her in?"

"We think that was a bluff to throw us off the scent."

"Pretty big bluff," I said. "Didn't the doctor fear for her life there for a while?"

"Maybe. Or maybe she's a better actress than anyone's given her credit for thus far in her nefarious career."

"Nefarious career. That's a good description of it," I muttered.

Sam, Pa, and I sat there, thinking, for a few minutes. Then I spoke.

"Isn't it generally men who kill their wives, and not the other way around? I mean, I've heard of Bluebeard, and Dr. Crippen, H.H. Holmes, and fellows like that who kill their wives. Aren't women more subtle? I mean, if they kill people, don't they generally use poison? Running husbands down in the street sounds like a…masculine thing to do. Or something."

"I think poison is generally a woman's weapon of choice, but there are all kinds of people in the world, and if her accomplice is a man, he probably drove the machine that ran down Michael Lippincott."

"Which belonged to Dennis Bissel. Do you think they wanted Dennis to take the blame for the murder?"

"Probably, but we know Bissel didn't do it because he was seen by several people at the moment the deed was done."

"I'm glad. I like Dennis and Patsy. And Mrs. Bissel, too, for that matter. She's been worried. I think that's one of the reasons she was so eager to have me perform the séance at her house."

"Could well be," said Sam.

"Sounds logical," said Pa.

"But who could possibly be Gloria's accomplice?" I asked, honestly puzzled. As far as I knew, nobody in the cast of *The Mikado*, except Gloria Lippincott, had any villainous tendencies. Mind you, Lawrence Allen and James Warden both seemed to have succumbed to Gloria's spell, but she was an expert at getting men to fall under her influence. Phooey. I didn't like to think that I'd been singing with a bunch of murderers. Or two murderers, anyway. "I hope it's not Max," I said, repeating myself.

"We'll probably find out on Saturday," said Sam. "I've talked to Mrs. Bissel, and she's having the Lippincott woman, the Allens, the Van der Lindens, and her son and his wife attend."

"Hmm," I mused. "That'll make a total of nine. That's manageable." I didn't like having more than eight to ten people at a séance, mainly because people in large groups were difficult to control. I'd perfected my craft—or was it an art? Oh, well, I don't suppose it matters—so well by that time that I never had trouble maintaining peace and quiet during my séances. However, I still didn't like large groups.

"We'll have officers stationed here and there at the house," said Sam. "So you needn't worry that anything will get out of hand when the culprit is unmasked."

"Unmasked?" I squinted at him.

Naturally, he frowned back. "You know what I mean."

"I guess so. Why did you pick those people in particular?" I asked, truly curious.

"After looking at everyone's background, we decided this would be the ideal setup. All the suspects will be there."

"They're all suspects?"

"Suspected suspects," said Sam, and he frowned again. I didn't blame him. Suspected suspects, indeed.

"Max and Connie, too? But Connie's the one being poisoned, isn't she? Oh. I guess you couldn't have Max without Connie, could you?"

"No," said Sam, giving me a look I don't think I deserved.

"I wish Harold would come," I said rather wistfully, "even though that would be a couple of people too many."

Sam shrugged. "Invite him. What's one more?"

Clearly he'd never had to conduct a séance.

Mrs. Pinkerton called upon me to do a tarot reading and an Ouija board session on Wednesday. Neither the cards nor Rolly told her anything they hadn't already told her about her life and her future fifty million times before. Perhaps that's a slight exaggeration.

"Oh, Daisy!" she cried as I picked up the Celtic Cross pattern I'd just dealt out and interpreted for her. "I just don't know what to *do*! I'd hoped the cards would help me, but they didn't. And now I still don't know what to do."

"About what?" I asked sweetly.

"About Christmas! Algie and I want to see Harold and you in *The Mikado*, but Stacy insists she wants to go to Santa Barbara before the holiday and stay until after Christmas."

If I were Mr. and Mrs. Pinkerton, I'd gladly send Stacy to Santa Barbara or anywhere else—Outer Mongolia sounded good to me—if only to get her out of my way. I couldn't say that, of course.

"Stacy doesn't want to see her brother perform? Harold is extremely good as the Lord High Executioner, Mrs. Pinkerton. I should think she'd be proud of him."

A wrinkle furrowed Mrs. P's powdered brow. "Well, I hate to say it, but I don't believe my children like each other very well."

I knew darned well they didn't like each other. *Hate* might be too strong a word, but it was a whole lot closer than *like*. "Perhaps you can see the operetta on the first weekend and then go to Santa Barbara," I suggested, wondering what Santa Barbara had to offer in the way of Christmas amenities. If the Pinkertons wanted to go there, it was probably home to a fabulous and ridiculously expensive resort. It was on the coast, wasn't it? I'd have to check the map.

"That's a wonderful idea, Daisy! See? I knew you could help me!"

An idiot could have come up with that suggestion, although I didn't say so. I did say, "Mrs. Buckingham has been filling in for Mrs. Lippincott, who has been ill. I don't know if she'll be in the final production. I suppose it depends on whether or not Mrs. Lippincott is well in time." Or whether or not she'd been arrested and incarcerated. I didn't say that, either.

"Mrs. Buckingham? You mean that Salvation Army fellow's wife?" Mrs. Pinkerton was glad her daughter no longer frequented speakeasies and got arrested all the time, but I know she'd rather Stacy had been "saved" by an Episcopalian than a Salvation Army person.

"That's the one, all right. She has a lovely voice."

"Oh." She sat there, looking bemused for a moment before she smiled and said, "I'm glad Stacy has some cultured friends at that church."

Cultured friends? A couple of years back, Mrs. Pinkerton was bemoaning—or perhaps bewailing would be a better word for it—the fact that Stacy was hanging out with Flossie. Of course, that was back when Flossie was under the influence of a violent gangster, but still....

"Oh, my, yes. Flossie is quite cultured."

It's a darned good thing liars' pants didn't actually catch fire, or I'd have been burned to a cinder years ago. Not that Flossie didn't have as much culture as Stacy Kincaid, who only had the kind of culture that grows in science laboratories and makes people sick, and Stacy was the one who had that kind, not Flossie.

That wasn't nice of me, was it? Well, heck, along with liars' pants catching fire, there's also an old saw about the truth hurting. And, since I didn't say it to Mrs. Kincaid, it would only hurt me, if God is keeping some kind of record on people's thoughts.

"I do wish I could come to the séance you're holding at Griselda's home on Saturday," said Mrs. Pinkerton pensively.

Nuts. She probably wanted me to fit her in somehow. "Would you like for me to speak to Mrs. Bissel on your behalf?" I asked, hoping she's say no. There were already too many people going to that séance, and if Sam had his way, it would be busted up by the cops before it ended.

"Oh, no. But thank you, dear. I talked to Griselda, and she said only people from the operetta will be there." Her brow creased again. "Although I don't believe Harold is going to be attending."

"I do wish you could both be there," I said, only half-lying that time. I really *did* wish Harold would be there.

"Perhaps Griselda will have some kind of party after the séance," Mrs. P said, brightening some. "I often do that. You know, have a little party and then have a few people take part in the séance." She tittered a little bit. "But of course, you know that, since you're always the one holding the séance for me."

I smiled at her because I couldn't think of anything to say. "Perhaps after Christmas, when you get back from Santa Barbara, you'd like me to have a séance for you," I suggested.

"What a wonderful idea!" said she, clasping her hands to her velvet-covered bosom. That day she wore a beautiful peacock-blue frock that must have cost a mint. It was festive, in keeping with the season, I guess, although that particular day was a bit before Thanksgiving, and I always think of Thanksgiving as an orange-and-brown sort of day. As for me, I wore black. Black fit my profession and my mood, so it was perfect. And tasteful.

"I'll be going now," I said, slipping my Ouija board and planchette into their lovely carrying bag.

I'd already tucked my tarot deck into the bag I'd made for it. My tarot deck was getting a trifle tattered around the edges, but I wasn't sure what to do about that. I doubted any stores in Pasadena would carry tarot decks. Maybe Chinatown in Los Angeles? Tarot wasn't a Chinese fortune-telling thing, but the Chinese were clever. Maybe they'd cottoned on to the spiritualist craze that had swept the nation after the Great War and the influenza pandemic.

Anyhow, it might be fun to visit Chinatown. I hadn't been there for years. Maybe Harold would go with me. Or Sam.

Sam?

Did I want Sam to visit Chinatown with me? He wasn't generally the fun, chipper companion Harold was. On the other hand, I hadn't often been with him except when he was working on various criminal cases. Perhaps he saved his fun, chipper side for things other than work.

He was generally friendly and happy when he came to dinner at our house, but who wouldn't be, what with Aunt Vi being the best cook in the entire United States of America?

"Thank you for coming, dear," said Mrs. Pinkerton, sounding sad that I aimed to leave her.

"You're more than welcome, Mrs. Pinkerton," I said with one of my more gracious smiles. "I'll be looking forward to your séance after the new year."

"Oh, my, yes!"

The new year. Merciful heavens, 1924 was just around the corner. It didn't seem possible somehow. This would be my second New Year's Day without Billy. I guess my family would all walk up to Colorado Boulevard and watch the Tournament of Roses Parade. And, if he wasn't working on some heinous crime, Sam would probably walk with us. Pasadena crowds were seldom unruly, and heinous crimes few, so he might be off that day.

I sighed heavily as I left Mrs. Pinkerton's drawing room and walked down the hallway toward the kitchen. It was around 3:30 p.m. Vi might be ready to come home for the day, and I'd be more than happy to drive her. When I entered the kitchen, however, she was elbow-deep in a bowl of dough. She turned and smiled at me.

"Good afternoon, Daisy! If you can wait a few minutes, you can drive me home."

"Only a few?" I eyed the bowl of dough doubtfully.

She laughed. "Daisy, Daisy, Daisy, I don't know why you can't seem to learn how to cook. You can sew and read those silly cards and play with the Ouija board, and you can sing like an angel. Cooking is much easier than all of those things."

It wasn't, either. I knew that from bitter personal experience. "I guess we all have our own talents," I said, keeping my voice as neutral as I could. I *hated* cooking. Worse than that, cooking hated me. Lowering thought. Anyhow, I knew darned well I didn't sing like an angel. Angels were all sopranos, weren't they? At church they were.

Vi picked up the bowl of dough and dumped it onto a floured surface. In a few deft movements, she'd flattened out the entire ball of dough and began plucking pieces from it. "I'm just making some dinner rolls. I'll be done in a jiffy."

And darned if she didn't create two entire baking tins' worth of leaf-shaped rolls in the jiffy she'd predicted.

"You're a genius in the kitchen, Vi," I said, looking on, amazed, at her creation.

"Nonsense," said she. But she was pleased. I could tell.

Even better, she brought some of her leaf-shaped dough balls home to our house, so that we could have them with the roasted chicken she aimed to serve us that night.

At which meal, Sam joined us. I was so accustomed to him being there for dinner, I didn't even blink when I answered the door and he came in.

"Hey, Sam," I said.

"Evening, Daisy," he said.

And we both trundled off to the dining room, where Ma and I had already set the table. Thanksgiving was the following week, so we'd set out a bowl of chrysanthemums in the middle of the table.

Thanksgiving fell on a Thursday, which was also both choir and operetta rehearsal evening. I wondered what we were going to do about that, but I needn't have. Others had thought these things through without my help. Figures.

TWENTY-FIVE

"Attention, everyone!" boomed Mr. Floy Hostetter in his best choir-director's voice the next evening when we'd all gathered for choir rehearsal. "Next Thursday being Thanksgiving, we're going to hold choir rehearsal on Monday night and rehearsal for *The Mikado* on Tuesday night." He gave us all a beaming smile. "I know all you ladies will be working hard on Wednesday evening, baking pies and so forth for the holiday."

Little did he know. At least about me. Vi wouldn't let me near the kitchen on major holidays unless I was walking to my bedroom, to do which I had to go through the kitchen. My job at holidays was to decorate stuff and set the table.

The other ladies in the choir tittered, so I guess they actually *did* bake pies and other foods for holiday dinners. I felt like such a failure.

However, that doesn't matter. Gloria showed up at rehearsal that Thursday evening, looking pale and wan. Mind you, I cultivate the pale and interesting look for my job. Gloria had no reason whatsoever to be pale, unless she wanted everyone to feel sorry for her.

I'm being catty again, aren't I? I'm sorry.

Flossie and Johnny showed up, too, so that made me happy. Flossie and I greeted each other with hugs and smiles, and I shook Johnny's hand. As soon as we turned loose of each other, Sam nabbed Johnny and hustled him off to a corner of the sanctuary. Plotting again, I was sure.

"Looks like Mrs. Lippincott is here today, Flossie," I said for the heck of it.

"That's all right. I enjoy listening, and Johnny said your choir director wanted me to come in case Mrs. Lippincott isn't feeling well enough to sing during the whole rehearsal."

I scanned her pretty face carefully, looking for any trace of sarcasm or cynicism. I didn't find any at all. Flossie, unlike me, is a very nice person, and she doesn't suspect people of underhanded doings, even after all her experience with the dark side of life. I kind of wished I could be more like her, although such a wish was futile. Which probably says a lot more about my own deficiencies than Flossie's abundance of spirit and love.

Anyhow, Mr. Hostetter called all of us to attention and made everyone go through the first scene of the first act, which didn't include any of the three little maids or me, so I decided to do some detectival stuff.

Smiling like a true spiritualist-medium, I walked up to Gloria after Mrs. Fleming began a spirited overture on the piano and said, "It's good to see you here tonight, Mrs. Lippincott. How are you feeling?"

Seated, drooping, in the first pew, she looked up at me with shadowed eyes. The shadows may or may not have had something to do with makeup. Now that I knew her history, I didn't want to give her credit for anything, even having been sick.

"Thank you, Mrs. Majesty. I'm feeling…better." She licked her lips. "Um, you didn't tell anyone about what happened, did you?"

"About you having ingested poison?"

She winced. "Yes. I didn't mean it when I said I thought someone had tried to kill me." Her words belied her expression, which was one of terror, and her gaze was focused plainly on Max Van der Linden. Hmm. Guess she really did aim to do in his wife so she could get her greedy little hands on his money. And would she blame the murder on Max?

Wait a minute. If she did that, wouldn't Max be arrested and charged with murder? How would that help Gloria's cause?

Pooh. I was confusing myself.

"I didn't tell anyone who mattered," I assured her, lying through my teeth yet again.

She heaved a gusty sigh. "I'm so relieved. I was so sick, you see, and I didn't know what I was saying."

"About Max being someone named Jack, you mean?"

Another really convincing wince on Gloria's part. "Yes. He isn't Jack. Jack is...someone else." Her voice dropped to a thrilling whisper on the last two words.

"Oh? Who? Do you know?"

She shook her head hard. Looked to me as if she'd had her hair bobbed and dyed at a hair salon since she left the hospital. She couldn't have been *that* sick then.

"It could be anyone," said she in yet another dramatic whisper. "But whoever he—or she—is, he's trying to do away with poor Connie, just as he tried to do away with me."

"Good heavens," I said not at all dramatically. "Um...How do you know his name is Jack?"

Gloria scanned the sanctuary as if searching for sequestered spies and whispered, "I overheard a conversation."

"A conversation? Between who and who? Or should that be whom?"

She tilted her head and gave me a quizzical squint. "I beg your pardon?"

"Never mind." Annoyed at myself for getting sidetracked, I said, "Who was having the conversation you overheard?"

"I don't *know!*" She still whispered, but she put special emphasis on that last word. "All I know is one man called the other Jack, and they talked about poisoning Connie."

"You should have told the police," I stated.

"Well...I wasn't sure who had spoken. I...I only heard one man call the other Jack."

"You know, the doctor who pumped your stomach"—this time it was I who winced, when I recalled that pump and that tube—"had to tell the police what he found in your stomach's contents."

She gaped at me. "You mean, *he* told the police?"

"I imagine so."

"Hmm. Well, that doesn't tell who made me take it, does it?"

"No."

"Then that's all right, then."

Huh? "I see." I didn't see a blessed thing.

That being the case, I only said, "Well, it's good to see you up and around again," and fled to the wings. Or to the choir room, which was one of the wings in this instance.

Although I didn't really trust Gloria not to be acting a part as she acted the part—so to speak—of Pitti-Sing, she did seem to drag and be slightly listless. Finally she said she couldn't go on, wept and apologized profusely, and Flossie took her place. That was fine with me. It was a lot more fun for me when I had to interrupt the revels in the town of Titipu in my role as Katisha this time, mainly because Flossie had to cover her mouth to hide her giggles. Guess she'd never seen me be mean and nasty before.

"'Your revels cease! Assist me, all of you,'" I sang, using my most elaborate gestures to indicate the character of Katisha, which was black as onyx and hard as flint. Not, perhaps, unlike Gloria Lippincott.

Have I mentioned how much I loved playing Katisha? Well, I did love it. For the first time in my entire life, I could be callous as a politician and not have anyone scold me for it. Bliss.

Sam must have noticed my delight because as he drove me home, he said, "You're enjoying yourself, aren't you? Playing that witch-woman?"

"Yes. It's more fun that I can remember ever having since I grew up." Only after I said the words, which were the truth, did I realize how sad they sounded. As an amendment, I said, "Well, except for when Billy and I were married. Our wedding was wonderful." And he'd been shipped overseas three weeks later.

"Yeah. Weddings are fun."

"You don't sound awfully convincing, Sam Rotondo."

He wrinkled his brow and twisted his lips. "You've never been to an Italian wedding, have you?"

"Can't say as I have."

"Let me just say that there are so many traditions and folderol involved that it takes all the enjoyment out of the occasion, at least for the groom."

"That doesn't sound right," I said, wrinkling my own brow.

"Doesn't sound right to me, either, but it's the truth. My God, you have to have the proper food, the proper colors and follow the proper superstitions. Poor Margaret had to wear a green dress at our rehearsal dinner, and it made her skin look yellow." He shook his head. "And I had to carry a piece of iron rod in my pocket at the wedding to ward off bad luck. Margaret even had to make a little tear in her veil."

"Those are all Italian traditions?" I asked, feeling slightly stunned. Heck, Billy had worn his uniform, and I'd worn a white dress and veil made by...well, me. And the word iron wasn't spoken at all, as nearly as I could remember. "Do your brides hold orange blossoms? I held orange blossoms. To this day, when I pass a blooming orange tree, I get all nostalgic."

"No orange blossoms. As we walked out of the church, everyone yelled *auguri* at us."

"That's pretty tame. They didn't throw anything?"

"They just hollered *auguri*. It means best wishes, which is nice, I guess."

"Huh. People threw rice at us when we walked out of the church. I guess that's one of our traditions, although, to be honest, I don't know which country it originated in."

"Hmm. You probably didn't have pasta and prosecco at the reception dinner. And I'll bet you got served a big cake baked by your aunt."

"We had ham and salads and Vi's wonderful dinner rolls, actually. And yes, we had a delicious cake." I sighed.

"Good for you. We got candy-coated almonds."

"Candy-coated almonds?"

"Italian tradition. Called *confetti*."

"Really? Is that where we get the word confetti? From Italian candy-coated almonds?"

"I guess so. I'd rather have had cake."

"Well," I hedged, "candy-coated almonds sound good."

"Yeah. They are good. So were Margaret and me, for a couple of years."

"Billy and I only had three weeks," I said, remembering.

ALICE DUNCAN

"Yeah, but both of our marriages ended the same way. More or less."

"I suppose so. More or less."

And if that wasn't a melancholy thought, I didn't know what was. I decided to change the subject. "So, you and Johnny were cloistered together during today's rehearsal. Is there anything else I need to know about Saturday's séance?"

"Nope. We were just firming up our plans. I gave Buckingham a photograph of Michael Lippincott, so he could do the best he can with makeup in order to look like him. I told him you'd help him with the makeup. Hope you don't mind."

"I don't mind, although it's difficult for me to imagine Johnny agreeing to this fell plot."

"We're trying to capture a couple of murderers, don't forget. Buckingham is all in favor of capturing murderers. He'll gladly help someone who's down and out, but he's not so keen on assisting folks who kill other folks for their own gain."

"True, true. Johnny is a good man."

"Yes, he is. And so's his wife. A good woman, I mean." Sam shook his head. "I've got to admit that when I first met her, I didn't anticipate her transformation."

I heaved a little sigh. "No. I didn't, either. And I still feel kind of guilty about foisting her on Johnny."

Sam turned his head and gaped at me. "You feel *guilty*? You probably saved the poor woman's life."

"Yes, I know. But I wasn't really doing a good deed at the time. I was trying to get rid of her, because she'd sort of attached herself to me. Why, she came to our house the morning after the raid on that first séance, beaten half to death."

"I didn't know that."

"No." Another sigh. "Nobody but Flossie and I know it. And now you. It's not something you normally advertise, I reckon. I hope that Jinx Jenkins character never gets out of the big house." Don't ask me why I called prison "the big house." I must have seen it at a motion picture or something.

"He won't," said Sam.

"How do you know that for sure?"

"He got shanked."

"He got what?"

"Shanked. A shank in prison terminology is a homemade knife. He can't get out of the 'big house,' as you call it, because he's dead."

"Goodness! I'm so glad!"

Sam looked at me again.

Feeling only slightly chagrinned, I said, "Well, I am. I was afraid he'd get out and come after Flossie."

"Now you don't have to worry. Some other thug took care of the matter for you."

"Good. What about the rest of Maggiori's gang?"

With a shrug, Sam said, "Can't say as I know for sure. New York wanted Maggiori, so he got sent back there for trial. I don't know what happened, but he probably got off."

"What do you mean, he got *off?* How can a murdering gangster get *off.*"

"Lots of ways. New York is relatively corrupt. He probably paid off a juror or a judge or something."

"That's terrible," I said, unable to comprehend corruption on such a large scale. "Are you serious? You're not serious, are you? You're kidding me."

Sam shook his head. "Nope. It's the bitter truth. That's another reason I'd rather be a policeman here in Pasadena than in New York City. Pasadena's a downright civilized place compared to New York. Hell, gangs used to run the city back there. Violent gangs."

"How awful." Dismayed pretty well describes my reaction to this news. I still couldn't quite make myself believe Sam's story.

"It was awful, all right. And the names those bozos gave themselves were stupid, too. The Dead Rabbits, the Whyos, the Five Points Gang."

"My Lord! Flossie was born and reared in the Five Points area."

"She's lucky she got out at all. Thanks to you and Buckingham, you really did save her life."

"Good heavens."

"Not a whole lot of heaven in New York these days, although the gang problems have changed. Now the Italian and Jewish bootleggers are taking over everything."

"Italians and Jews? I don't think I ever heard of a Jewish gangster."

"Yeah, well, they exist. Burns me up that the Italians are so big into bootlegging. Besmirches my heritage, you know?"

"I guess so, but you're one of the good guys, so you shouldn't take it seriously."

"Hard not to," grumbled Sam. "I'm pretty sure one of my sister's kids is in with a bootleg gang. Oh, and the Irish and Negros have their gangs, too. Harlem is a big bootleg area."

"Good heavens."

"Back to heaven, are we?"

"I don't know. Pasadena sounds like heaven compared to New York City."

"Trust me, it is."

"I trust you. But how sad."

"Yeah. I'm going to kill that kid if I ever get back to NYC."

"Your sister's boy?"

"That's the one, all right."

"That'll help a whole lot," I said dryly.

"It'll help my sister. She doesn't need that son of a...dog dragging the family name in the dirt."

"And you think it would help her if you killed her child?"

"He's headed straight to jail or getting shot down with a Tommy gun."

"Oh, that's awful. But your poor sister. Wouldn't she be grieved by her son's death?"

"Probably, but it would cause her less trouble in the long run if someone just did away with him now."

"That's terrible, Sam."

"Yeah, well, I don't know any Johnny Buckinghams back in New York City, so options are limited."

He had a point there.

TWENTY-SIX

Saturday morning's rehearsal of *The Mikado* went quite well. Again, Gloria wasn't well enough (she said) to endure the entire rehearsal. That was all right by me. Flossie, Lucy Spinks, and Connie sounded great together. I decided that Flossie made a better Pitti-Sing than Gloria, anyway, because she wasn't such a sophisticated snob. Or maybe that's only my imagination. About Flossie being a better Pitti-Sing, I mean. Gloria was still a sophisticated snob. And a murderous one, if Sam was correct, and I could think of no reason to doubt him.

It just occurred to me that I didn't doubt him on the Gloria issue because I didn't like Gloria. If he'd told me Flossie was an evil murderess, I'd doubt him to the skies. Which just goes to show how much one's emotions have to do with one's common sense, I reckon.

At any rate, rehearsal ended about one o'clock, and Sam treated me to lunch at a little soda fountain in Altadena at Webster's Pharmacy. I had a tuna-fish sandwich, and Sam had roast beef on pumpernickel. I didn't believe I'd ever seen pumpernickel bread before that day, and I told Sam so.

With huge eyes, chewing, he stared at me. After he swallowed, he said, "Are you telling me the truth?"

"Well…Yes. In fact, until you ordered that sandwich"—I pointed at same—"I'd never even *heard* of pumpernickel bread. It looks dark. Does it taste like...what's that other bread that we had at the Tea Cup Inn? Rye?"

"You don't eat rye bread either?"

"Well, only at the Tea Cup Inn when we ate there with Harold. We just eat Vi's bread at home," I told him. "She makes good bread."

"And your family is from Massachusetts?"

"What's that got to do with anything?"

"Nothing, I guess." He sighed. "You know, I don't much care for New York City, but you can get every kind of food known to man there. Rye, pumpernickel, white, whole wheat, pita—"

"Pita? Is that a joke?"

"It certainly is not. In fact, you had pita bread in Egypt and Turkey."

I cast my mind back to my not-awfully-successful trip to Egypt and Turkey. "I don't remember," I told him.

"Huh. You stayed at tourist hotels."

"Yes, Sam. Harold took me, remember? Only the best for Harold Kincaid."

"I remember." From the tone of his voice, he didn't like remembering, either. "You never had anything rolled up in a flat piece of bread? That's pita. The bread. Not the stuff inside it."

"Nuts. Now I feel as though I missed something during that horrible trip. Is pita bread tasty?"

"Tastes like bread. Chewy bread. The good stuff is inside it. My buddy Jamir used to invite me to his place for lunch, and his mother made us falafel sandwiches."

"Ah. I think I remember you telling me about falafel once. What are they made of?"

"Garbanzo beans, garlic. Stuff like that."

"No meat?"

"No meat. Although you can get lamb on a pita, too. That's delicious."

My mouth watered, so I took a bite of my sandwich, which came complete with a pickle spear. I love dill pickles. I kept eyeing Sam's sandwich, however, and almost wished I'd been more daring.

Sam must have noticed, because he took his knife, carved a corner off the sandwich half he hadn't yet bitten into and transferred it to my plate. "Try it. It's good. Got mustard."

"Thanks, Sam!" Mustard wasn't my favorite food, but what the heck. I picked up the sandwich tidbit and popped it into my mouth. "Oh, my, this is good!" I exclaimed once I'd swallowed. But honestly. How was I supposed to know that roast beef and pumpernickel bread would go so well together? I was a Southern California girl, for Pete's sake.

"Maybe your aunt can make pumpernickel. Or rye bread." He shrugged. "Can't be too difficult. All the Germans and Poles and Rumanians in New York make the stuff."

"Rumanians?" The only thing I knew about Rumania was that it was near Hungary, and Count Dracula lived there, according to Mr. Bram Stoker. I loved that book, *Dracula*. It was really creepy.

"I'd bet, if I were a betting man, which I'm not, that you can find someone of every country on this green earth somewhere in New York City. Oh, the Rumanians have this kind of cured meat called pastrami that's delicious. Pastrami on rye used to be my favorite."

"Pastrami, eh? I think I'll have to go to New York City someday, just so I can stuff myself with new food."

Sam grinned a little and said, "Maybe we can—Never mind."

What had he been going to say? That maybe he and I could go there together someday? Did that mean he still loved me? Bother. I was too tired to think about deep stuff anymore that day, so I reverted to my normal self.

"I'll go to the library and check out a cooking book for Vi," I said, feeling determined and more sorry than ever that I hadn't dared pumpernickel that very day. Or pastrami on rye. Not that Webster's carried such exotica as pastrami. Ah, well. Learn something new every day, is my motto. Actually, it isn't, but it seems appropriate regarding foodstuffs.

So Sam took me home after our delicious lunches, and I lay down with Spike for a bit, in anticipation of the séance to come later on that day. I wanted to be fully fresh and alert so I could remember it all later and be able to tell Ma, Pa, and Vi precisely how the police and I thwarted two dirty crooks.

———

The séance was set to begin at eight-thirty, and I had to drive myself to Mrs. Bissel's house, because Sam would be there on professional duty, doing policemanly things. I could hardly wait to find out the identity of Gloria's evil assistant. Of those who were going to be present, I didn't feel inclined to choose one. I didn't want it to be Max. And, however much I loathed Lawrence Allen spurning his own wife in favor of Gloria Lippincott, he was merely a weak-minded male, after all. Gloria seemed adept at spinning her web. If Lawrence got caught in its sticky tendrils, he'd learn a hard lesson this evening. Whether Sylvia would forgive him or not was anyone's guess.

I knew the cohort wasn't Dennis Bissel because he just wasn't the type. Whatever the type is. But I had yet to detect a malicious bone in his body. Not that I knew anything about his body; I'm only using a figure of speech.

I drove into Mrs. Bissel's circular driveway in back of her house at about seven-thirty that evening. I figured that would give me lots of time to get any instructions Sam might want to impart. I wore one of my lovelier black ensembles. Feeling a little silly, but not awfully, I also wore my juju, which I tucked discreetly out of sight. The skirt reached my ankles, so I also wore black shoes with a Louis heel and carried my black bag. I'd stuck a couple of black feathers in my hair in lieu of a hat for a change.

Keiji Saito, Mrs. Bissel's houseboy, met me at the back door. He'd taught me all sorts of stuff about his own Japanese culture and was at this time attempting to teach me a way of folding paper into interesting objects via an art form called origami. Keiji'd made me a charming origami crane. Just by folding paper! I wasn't great at it yet, but I was trying. My mother would say I'm very trying, but I think she means it as a joke. Ma isn't a great jokester as a rule, but I'd walked right into that one a time or two.

"You look very nice this evening, Daisy," said Keiji.

"Thank you," I said.

"You look like a black crow," said Sam Rotondo, who stood right behind Keiji. "What are those feathers for?"

Trust Sam. "Why, thank you very much, Sam. Say anything else rude, and I'll peck your stupid eyes out."

Sam smiled, drat the man.

Keiji tried not to laugh.

"But you'd better come with me, and I'll show you what's going to happen when," said Sam.

"Let me take your shawl and handbag, Daisy," said Keiji, doing same. At least he was nice to me.

"Thanks, Keiji." I turned to my nemesis. "All right, Sam. What's going to happen when?"

"Come here." He walked from the sunroom, where the back door was located, to the right, where sat the breakfast room. A suite of rooms leading from the breakfast room was where Mrs. Bissel's housekeeper/cook lived. Sam turned the knob and walked right in, from which I assumed he'd confiscated Mrs. Cummings' quarters for the evening. I felt kind of sorry for Mrs. Cummings, the housekeeper/cook, but oh, well. The police had a job to do and so did I.

"Buckingham will come out of this room at the appropriate time," Sam told me.

"When's the appropriate time going to be?"

"Whenever you get around to conjuring him."

I frowned at him. "You're not very helpful, Sam. Can you give me a hint? What do you want me to say?"

"Hell, you're the spiritualist. Do it when it feels right. Don't you go through some rigmarole first and then swoon or something?"

Blast the man! "All right. I'll follow my instincts."

"Don't get carried away," he said in a warning tone.

"I do *not* get carried away, Sam Rotondo! I'm a professional spiritualist-medium, and I know what I'm doing."

"Yeah, yeah. Whatever you say."

Sam Rotondo could drive me crazy in less time than any other human being on earth. Johnny Buckingham showed up at that moment, so I couldn't tell Sam so.

"Hey, Johnny."

"Hey, Daisy. How-do, Sam," said Johnny.

They were on a first-name basis, were they? Hmm. Not sure how I felt about that.

"Doing great here, Johnny," said Sam. "Did you bring the makeup and powder?"

"Right here," said Johnny, holding up a cardboard box.

"Good. Daisy, will you help Johnny use makeup to look approximately like this fellow, only dead? This is Michael Lippincott." He handed me a photograph.

Michael Lippincott had been an ordinary looking bloke. Not awfully handsome, but he had kind eyes. Unless that was my imagination, which leaps to unwarranted conclusions from time to time. Just by looking at this picture, however, I sensed I'd have liked him a lot better than I like Gloria. Poor guy.

"I'll do my best," said I. "Although I really don't know much about makeup. I only use white rice powder on my face to make me look the part of a spiritualist-medium."

"Which you do to perfection," said Johnny, giving me a good once-over.

I think Sam snickered, darn him.

"Maybe you should have had Flossie help you with this, Johnny. She's ever so much better at makeup than I am." As soon as I spoke those words, I wished them unsaid. I'm sure neither Johnny nor Flossie liked remembering the bad old days.

Thank goodness Johnny had a good sense of humor. He only laughed. "Flossie's got baby duty tonight, Daisy, so it's up to you. Make me look like a ghoul."

"White powder should do the trick," said Sam. "It works on you, Daisy."

Shooting him a hot scowl, I said, "I do *not* look like a ghoul, Sam Rotondo. For your information, I cultivate the pale and interesting look for my job."

"Whatever you say," said Sam, holding up his hands as if in surrender.

"Let's get this show on the road," said Johnny, interrupting our little spat. "Flossie told me to put on a little greasepaint under the powder so the powder will stick, and to make sure my eyes look sunken. She gave me some of this gunk for that." He reached into the cardboard box and lifted out a small jar filled with what looked like black cream.

"My goodness. I wonder what Flossie ever used this for," I said as I took the little jar from Johnny.

"She said it was all the rage to draw black lines around a lady's eyes," said Johnny, sounding not in the least embarrassed by his wife's tawdry past. Well, there was no reason he should be embarrassed; after all, he knew all about Flossie, and she probably knew all about him and how he hit the gutters after the war, addled from shell shock, bitterness and alcohol. That happened to a lot of men who fought in that ghastly conflict.

Pooh. I was almost in tears. I screwed on the little jar's lid and began ordering Johnny about. "Go into the dressing room there, Johnny, and sit on the bench. I'll see what I can do."

The first thing I did was stick Michael Lippincott's photograph under the upper frame holding the mirror to the dressing stand so I could study it as I worked on Johnny.

Perhaps I missed my calling and should have pursued a dramatic career, because, by the time I was through with him, Johnny looked as though he were Michael Lippincott, and he'd just climbed up the stairway from hell. I stood back, proud of my efforts.

"There," I said. "What do you think?"

Shaking his head in admiration, Johnny said, "I've never looked worse in my life."

"Wish I had one of those Kodak cameras. I'd take your picture so you could show Flossie."

"That's all right. I wouldn't want to scare her," said Johnny, chuckling.

"We can have a newshound snap your photo if you like," Sam offered.

"No, thanks. My flock would disown me if they knew I was mixed up in this adventure."

"Why would they do that?" I asked, indignant. "You're looking like a ghoul for a good cause!"

"I'm ribbing you, Daisy. My flock pretty much always gives other folks the benefit of the doubt, mainly because they've been in some bad fixes themselves."

"I really admire the work you do," I told Johnny sincerely.

"Yeah. Me, too, but it's a little after eight now and the culprits are arriving, so you'd better get on out there, Daisy," said Sam, pulling out his pocket watch and squinting at it. He wore eyeglasses for reading, but I guess he didn't need them to read his watch.

I'd heard the doorbell ring a couple of times while I'd been fiddling with Johnny's face—that sounds odd, but it wasn't meant to—so I was sure Sam was correct.

"All right. I'd better take advantage of the facilities before I face the mob."

"Don't use this bathroom," said Sam. "We're locking this place up right now, and nobody can come in or out until Johnny's grand entrance."

"All right. I'll grab my handbag and go to the upstairs bathroom." There were actually two upstairs bathrooms; one at the head of the grand staircase and the other at the west end of the house near the servants' stairs.

"Don't go through the main part of the house," warned Sam. "I don't want anyone seeing you yet."

"How am I supposed to get my handbag? It's hanging in the sunroom."

"You don't need it. Just wipe your nose with a tissue, and it won't be shiny any longer."

"My *nose* is shiny?" I screeched. But honestly. I applied my spiritualistic makeup with great care, and my nose *never* shone.

"He's teasing, Daisy," said Johnny. "You don't shine anywhere. Well, except for those beady things on your gown."

"Yeah," said Sam. "You look kind of like the ghost of Christmas Yet to Come."

"Good," I snapped. "Then I'm perfect for my role." I left the men to their chuckles and went up the servants' staircase on the west side of the house. The bathroom was nearby and a door from the hall led into it. The house was full of suites of rooms. On this, the west side of the house, there was a huge room that might have been used as a bedroom, a dressing room, a bathroom, another dressing room, a sitting room, and a small bedroom. The moment I opened the door to the bathroom, I heard angry whispery voices coming from the dressing room at the northern end of the bathroom. Puzzled, and clutching my juju through my dress, I tiptoed over to the door. What was going on in there? wondered I.

It took me a few minutes to find out, and then all heck broke loose.

TWENTY-SEVEN

"Why the devil did you give me so much of that damned stuff?" a woman asked as if she were sorely irked.

"Because it needed to look real, sister dear," a man answered. He sounded irked, too.

I didn't recognize his voice. Mind you, they were whispering, but I recognized Gloria's voice as that of the woman. But who was the man? And was he really Gloria's brother?

"It more than *looked* real," snarled Gloria. "I damned near died. Then where would you be?"

"Still pretty damned rich, although I'd also still be married to the most insipid woman in the universe."

"That's going to happen anyway."

"I guess." The man heaved a sigh.

"If we ever do this again, I'm not even going to entertain the notion of poison," Gloria declared in a passionate undertone.

"You will if there's a rich widower to snatch out of a wealthy dead wife's hands."

"I don't know about that. I was so sick, Jack. It was horrible."

Jack! *Jack?* The person whispering to Gloria was *Jack?* Whoever Jack was, he wasn't Max Van der Linden. I could tell by the quality of his voice, which maybe sounds nuts because they were whispering, but trust me, you can recognize a familiar voice, even in a whisper. But who the heck was he? I didn't dare open the door and look. I did, however, listen harder.

"And then there was that cursed paving stone. I pulled the rope attached to it, and almost got brained!"

"Nuts. That went off perfectly. I ran over to you and untied the rope, and nobody ever suspected you'd pulled the stone down yourself."

"Huh. I'm not doing *that* again either. I had to leap out of the way, and leaping in a corset and heels isn't easy."

"Yeah, but we made a great spectacle of ourselves. Everyone thought we were lovers." The man chuckled softly.

"Well, I don't like being a target. If we do this again, no stones and no poison," said Gloria, sounding as if she meant it.

"As soon as this idiotic séance is over, Malcolm Miller will be fingered as the culprit and then you can ply your wiles on dear Max after we get rid of poor little Connie. And then we can get rid of Max, too."

Good Lord Almighty. I'd never heard such coldblooded words issue from a human throat.

Actually, that's a lie, but never mind that now. These two, Gloria and whoever Jack was, were two of the most merciless characters I'd encountered in my career as a spiritualist-medium who occasionally gets caught up in crimes. Unintentionally, I'm sure I need not add.

"I hope so," said Gloria. "I think this is an idiotic way to go about it. Daisy Majesty might well be a fake, but she's a good one, and I don't know how we're going to finger Malcolm during the séance."

"Never you mind about that. I haven't forgotten our dear father's teachings. I can still throw my voice like nobody's business. Poor sweet Connie nearly fainted one day at rehearsal. I do believe the poor dear thinks she's going crazy."

"As planned," said Gloria.

"As planned," the fellow affirmed. "Daddy was good for something, I guess."

"Vaudeville," said Gloria in a repressive tone of voice. "Good old Daddy. A barrel of laughs, he was."

"Mother didn't think so."

"No. She didn't. Good thing I shot him for her."

Good Lord Almighty again! Gloria had shot her own father? And it sounded as though these two really *were* siblings! My mind boggled and my body went kind of limp. I've meet my share of crooks, but boy, this callous couple took the cake. A poisoned cake, if somebody'd allow me to be in charge of its creation. I neither gasped nor cried out, but I felt like doing at least one of those things.

"Anyhow, don't worry about the séance. When your little friend begins babbling about Michael, I'll take over for her."

"Daisy might object," Gloria pointed out. "From what everyone says of her, she has her art of séance down to a science, and she doesn't tolerate much nonsense."

She was right about that!

"We've garnered hundreds of thousands of dollars thanks to our own science, don't forget."

"How could I forget?" Gloria sounded pleased. What a totally despicable human being. Or maybe she was some alien life form come to earth to torment us normal people.

Or maybe I'd been reading too many of Edgar Rice Burroughs' *John Carter of Mars* books recently.

"Anyhow, don't forget that I planted Malcolm Miller's scarf in that idiot Dennis Bissel's Rolls."

"Why haven't the coppers cottoned on to the fact that the scarf didn't belong to Dennis?"

"I haven't a clue, but I can drop more evidence to pin the deed on Miller. He's a dope."

"You think they're all dopes, but I'm not sure about Daisy Majesty."

"Oh, hell, she doesn't matter. That clunk of a copper is a big dope."

If whoever spoke those words was referring to Sam Rotondo, he was dead wrong. Sam might look like granite obelisk, but he was smart as a whip.

"I have to go to the bathroom before this performance begins, so I'll meet you downstairs," said Gloria to her cohort.

Yeeks! That meant she was going to come right into this room. As she turned the doorknob on the other side of the door at which I'd just been listening, I scrambled as quietly and quickly as I could to the door that led from the bathroom to the hallway. I got out just before Gloria entered the bathroom.

However, I guess she saw the door close, because she hollered, "Someone was in here listening to us!"

"What? Damnation!"

And I pulled my lovely long dress up to my thighs and hightailed it to the main staircase, and that meant I had to traverse the long upstairs hallway—which was wide enough to hold a ballroom dance contest—and clear on the other side of the house. Darn, darn, darn, darn, darn! Why hadn't I taken the servants' stairs? Idiocy, I reckon.

I heard footsteps thundering after me, so I know whoever chased me wasn't Gloria. But who was it? Although I knew it was a big risk, I looked over my shoulder and lo and behold, if it wasn't Lawrence Allen himself chasing me!

Lawrence Allen? Was *he* Gloria's brother? Was he the other murdering maniac of the Gloria-and-fiend pair? And was his name really Jack?

Dang, he ran fast.

"Come back here, Mrs. Majesty," Lawrence called cajolingly.

He was catching up with me. I wished in that moment that I were six feet tall and had really, really long legs. But I wasn't, and I didn't. I did spur myself on to greater speed, however.

"You misunderstood what you heard in there," said Lawrence. "We were going over roles for our next production."

Did I believe that?

After giving myself approximately half a second to think about it I decided I didn't.

Just as I made a skidding turn at top of the staircase, Lawrence almost grabbed me by the shoulder. Since he couldn't quite do that, he did the next best thing, reached out, and gave me a hard shove, making me stumble and teeter at the top of the stairs. He wanted me to fall to my death down that blasted staircase!

To heck with it. I screamed bloody murder. I also grabbed hold of the staircase railing to keep from falling. The stairway was steep, and I was at the top of it. If Lawrence got another chance at me, he might just fling me over the banister and down to the hall below. After struggling and struggling—later I'd think of me in those moments as akin to one of those trick riders in circuses, but not nearly as graceful—to lift myself to a sitting position without falling completely overboard, at last I achieve success. Darned if I didn't sail down Mrs. Bissel's banister as if I'd been doing stuff like that all my life. Mind you, I'd always kind of wanted to slide down Mrs. Bissel's banister, but, being a dignified spiritualist-medium with a professional reputation to uphold, I'd never done it—until sliding down the banister was the only way to save my life.

As luck would have it, everyone in the whole darned house had heard me scream. As I reached the bottom of the banister and bumped my fanny, hard, against the newel post, an entire gang of spectators was there to see me do it. At the moment, my skirt was up to my waist, and everyone had a splendid view of my black silk stockings, garter belt, supporters, and combinations.

Huge hands plucked me off the banister before I could even catch my breath.

"What the devil are you doing?" demanded Sam. It would be he, wouldn't it?

Still frightened out of my wits, I turned in his arms and flung my own arms around his neck. I felt my skirt slide down and only then realized what a spectacle I must have made of myself. I sure heard a lot of buzzing and chatter around me, though.

"Oh, my, whatever is going on?" asked Mrs. Bissel. "What's the matter, Daisy?"

"What was that horrible noise?" asked Mrs. Cummings, appearing from the dining room. She'd probably been in the kitchen.

"What's the matter?" asked Keiji, joining the mob.

"It's...It's..." I sucked in a gallon or two of air to try and calm myself. "It's Gloria Lippincott and Lawrence Allen!" I cried onto Sam's shoulder blade. "They're the ones who killed Michael Lippincott and are poisoning Connie Van der Linden. I heard them talking about it in the dressing room next to the bathroom!"

Gasps and more chatter all around.

Connie squealed, "Poison?"

Max said, "I'll kill them both!"

"Everyone, stay exactly where you are!" Sam dumped me onto the floor in the hall and hollered, "Doan! Pickett! They're upstairs!" He turned to Mrs. Bissel. "Is there a way out of the house from up there?"

Poor Mrs. Bissel. She wasn't accustomed to policemen asking her abrupt questions. She stood there, her mouth opening and closing, looking a bit like a landed trout for a few seconds, before Dennis rescued her.

"The only way out of this house is through the downstairs. There are no exits from the second or third floors." He turned to his mother. "That's a fire hazard, Mother. You should install a staircase leading down to the patio or something."

"Never mind that right now," growled Sam. "Doan and Pickett, go upstairs and arrest the woman who calls herself Gloria Lippincott and the man who calls himself Lawrence Allen."

"Lawrence? *Lawrence*! Lawrence isn't involved in anything!" screeched Sylvia Allen, whom I hadn't noticed before. I could have set her straight, but I'd begun shaking and my tongue had stuck itself to the roof of my mouth. Anyway, how could she say Lawrence wasn't involved in anything? She herself thought he was involved with Gloria Lippincott. Or the woman who called herself Gloria Lippincott. I'd seen Sylvia sulking at all those *Mikado* rehearsals with my own eyes.

Oh, golly. *The Mikado*. Now we were short not merely Pitti-Sing, but also Go-To, a noble lord of Titipu. Flossie could play Pitti-Sing, but Go-To was a bass part, and basses weren't all that thick on the ground.

"Cuff them!" hollered Sam, and I looked up to see Gloria and Lawrence, appearing at the top of the stairs like a couple of frightened and furious something-or-others.

Doan and Pickett pounded up the staircase. Doan reached Gloria and caught her arm to stop her sudden turn and mad dash to nowhere.

Gloria snarled, "You put cuffs on me, and you'll die, copper!"

Doan evidently didn't believe her, because he grabbed both of her arms, yanked them behind her back, and I heard the satisfying sound of handcuffs being clamped around her slender wrists.

The other officer, Pickett, was having a struggle with Lawrence

Allen, who didn't seem to want to go gently into those metal cuffs. He actually clipped Pickett on the chin with his fist and turned to run the other way. Not quite sure what he aimed to accomplish by doing that since he was headed straight for Mrs. Bissel's upstairs sitting room. Anyhow, according to Dennis, who ought to know, there was no way out of the house from the second floor unless he wanted to leap from a window. I didn't think he'd want to do that. He clearly had no qualms about causing the deaths of others, but, as I'd noticed before when reading articles about black-hearted murderers, they held their own worthless lives as precious.

None of that mattered, though, because Pickett tackled him, and Lawrence Allen—or the man who called himself Lawrence Allen—went flying face first on the hardwood flooring. He missed the rug and made quite a thump, yelled "Ow!" and I was glad. Officer Pickett leaped upon his back, yanked his arms behind his back and clinked the cuffs on him, too.

So the bad guys had been caught. And we didn't even need a séance to accomplish their capture. Although I'd recently been frightened almost out of my mind, I was now a trifle disgruntled that I'd played so paltry a part in the denouement of the action. Well, maybe not precisely a *paltry* part. If whoever Lawrence Allen was had caught up with me, I'd have been a dead Daisy.

"What's all the uproar going on out here?" And at that very moment, Johnny Buckingham, who, I guess, had become bored and wondered what the excitement was about, put in an appearance through the walkway from the breakfast room to the gigantic hallway where the staircase ended.

Sylvia Allen screamed and fainted. No one was nearby to catch her.

Griselda Bissel screamed and fainted, but Keiji, gallant lad that he was, absorbed her weight. Mrs. Cummings (she screamed, too, but she didn't faint) helped him lay her out on the hall carpeting.

Connie Van der Linden, who had been held tightly in her husband's arms, forewent the scream and merely fainted.

Gazing at Johnny, I had to admit I'd done an admirable job in turning him into a ghoul. He looked like a demon from hell.

I was darned proud of myself!

Not only that, but I recalled in that very instant that Sam Rotondo had a simply superb bass voice.

Heh, heh, heh.

TWENTY-EIGHT

Doan and Pickett took the pseudo Gloria Lippincott and the pseudo Lawrence Allen down to the Pasadena Police Station. I probably should mention here that Altadena, where Mrs. Bissel lived, operated under the jurisdiction of the Los Angeles County Sheriff's Department but, as Sam once snidely put it to me: "We cooperate." So I guess the Altadena Sheriff was happy to be rid of the dastardly duo.

Keiji had the presence of mind to telephone Dr. Dearing, who lived across Maiden Lane from Mrs. Bissel, and the kind doctor trotted over to see to the fainting victims and, most especially, to Connie Van der Linden.

"Poison? Good Lord, what kind of poison?" he asked as he listened to her heart with this stethoscope. We had gathered in Mrs. Bissel's gigantic living room by that time.

Max Van der Linden, who didn't seem to want to leave his wife's side, said, "I don't know. I hope to heaven Gloria and Lawrence—or whatever their names are—will tell us."

"I can't believe they wanted to murder me," whimpered Connie, who'd begun to look sickly again. At present she lay on one of Mrs. Bissel's sofas. There were a bunch of them in that huge room.

"According to what I heard," I said before Sam could tell me to be quiet, "Gloria aimed to get her clutches into Max after they'd managed to do you in. They said you have a lot of money."

"How horrid!" whispered Mrs. Bissel, who, at Dr. Dearing's insistence, was sipping a restorative glass of brandy. It was all right to drink alcohol for medicinal purposes during Prohibition. I have a feeling many doctors prescribed strong drink to a lot of their patients back then, if only to keep them from finding more accommodating physicians. But Dr. Dearing wasn't one of that breed. At least, I don't think he was.

Standing up again, Dr. Dearing said, "Well, my dear, according to the symptoms you described to me, I think you'll be all right. Sounds as if you've been given several small doses of arsenic."

"*Arsenic!*" cried Max. He leaped to his feet. "Dammit, I *will* kill those two!"

Sam put a hand on his shoulder and shoved him down. "Don't bother about that. We'll kill them for you, in all probability. The electric chair is good for solving just such problems as those two."

Connie had begun crying weakly. "No wonder I've felt so horrid for so long."

"Indeed," said Dr. Dearing in a voice meant to cheer. "The Victorians used to call arsenic 'inheritance powder' because it was so hard to trace back then. Testing methods have improved considerably since the eighteen hundreds, and we'll be able to tell for certain if arsenic, which is what I suspect, was used. We'll have you right as rain pretty soon." He glanced at Mrs. Bissel. "May we have some bicarbonate of soda in some water, Mrs. Bissel? That should ease any existing cramping."

"Oh," said Mrs. Bissel, getting to her feet but sounding and looking confused.

Keiji, who had his wits about him, said, "I'll get some right now."

"Oh. Thank you," said Mrs. Bissel, who seemed to be catching on, although I'm not entirely sure about that. She sat again and sipped some more brandy.

"Then, my dear," Dr. Dearing said, smiling at Connie, "be sure to drink lots of milk."

"Milk?"

"Yes. It helps to counteract the effects of the poison." He squinted at first Connie and then Max. "Do you have any idea how the villains were giving her the arsenic?"

"Drinks, I guess," said Max. "Gloria was always pressing Connie to take some kind of thing she called an elixir."

"It tasted horrid, but I felt so bad, I drank it anyway, thinking it might do me some good. How stupid of me!"

"Nuts," I said bracingly. "How could you know what was in the stuff?"

"I gave her lots of vitamins," said Max, sounding as if he felt his treatment might have been a tad lame. I agreed with him, but I acquitted him of wanting to harm his wife.

"I...I can't believe Lawrence did those dreadful things," whispered Sylvia Allen, who had also been given a glass of brandy. She appeared pale and wan, too, but not from poison. I suspected her condition was caused by shock. "I...Well, I knew he wasn't a nice man, and he'd been carrying on with that...Oh, my Lord! Is Gloria *really* his sister? They couldn't have been—" She stopped speaking abruptly and gulped. It was all right. We knew what she'd been thinking. "Could they?" she asked finally in a pathetic whisper.

"No," said Sam, who seemed to have no qualms about much of anything. "They were only pretending to be having an affair so they could throw people off the mark. They wanted Mrs. Van der Linden out of the way, and then the female of the pair would sink her teeth into Mr. Van der Linden."

"Do you know what their names really are?" I asked of Sam.

"I think so, but I'm waiting for a call from the station. Chief Kelley."

"The chief himself is involved?" I said, startled.

"Yes, indeed. These two crooks have committed at least three murders, and they're wanted in New York, Missouri, and now in California. Kelley wants first dibs on them."

"Th-three murders?" Connie moaned. "Oh, my land."

"No!" cried Sylvia Allen. "It can't be true!" Poor thing. I felt sorry for her. She whispered, "We moved from Kansas City two years ago."

Huh. About the same time Gloria and Michael Lippincott moved to Pasadena from the same place. Coincidence? I think not.

The telephone rang, and I swear every person in that room, including Sam and Dr. Dearing, jumped a yard in the air. Keiji was the first to recover his equilibrium, and he dashed to the 'phone room under the staircase to answer the call. A second or two later he returned.

"Detective Rotondo, the call is for you."

"Ah. Good. Maybe I'll be able to give you some answers now." Sam marched to the telephone room.

Silence prevailed in the room for the first few minutes as we waited for Sam to get through with his telephone call. I glanced around at the assembled company. Johnny was there, no longer looking ghoulish. He'd apologized for scaring everyone and told us he'd forgotten all about his makeup when he heard the ruckus in the hall. I took him back to the dressing room in Mrs. Cummings' quarters, gave him some cold cream, and made him wipe off the makeup and wash his face. He looked fine now. We all forgave him because, as everyone now knew, he'd been prepared to perform an act of…well, acting, for the sake of truth and justice.

At the moment, he sat next to Sylvia Allen, trying to offer her support and comfort, two qualities he possessed in abundance and gave freely. I'm not sure if Sylvia appreciated his efforts. She kept saying things like, "I don't believe it," and so forth, although I got the strong impression she really *did* believe it.

After five minutes or so, the natives began to get restless.

Mrs. Bissel said, "What's taking him so long?"

Her son said, "It can't take this much time for someone to tell him the names of the crooks."

Patsy, clinging tightly to his arm, nodded with vigor.

"I'm sure the chief is telling Detective Rotondo much more than their names," I said in peevish defense of my…whatever he was to me. "They're investigating more than one crime, don't forget, and in more than one state."

"I'm sure you're right, Daisy," said Mrs. Bissel. "It's just so…awful. And terrifying. And to think those monsters used my son's machine to kill a man and they aimed to pin the crime on some poor innocent soul! Why, it passes all understanding!"

"Noooo!" wailed Sylvia. "It can't be true!"

Oh, boy. She was in for a hard time of it. I felt sorry for her, but I felt sorrier for the people her miserable husband had killed. However, it must be difficult to comprehend having been married to a monster for however many years they'd been hooked up. From what I'd eavesdropped upon in that upstairs bathroom, her husband hadn't valued her or loved her. She'd almost certainly be better off without him, stigma or no stigma. And there definitely would be a stigma. One didn't overlook other people's foibles in those days as they do in these loose times. Heck, poor Sylvia would probably not be invited to anyone's parties any longer, and not for anything she'd done, but because she'd had the bad luck to marry a disgusting man.

It was probably a good thing she had Johnny with her. Maybe he'd bring her into the Salvation Army fold. They never turned up their noses at anyone.

We were all on edge and fidgety when Sam finally returned to the living room. Instantly, I asked, "So who are they really?"

"They're originally from New York City. They were part of their parents' Vaudeville act for years, then their father was gunned down—"

"By Gloria," I said, interrupting him. Impolite, I know. "She said so."

"When?"

"I don't know when. She just said she shot him. She didn't give a date."

"No," said Sam with a frown. "When did she tell you this?"

"She didn't tell me anything. When I was in the upstairs bathroom listening to her and her brother talk about their foul careers, she said she shot their father because he was mean to their mother. And them, too, probably. Oh, and she also pulled on a rope attached to the paving stone that nearly brained her. Evidently Lawrence—or whoever he is—got to her first, untied the rope, and stuck it in his pocket. Then they pretended to be lovey-dovey to throw everyone off the scent." I frowned. "Or something like that."

"Good God," said Sam. Then he shook his head and went on. "Their birth names are Johannes and Ingeborg Niederhauser."

I leaped to my feet. "They're *Germans!*" Oh, boy. My list of reasons to hate Germans just grew longer by two names. Never mind that people are people the world over, and there's nothing inherently wrong with most Germans. They'd killed my husband, damn them all! I sat down again, feeling kind of silly for my outburst.

"Their parents were from Germany," said Sam, as if he didn't want to admit as much. "They had a singing and dancing act and used their kids as little singers and dancers. I guess the father had a drinking problem."

"Ah," I said. "No wonder they can both sing well. I guess their parents trained them."

"Probably."

"So you're going to arrest them and stick them in jail, and eventually they'll pay for their crimes, right? I mean, I heard them both confess to murder and attempted murder."

Sitting down and taking his notebook from his coat pocket, Sam opened it and gazed at it for a moment or two before answering my question. "We need hard evidence, Daisy. What you heard is just that: hearsay."

"*What*?" I cried.

"No need to holler," said Sam. "We have fingerprint evidence on Mr. Bissel's Rolls-Royce, and right now there's a search being made of both Mrs. Lippincott's house and Mr. Allen's home."

"The police are searching my *home*?" squealed Mrs. Allen. Or Mrs. Niederhauser. "They can't do that! Can they?" She'd taken to wringing her hands. I didn't know people really did that until then.

"We got a judge to sign a warrant, Mrs. Allen," said Sam, clearing up the last-name issue, at least for the time being. "We're talking about several murders here. I know you don't want to believe your husband is involved in the crimes, but evidence points to him and to the woman who called herself Gloria Lippincott. The chief has a preliminary report on an arsenic bottle found in your husband's pocket. It has his fingerprints on it. His fingerprints are also all over Mrs. Lippincott's house."

"She was mad at him for giving her so much of whatever kind of drug she took when she went to the hospital," I told everyone. "She said so. He said her condition had to look real, and she said she almost died, and she was angry about it."

229

"Can't say as I blame her," said Sam. "But evidently the police are finding good, solid evidence at the two residences." He gazed at Sylvia. "I'm sorry, Mrs. Allen. This must be very hard for you."

See? Sam could be nice sometimes.

Sylvia began crying quietly, and Connie, who still looked sick, went over to her. "I'm so sorry, Sylvia. I know you had nothing to do with what the two of them were doing."

That was more than I knew, although I had a feeling Connie was correct. Sylvia seemed too distraught to be part of her husband and sister-in-law's cruel schemes, unless she was a much better actress than I believed her to be.

Sam gave us some more information regarding the crimes the deadly duo was believed to have committed in New York City and Kansas City. He ended with, "If they're tried and found guilty in Pasadena, they will probably have to face charges in Kansas City and New York, too. They'll be extradited to those states unless the court here decides on the death penalty. Then they'll probably end up in our electric chair and save the time and money to ship them elsewhere."

Sylvia Allen uttered a ghastly moan and crumpled to the floor.

Sam could also be a trifle blunt sometimes. Although I felt sorry for Sylvia, I couldn't really fault him for telling the truth.

Mrs. Bissel downed the last of her brandy and held out her glass for a refill. Keiji obliged.

TWENTY-NINE

As you've probably figured out by this time, I didn't hold a séance that night. I ended up driving home shortly after Sam had delivered his news. Pa, Ma, Aunt Vi, and perhaps even Spike, were surprised to see me so early in the evening.

So we gathered in the dining room, sat in the various chairs, and I told them what had happened. Shocked gasps and exclamations ensued.

"Now all I have to do is try to figure out how to get Sam to play Go-To, a noble lord of Titipu, since Lawrence Allen—I mean Johannes Niederhauser—is in the clink. Flossie can play Pitti-Sing."

"Will he have enough time to prepare for the part?" asked Pa.

It was a good question, and one to which I didn't really have an answer. I shrugged and said, "He'd better. I don't know anybody else in Pasadena who can sing a bass role like he can."

A knock sounded on the front door. We all looked at each other. As I walked to the door, Spike by my side in happy, tail-wagging, greeting mode, I heard Pa said, "Guess we'll find out soon." Although, in my opinion, this was no laughing matter—after all, I'd been practically forced, kicking and screaming, into playing Katisha—they all laughed.

Sure enough, Sam stood at the front door, his hat pulled down because the night was cold, and his overcoat buttoned up. I stepped aside, and he entered. Knowing where his duty lay, he instantly knelt to give Spike a healthy greeting. He creaked when he rose from the floor.

As he hung his hat and coat on the stand, I said, "We were just talking about you, Sam."

He eyed me warily. "Yeah? Why?"

"Because I think you're the only one who can play the part Lawrence Allen—I mean Johannes Niederhauser—was going to sing in *The Mikado*."

He scowled hideously as he walked into the dining room to greet my folks, who were gathered around the table where we'd been yakking. "Oh, no, you don't. I'm not going to sing in that blasted operetta."

"You'll have to, because you arrested Go-To, the noble lord of Titipu. If you don't sing his part, we won't have a Go-To. And we *need* a Go-To."

"I'll fix some tea," said Vi, grinning as she went to the kitchen to do so.

"What about Buckingham? He can sing, can't he?" He still scowled, but he added, "Thanks, Mrs. Gumm. I could use a strong cup of tea." He'd probably rather have had a glass of brandy, but we didn't have a helpful prescribing physician nearby to authorize one for him.

"Johnny's a tenor. Go-To requires a bass. The only other bass is playing the Mikado."

"You've got to have other basses in your choir," said Sam, beginning to whine and sound churlish.

"You have the best bass voice. If you won't sing the role when I ask you, you're going to have Mr. Hostetter and the rest of the cast hounding you until you agree."

"This isn't fair," said Sam, sounding a wee bit like me, actually.

"It wasn't fair when everyone forced me into playing Katisha, either, but I'm doing it."

"I have enough to do with my job."

"So do I."

We continued to argue even after Vi brought out a pot of tea, some teacups and saucers and a plate of oatmeal cookies, and we hadn't reached a satisfactory conclusion—a satisfactory conclusion being Sam agreeing to play Go-To—when Sam stifled a huge yawn and said, "I have to get home. It's been a hellish couple of days."

"At least you caught the crooks," said Ma.

"Thanks in large part to me," I said.

Sam said, "Huh."

"Nuts. You know it's true."

"Maybe," he said, conceding more than I'd expected him to.

I decided not to needle him. He did look tired. "I'll walk you to your car, Sam."

"Thanks." He put on his coat and hat, and I got my raggedy old sweater that's warm as toast, and Sam, Spike, and I went out the front door.

"You really do need to sing that part, Sam," I said when we reached the Hudson.

He heaved a sigh, turned, and gazed down at me, his heavy eyebrows making a V over his nose. "I'll do it on one condition," he said after several tense seconds of silence.

"What's the condition?" I asked with much trepidation. If he was going to ask me to quit my job or anything, we'd just have to find another Go-To.

"That you marry me."

It took me a second or two to take in the meaning of that sentence. Even after I was pretty sure I knew what he said, I couldn't quite believe it.

"What?" I asked. Stupid, I know.

"You heard me."

"I…I…Oh, Sam, I don't know. I mean, I have deep feelings for you."

"You have?" He didn't sound convinced.

"Yes, I do. But…but it's only been a little over a year since Billy died. I don't think I'm ready to take on another…marriage."

"I love you, Daisy. You know that."

Did I know that? I guess I did. "I know. I…I…love you, too, Sam." Boy, I hadn't thought I could get that sentence out into the air without bursting into tears, but I did it.

"Do you?"

I swallowed a lump in my throat. "Yes. Yes, I do."

"We don't have to get married right away. We can be engaged for ten years if you want to be. I just want to know that you'll marry me when you're ready."

"Oh, Sam!"

I hurled myself at him, and he engulfed me in the biggest, warmest hug I'd ever felt in my life.

The big lug.

He made a fabulous Go-To.

The End

UNSETTLED SPIRITS

A DAISY GUMM MAJESTY MYSTERY, BOOK 10

January 1, 1924, fell on a Tuesday. The week following that colorful parade day progressed at a slow, dignified, Pasadena-like pace. I had no séances to perform for anyone, probably because most of my clients were recovering from their Christmas and New Year's celebrations.

As for my family, my mother and aunt resumed their duties at their different workplaces, and I went to the library and picked up books for everyone to read. My favorite librarian, Miss Petrie, had taken some time off, so I had to search the shelves for reading material on my own —Miss Petrie liked to put aside books for my family and me to enjoy. Pa and I walked Spike every day, and Sam came to dinner most evenings. In other words, our lives were as normal as normal could be.

Then came Sunday, January sixth, when the elderly widow, Mrs. Theodore Franbold, dropped dead right after taking communion at our church. My family attended the First Methodist-Episcopal Church on the corner of Marengo and Colorado, and Mrs. Franbold's demise provided a whole lot more excitement than most of our Sunday services could offer. Not that I wanted people dropping dead in church; I only mention the matter as interesting.

At our church, we take communion once monthly, on the first Sunday of each month. I sang alto in the choir, and we choir members

235

sat in a space reserved for us on the chancel. We were served communion separately from the rest of the congregation, so I couldn't rush to
see what had happened when I saw Mrs. Franbold keel over right in
front of Mr. Grover Underhill. Rather than trying to help her or catch
her, Mr. Underhill jumped out of the way, bumping into several other
people. I frowned, thinking this behavior was typical of him. He was a
certified meany, as far as I was concerned. Not that I knew him well, but
what I did know of him, I didn't like.

Squinting, I saw the folks around Mrs. Franbold steady themselves
after being bumped by Mr. Underhill and gasp when they saw the
reason for his ungentlemanly behavior. A few seconds later, I saw several
people, including Sam Rotondo, who had taken going to church with us
even though he'd grown up in the Roman Catholic Church, gather
around the fallen woman. I lost Sam in the crowd when he knelt, probably to organize things and see what he could do for the Mrs. Franbold.

A general buzzing ensued. Mr. Underhill looked irritated, as if he
didn't approve of people collapsing in church. Lucy Spinks, a soprano
who was engaged to marry an older gentleman named Albert Zollinger,
whispered in my ear, "What do you think is happening?"

As much as I squinted, I couldn't see much because there were so
many people in the way, so I said, "I'm not sure. It looks as though Mrs.
Franbold fell down."

"Oh, dear. Poor sweet thing. I hope she didn't break anything."

"Me, too."

A scream erupted, and I winced, as I'm sure the rest of the choir
did, also. This time, I decided to heck with convention and stood in an
effort to discover who'd screamed. It was then I noticed Miss Betsy
Powell, who had been assisting with communion, cover her face with
her hands and give out short, sharp, piercing shrieks. At that point our
minister, Merle Negley Smith, decided to abandon his position behind
the communion cups and assist the afflicted, because he hurried down
the chancel steps and rushed over to Miss Powell. She had by this time
broken into noisy sobs, and Pastor Smith gently guided her out of the
church via a side door.

"What's the matter with whoever that is?" whispered Lucy.

On tiptoes, trying to see around the podium used by our lay speak-

236

ers, I said, "I'm not sure. Maybe Mrs. Franbold is dead or having a fit or something. It was Miss Powell who was screaming. Now it looks as if she's crying hysterically. Pastor Smith is leading her away from the mess." Darn, but I wished people would get out of my line of vision!

"Why would she scream?"

"Maybe she's not used to seeing people fall down in front of her?" I shrugged.

"Maybe."

Mr. Floy Hostetter, our choir director, abandoned the chancel then, and rushed over to the crowd clustered around Mrs. Franbold. Lucy and I exchanged a speaking glance, but I guess we both decided not to add our presence to what was already a chaotic scene.

Suddenly Sam Rotondo stood up. His voice rose over those of the masses. He didn't holler. He didn't have to. "Everyone, please take your seats. I'll handle this."

Nobody moved.

"Take your seats," said Sam in a voice I doubt anyone could ignore. He sounded like a general giving instructions to a firing squad.

The well-behaved congregants of the First Methodist-Episcopal Church on the corner of Marengo and Colorado in Pasadena seemed inclined to obey him, because everyone straggled back to their seats. This was probably a good thing, although communion hadn't ended yet, so many of the sittees were as of that moment un-sanctified. Or something like that.

After a brief conference with Sam, Mr. Hostetter trotted back to the chancel, climbed the steps, and walked to the preacher's podium. He held up his hands, and all murmuring stopped. I sat down. Darn it, I wanted to know what had happened!

"Dear ladies and gentlemen, please remain seated for a moment or two more. Mrs. Franbold has been taken ill, and some kind fellows are assisting her out of the sanctuary."

What he meant was that Sam and Dr. Benjamin were picking the woman up off the floor and aimed to take her somewhere else. My guess was that they would aim for Mr. Smith's office, where there was a convenient couch. Lying on a couch must be more comfortable than lying on the floor of a church sanctuary. Of course, at that point in time, no one knew for sure that the dear woman was dead. Well, I kind of did, but that's only because stuff like that seems to happen in my vicinity. Not necessarily people dropping dead but, as my father once told me, "Strange things happen around you." I'd resented his words at the time, but he was right, whether I resented his saying them or not.

After another few minutes, during which Sam and Dr. Benjamin, each with one of Mrs. Franbold's arms around their shoulders, escorted the woman from the sanctuary, Mr. Hostetter said, "Er... We shall resume communion at this time." He glanced frantically around the church. "Um, may we have a couple of volunteers, since our minister and Miss Powell are indisposed?" He then turned, gestured to Lucy and me and said, "Miss Spinks and Mrs. Majesty, perhaps you might be of service now."

Lucy and I looked at each other, shrugged, and went to take over the giving of communion in place of Mr. Smith and Miss Powell. Communion isn't difficult to assist with, since all you have to do is hold out a plate with communion wafers on it, and then offer each congregant a little glass cup filled about halfway with grape juice. Folks eat the wafer, drink the juice in the cup, and then—if they're doing it right—kneel prayerfully at the front altar or go to their seats. I regret to say my mind often wandered when it was supposed to be contemplating the state of my soul.

It sure wandered that day. I could hardly wait for the service to end so I could ask Sam what was wrong with Mrs. Franbold. If she was dead, how'd she die? If she was merely sick, what had made her sick? Had she suffered an apoplectic stroke? Heart attack? Perhaps she'd been ill and had come to church with walking pneumonia, although that sounded far-fetched. If a person is *that* sick, he or she should stay home, sleep and drink lots of hot tea with lemon and honey. At least that's what my mother always made me do when I was sick. Oh, and she'd give me cod-liver oil, too.

The mere thought of cod-liver oil made me shudder.

Lucy asked, "Are you all right, Daisy?"

"Fine, thanks." I decided she didn't need to know my thoughts.

After communion was over, the congregation, led by Mr. Hostetter, began singing our final hymn of the day, "O For A Thousand Tongues to Sing," which is a nice hymn. It's also the first hymn in every Methodist hymnal I've ever seen, although I'm not sure why. It was written by Charles Wesley, so maybe that's the reason, the Wesley brothers having begun Methodism in the 1700s.

Because Pastor Smith hadn't returned by the time the hymn was finished, Mr. Hostetter gave the final benediction and bade the congregants God speed.

Fortunately for us, Lucy and I didn't have to pick up the leftover communion stuff. Ladies from the Communion Committee did that. So we both hightailed it to the choir room, removed our choir robes, hung them up, and hurried to Fellowship Hall, where tea and cookies would be served.

We never stayed long at fellowship because Aunt Vi always had a delicious meal cooking for us at home. Therefore, I rushed around asking people if they knew what had happened to Mrs. Franbold. Nobody knew. And Sam, darn him, didn't show up at fellowship.

"We'd best be getting on home," Ma said not ten minutes after I'd appeared in Fellowship Hall. "Do you suppose Sam is still busy with Mrs. Franbold?"

"Don't know," said Pa.

"Probably," said Aunt Vi. "That poor woman. How old is she, anyway?"

"I don't know," I said. "Old. Well, elderly," I amended when I saw my mother's black look aimed at me. She expected her daughter to be polite and courteous all the time, even though her daughter—me—was all grown up and earning a living. I sighed. "Maybe he's in Pastor Smith's office. I'll go look."

"I'd like Sam to come to dinner," said Aunt Vi. She loved anyone who loved her cooking, and Sam lavished praise upon her every time he dined with us. Not that she didn't deserve his accolades, but I suspected him sometimes of going overboard just so she'd ask him to dinner more often.

"Right. I'll be back directly." And before anyone could stop me, I hurried out of the fellowship hall and to the pastor's office, which was just up the hall a few feet. I knocked softly on the closed door and wished curtains hadn't been drawn across the window.

A few seconds elapsed, and then I nearly leaped out of my skin when the door suddenly opened, and a scowling Sam glared down at me. He took up most of the doorway, so I couldn't see past him.

"What?"

"Aunt Vi wants to know if you're coming to dinner with us," I said, deciding not to bellow at him for his rudeness. We were, after all, in a church.

"I don't know yet."

Well, wasn't he just a load of joy and helpfulness? "Sam, what happened to Mrs. Franbold?"

Before Sam could tell me it was none of my business, I saw a hand descend upon Sam's shoulder, and Pastor Smith said, "Perhaps Mrs. Majesty can help console Miss Powell, Detective."

So. Miss Powell needed consolation, did she? I wondered why. Rather than ask, I said, "I'll be happy to help." It wasn't even a fib. If I could get into the pastor's office, maybe I could finally learn what had happened to the poor old woman. And why it had so upset Betsy Powell.

Sam, who knew me very well, scowled even harder and said, "She only wants to nose around."

"I do not!" Very well, that was a little fib. I also wanted to be helpful.

"I do wish you'd step aside and let her in, Detective Rotondo. Miss Powell is having hysterics." Pastor Smith sounded rattled.

After heaving a sigh about the size of Mount Wilson, Sam said, "Very well. Come in. But sit with Miss Powell and don't get in the way."

"I won't get in the way," I told him in a voice that clearly conveyed my annoyance with him. Get in the way, my foot.

"Right," said Sam, unconvinced.

Nevertheless, he stepped aside, and I entered the pastor's office. I was surprised to see a couple of uniformed police officers standing at the sofa that held Mrs. Franbold. I shot a quick look at Sam and whispered, "Is she…"

"Yes. She is. Now go comfort that other lady."

Oh, my. Poor Mrs. Franbold! What could have happened to her?

Betsy Powell sat sobbing on an overstuffed chair not far from the minister's desk. I walked over to her and knelt beside her. "Miss

Powell? Betsy, please tell me what's wrong. Is there anything I can do for you?"

She lifted her head, and I saw that she, too, failed to look good when she cried. Her eyes were swollen almost shut, her face was red, and she was gasping and sobbing and generally looking like a mess. I feared she might faint if she kept that up.

Putting an arm on her shoulder, I said, "That's enough now. You needn't cry. Poor Mrs. Franbold was an elderly woman, and she's now in a better place. If God decided to call her during communion... Well, what better time to do it?" I thought that was kind of a nice way of putting it, but Betsy only gasped loudly and sobbed harder.

"No!" she cried, her words thickened with tears. "No! It wasn't her time! Oh, oh, oh!"

Great. Now what was I supposed to do? I'd heard that one could cure a hysterical person by slapping the person's face, but I didn't think church would be a good place to do that. Therefore, I shook Betsy's shoulder rather hard.

"That's enough now, Betsy Powell. Get hold of yourself. This is no time and no place to get the galloping glooms." Don't ask me why I used those words. I think I'd read them in a book or something. "This is Pastor Smith's office, and I'm sure he has better things to do than listen to you have fits while he's trying to deal with the death of a long-time congregant. Now buck up." I spoke sternly, for me. I generally try to convey a gentle waftiness, but I was dealing with hysterics here, so I believed firmness was called for.

Evidently Betsy Powell wasn't so sure, because she stared at me for about thirty seconds, and then crumpled into a faint. Oh, goody. Just what everyone needed: another body to contend with.

But no one else seemed to mind. In fact, Pastor Smith actually said, "Thank God."

Sam said, "Thanks, Daisy. She was driving us nertz."

Dr. Benjamin said, "She fainted? Good."

Well, there you go. I'd been mean, and everyone appreciated me for it.

"What happened to Mrs. Franbold," I asked after making sure Betsy still breathed. She did.

"Don't know," said Sam. "That's why the uniforms are here."

"Oh. I wondered why you'd called the cops."

Sam gave me a frown I don't believe I deserved. "Any time there's a sudden, unexpected death, it's a good idea to get medical opinion. Dr. Benjamin is the one who suggested we call the uniforms."

"Really?" Still kneeling, although my knees were beginning to object, I turned to Doc Benjamin. "Why's that, Doc?"

He didn't answer me for quite a few seconds, and his lips pursed in and pooched out, as if he were determine whether or not to answer my question. I held my breath and slowly got to my feet, making sure Betsy Powell was firmly attached to her chair and wouldn't fall out of it.

At last, the doctor looked at me and said, "From the signs, it looks to me as if Mrs. Franbold has taken or been given some kind of poison."

As luck would have it, Betsy Powell opened her eyes in time to hear Dr. Benjamin's words. She let out a screech that could probably have been heard in Illinois. Fortunately, she fainted again instantly.

Available in Paperback and eBook From Your Favorite Online Retailer or Bookstore

ABOUT THE AUTHOR

Award-winning author Alice Duncan lives with a herd of wild dachshunds (enriched from time to time with fosterees from New Mexico Dachshund Rescue) in Roswell, New Mexico. She's not a UFO enthusiast; she's in Roswell because her mother's family settled there fifty years before the aliens crashed (and living in Roswell, NM, is cheaper than living in Pasadena, CA, unfortunately). Alice would love to hear from you at alice@aliceduncan.net

www.aliceduncan.net

 facebook.com/alice.duncan.925

www.ingramcontent.com/pod-product-compliance
Lightning Source LLC
Chambersburg PA
CBHW020550020726
47494CB00006B/2011